ALSO BY KATHLEEN EAGLE

wm

WILLIAM MORROW

75 YEARS OF PUBLISHING

An Imprint of HarperCollins*Publishers*

You

Never

Can

Tell

KATHLEEN
EAGLE

HarperCollins books may be purchased for educational, business, or sales promotional use. For information please write: Special Markets Department, HarperCollins Publishers Inc., 10 East 53rd Street, New York, NY 10022.

FIRST EDITION

Designed by Jessica Shatan

Printed on acid-free paper

Library of Congress Cataloging-in-Publication Data

Eagle, Kathleen.
  You never can tell / by Kathleen Eagle.—1st ed.
    p. cm.
  ISBN 0-380-97816-4
    1. Women journalists—Fiction. 2. Indian activists—Fiction.
 3. Minnesota—Fiction. I. Title.

PS3555.A385 Y68 2001
813'.54—dc21

                 2001016261

01 02 03 04 05 RRD 10 9 8 7 6 5 4 3 2 1

This book is dedicated

to my favorite aunt,

Margaret Garner Lennon,

and in loving memory of

V. S. Garner, my uncle Biven

ACKNOWLEDGMENTS

I am long overdue in publicly thanking Steven Axelrod, the best agent in the business; Lucia Macro, editor extraordinaire; and Carrie Feron, whose editorial insight and guidance have been indispensable to all of us. It's a pleasure to work with all of you.

Thanks also to Connie Brockway, who said the magic words when I was stuck on this one. She remembers what they were.

You

Never

Can

Tell

1

The man she wanted was sitting kitty-corner across the bar, big as life.

Heather Reardon felt hot and damp all over, her gut gone goosey, like a silly teenage groupie, but one with no friend along to poke her and remind her not to stare. The tinny chords from a steel guitar looped round and round her, while a dying bulb in a beer sign above the door marked "Can" did a crazy dance.

Can, indeed, she thought giddily. Can and did. Searched and found. She had followed her leads and her instincts deep into the backwoods, nearly to the Canadian border, and found the man she'd been looking for perched on a run-of-the-mill bar stool.

She wasn't staring. She didn't have to. Heather Reardon was a professional. She had the eavesdropping ear of an owl and the peripheral vision of a horse. Staring was no way to get what she'd come to the Minnesota backwoods for, which was not so much the man as his story. But the man—seeing him in the flesh, hearing his voice live, remembering his public deeds as well as the personal stories she'd been told—the man was something else.

His name was Kole Kills Crow, and he was acting remarkably ordinary, sitting there, minding a beer on the stained bar, the sportscaster on the small screen above the fat bartender's head, and the occasional comment from the younger Indian man sitting two stools down on his far side.

He didn't resemble any fugitive she'd ever encountered—and she'd met a few—nor did he strike her as a martyr. He didn't look like a rabble-rouser or a terrorist or a messianic leader of Native people or a convict. He certainly didn't look like a murderer, but Heather had interviewed enough murderers to know that you couldn't tell by looking at them.

And he knew she was looking at him, if furtively. That much she could tell by the way he studiously ignored her.

She was fairly certain that being the only woman in the Cheap Shot Saloon rendered her somewhat noticeable. She was also the only Caucasian, although the bartender was probably more white than Indian. He was the only person who'd said anything to her so far—"What'll it be?" and then "Never heard of it. You got a second choice?" She'd ended up with red wine vinegar in a juice glass.

"How is it?" the bartender asked her after he'd delivered a couple of beers at the other end of the bar. "The wine."

Heather looked down at the glass. Not that she'd forgotten, but she couldn't bring herself to look the guy in the eye when she said, "Fine."

"Didn't know if it would keep. Opened it up for a lady last month."

"Last month? Well . . ." She flashed a tight smile. "As long as you keep the cap screwed on tight."

"Lost the cap, so I just—"

"Are you palming off some of that stuff you make yourself, Mario?"

The bartender raised his voice as he shot the younger man a scowl. "Put a cork in it."

"Damn, we lose more tourists that way."

The exchange drew a chuckle from the reticent Mr. Kills Crow as he set his beer down after taking a sip.

"They come all this way to soak up the flavor of, uh, the native . . ." The young guy made a rolling gesture. "What do you call it, Kola?"

"Hooch."

"Not that. The atmosphere. The whole cultural—"

"That ain't hooch, hey. That there's genuine—" The bartender grabbed the bottle, checked the label, then shoved it under the younger man's nose. "Italian. It's Italian wine. Imported from Chicago. I got a cousin there."

Heather slid Kills Crow a quick glance. She had the edge. She knew who he was, knew from her reading that *kola* was the Lakota word for "friend," knew that they were both visitors to the woodsy Northern Minnesota Blue Fish Indian Reservation that was home, not to the Lakota, but to their traditional rivals, the Chippewa. He, on the other hand, knew nothing about her.

Not that he was interested. Clearly he meant to spare her no more than a glance as he lifted his beer, but he stopped short of a sip and lowered the bottle. A spark flashed in his dark eyes, like a secret smile. "You're supposed to let the lady check the cork, Mario," he said.

He no longer wore his hair in the braids he'd sported when he'd waved an assault rifle above his head and defied the South Dakota National Guard with a chilling whoop that echoed across the airwaves into living rooms across the country. Heather had only had a passing interest at the time—much like that reflected in the look he was giving her now—but she'd since gathered every piece of news he'd made. His hair had been jet-black then. It was shorter now and streaked with an abundance of silver for a forty-year-old man. She could count the years in his tawny face, too, but he wore them well. And his eyes promised a fascinating story.

"Ain't nothin' wrong with the cork. See? Just a cork." Mario snatched it out of the sink and thrust it under each nose along the bar, as though he wanted them to sniff for spoilage. "Damn, you guys," Mario said, flicking the cork in the young man's face when he grimaced. "She said herself, it's good wine. Right?"

"I said it was fine." She offered another tight smile to the bartender as she grabbed the glass, then cast a quick glance at the man she'd come two thousand miles to find.

Dare ya, said the eyes with the secret smile.

She drank, willing her tongue to let the stuff pass quietly, finishing off by turning a sour pucker into a savory lip smack, then a grin. "Mighty fine wine," she declared.

The secret smile turned public.

The younger man applauded.

Bartender Mario looked worried. "You're the wine expert, Jack. How many days does it have to age before it's safe to chug like that?" He laughed when Heather's face fell. "Just kidding. You're a good sport."

"What is your sport?" Kole's friend, Jack, asked. "Hiking, fishing, canoeing? What brings you way out here from way over . . ."—he gestured with a revolving index finger—". . . yonder?"

"East," she said with a nod as she lit a cigarette. "A little of each, along with the fact that I've never seen this part of the country."

"Did you know you're on an Indian reservation?"

"Yes, but it's not closed to non-Indians, is it?" She glanced at Kole through her smoke. "I actually have a little Indian blood. Cherokee, I think."

"That puts you in with about ninty-nine percent of the population," Jack said.

"I suppose that sounds . . ." She waved her own claim away with cigarette smoke, embarrassed to have made it to these people in this place. "Family fable, I guess. Am I not allowed to be here? I'm staying at the lodge, which was advertised on the Internet."

"What kinda net?" somebody beyond the bar put in.

"Internet," Jack said. "They use it to fish for tourists."

"It's legal," Mario reported with a grin. "No limits, no season."

"Is it covered by treaty?"

"Some white guy invented it," another voice reported, the conversation spreading like ripples from a pebble plunk.

"Then we're safe. You've got a home page, Mario?"

"They gave it to me free with the Internet service."

"You got a computer?"

"No, but I'm gonna get one pretty soon."

"He uses mine," Jack said.

"It's the cheapest kind of advertising you can get, and it works." Mario jerked his chin in Heather's direction. "Reeled in a real nice one."

"Without even mentioning the fine wine," Heather said.

"Mighty fine wine. Would you care for another hit?"

With a quick hand she covered the glass. "Oh, no, thanks, I'm fine."

"Mighty fine." Mario winked at her, went to brace an arm on the bar and tipped over a bowl of peanuts, which he quickly brushed onto the floor behind the bar. "What are you fishing for?"

"Well . . . *fish.* Whatever bites."

"You've got three or four of us swimming around the hook here," Jack said, grinning. "But Mario can't do any serious biting since his ol' lady wired his jaws."

Other baiters chimed in.

"Stuffed and mounted is what he is."

"When Mario has a few beers, his ol' lady does all the pissing. That's how close they are."

With lips rather than fingers, Mario pointed past the bar. "What about you, Dogskin? You're caught, too."

"But I'm about to be released. She kicked me out two days ago."

"I have a feeling I'm in way over my head here," Heather said with a laugh. "But I really do need a guide." As long as everyone seemed easy with her now, she slid Kole a look to complement those he'd given her. "Would you be interested?"

"That's not my line," he said quietly.

"Mario knows every trail around here," Jack said. "But if you're looking for an outfitter, you probably should have—"

"Is that what you're looking for?" Kole asked, his eyes telling her he knew better. "An outfitter?"

"Well, all right, maybe I will have something in a sealed bottle," she said with a pointed glance at his beer.

Kole signaled the bartender, who served her a bottle and a glass. The glass appeared to be Mario's special favor to her, since no one else had one. She figured the bottle was safer, but she didn't want to hurt any feelings or cause any offense, so she poured, sipped, grimaced—she wasn't a beer drinker—nodded, smiled, and thanked them both. She was, she decided, making progress.

"I'm Heather Reardon, from New York. I'm a writer, and I'm here for a much needed getaway and a little of that ambiance you mentioned."

"*I* mentioned? That must be something you saw on the Internet, Heather Reardon from New York." Kole Kills Crow had a formidable scowl. "Did you advertise our ambiance, Mario? Is that what we're selling these days?"

"There's plenty here," she said.

He laughed. "Yeah, but you gotta pay for it. We're not giving it away. Not even to the great-great-granddaughter of a Cherokee princess."

"I'll pay." She laughed, too, because he couldn't drive her away with a stick, not when his eyes kept inviting her back. She stubbed her cigarette out in the black plastic ashtray. "What would a dance cost me?"

"You want a guide or an escort service?"

"Just a dance."

He tipped his head to one side, drew his mouth down, considering.

Jack slapped him on the shoulder. "Where are your manners, Kola? The lady's askin' nice."

He surprised her when he slid from the stool. "I'll risk it if you will. No charge."

"The man is priceless," Jack said.

Not as a dancer, she thought as their feet tried to agree on the steps. The honky-tonk rhythm was foreign to her, but at least she had him to herself for about a minute and a half. Somehow she had to parlay that into about a month and a half. Once he agreed to work with her, she would need that much time to get to know him well enough for the story to emerge. This would be more than an interview. She believed him to be one of a rare breed, maybe even a dying breed of men. He was, unless she was badly mistaken, a true champion of the people.

Breed was probably not the best term under the circumstances, and she was using *men* in the universal sense, of course, the gender-neutral sense. Except that his arm around her, his hand riding her hip, his hard shoulder under her hand—these were things she had thought about over the years, watching him in news clips and listening to the musings and memories of her friend Savannah Stephens, who had known Kole Kills Crow when he was a teenager. These things, once imagined and titillating, were suddenly real and titillating, hardly gender-neutral. But they weren't part of the story.

"Did you come all the way out here alone?"

Was he serious? She glanced up, checking his expressive eyes for a clue. She found none.

"I get around pretty well on my own," she said, "as long as there are roads and I have a map. When I get lost, I'm smart enough to ask for directions, and when I run out of road, I'm smart enough to look for a guide. Someone who's native . . ." She smiled. "To the area."

"You're barkin' up the wrong tree there. I may look native, but I'm not from this area."

"Where are you from . . . Kola?"

"All over."

"Originally."

"West of here. South and west."

"I'm pretty good with geography. Mention a country, state, even a town, and I'll probably know where it is."

"Indian country."

"Are you the same Kola who makes the flutes?"

"Among other things. Are you a musician?"

"I'm an avid listener." She smiled again. She'd cracked her share of tough nuts. "And a writer. I know a little bit about a lot of things, but I'm always trying to learn more. Your flutes are very much in demand."

"I'm getting tired of flutes. I make a lot of stuff. Workin' on my first canoe now." He looked her in the eye and returned the smile. "What are you workin' on?"

"I've got several things in the works right now."

"Fiction?"

"Not if I can help it." She was getting the hang of his two-step, beginning to relax a muscle or two. "If I can find my way through the woods, I might write a travel piece. *That* would be free advertising. Even cheaper than the Internet."

"Talk to Mario. He's the one who needs the advertising." He glanced toward the bar. "I don't know if I'd follow him into the woods, though."

She followed the direction of his glance and counted five pairs of eyes looking back. They were the only show in the place.

"I think I'd rather follow you. I could do an artisan piece. Couldn't you use the advertising?"

"I can't keep up with the orders now. New Age musicians love Indian flutes. There's also a big demand in Europe." He raised his brow. "But don't let that stop you."

"From writing about you?"

"From following."

"You're available, then?"

"Sure." He tripped her up with a quick turn, putting his back to their audience. "My place or yours?"

"I meant to take me, *guide* me on a . . ." Damn, where was her clever quip? She should have been ready, undoubtedly would have been if he'd been anyone but Kole Kills Crow.

"If you want me to lead, try movin' with me, okay?" He indulged her with a smile. "If you want me to lead you, expect to encounter some temptation."

"Where? On the garden path?"

"Not around here. You're sojourning in the wilderness now. Or maybe the Garden of Eden." The smile fell away. "You wanna go someplace else?"

It was a natural question, and she knew it, but she wished he hadn't come out and asked. "I want to go hiking, but seriously, I need a guide."

"Like I said, that's not my line. Especially the serious part." He drew away as the music ended, letting her make the first move toward the bar. "Thanks for the dance," he said to her back. "It's been a while."

She turned, assured him with a smile, "For me, too."

"That's what I meant." He gave a cocky wink. "Enjoy the ambiance, Heather."

He said something to Jack, still sitting at the bar, and then he left.

Stinging, she waited only a moment before she left, too, just in time to catch sight of his pickup's taillights. The men in the bar would assume she was meeting him, but who cared what they thought? She had come to this neck of the woods to find Kole Kills Crow, who was about to disappear into its bowels, thinking he'd gotten in the last and best word. The arrogant . . . like he was some kind of Fred Astaire.

She followed him in the four-wheel-drive mountain-man vehicle she'd rented at the Minneapolis airport that morning. She hadn't been able to pass up the opportunity to try one out, in case she had to go "off-roading." It was late September, and this was northern Minnesota. Who knew when the first snow might fall, or what some of these unpaved roads might be like when it rained? Heather was prepared to find out.

Now that she'd seen the man, it would be handy to know exactly where he lived. She turned on her tape recorder and talked herself down the road, referring often to the car's odometer and to the glow-in-the-dark compass that had been part of her gear since she'd traveled into the Arkansas outback to interview the deposed leader of the Aryan Nation. She'd gotten to him two weeks before he'd pitched over the edge of a cliff and tumbled into a picturesque gorge. *Time* magazine had already had her interview in the pipeline. Fortunately she'd been able to attach a postscript.

But this north woods reservation was even more remote than the Arkansas hill country. Scoping out her subject's digs was a wise move, if she could just keep those red taillights in sight. The man drove like a demon, the road was a meandering moose trail, and the forest was dark and deep—all of which she reported on tape as the two red lights disappeared over a hill. When she topped the hill, the lights were gone. She proceeded through the tunnel of low-hanging branches as the moose trail turned into a rabbit path. The trees seemed to come alive, closing in on both sides of the car and bending low to snatch at the door handles and snap the antenna. She'd driven into her worst childhood nightmare. There wasn't even enough room to turn around, which suddenly seemed like a wise thing to do. Wiser than scoping out any digs.

Heather threw the Explorer into reverse and started to back out. She'd always had trouble driving in reverse. She'd failed her first driver's test because she was such a crooked backer. "Just take it slow and easy," she told the tape recorder. "Hold the wheel steady. Can't be more than a mile or two. Those two Indian chicks in that *Smoke Signals* movie drove this way all the time."

She laughed. She'd loved that movie—Indian people enduring all kinds of adversity—and now it had her smiling through her own dark moment. But her smile slid away when the headlights flashed behind her. Thank God, another human being.

Oh God, let it be one of the good ones.

She locked her doors and waited. The lights shone through her back window, but no face appeared. She rolled down her window and stuck her head out. "Am I trespassing? Forgive me, but I seem to be . . ." Not *lost*. That was the last word you ever want to say in a dark alley. ". . . in the wrong . . ." Shifting shadows. Did somebody move? "I was just trying to . . ." She shut up and listened to the rumbling motors. "Hello?"

"Hello."

"Kola?" It sounded like his voice, but how could he have slipped behind her? "It *is* you. Isn't it?"

"If you want me to forgive you your trespasses, you'll have to confess." Coming from the bright light, it sounded more like the Great Oz.

"To what?" Heather barked back. Be damned if she'd be the small and meek.

"Whatever it is you're up to, lady."

"I seem to be up to getting lost."

"Told you I wasn't much of a guide."

"You got me lost on purpose."

"If I did, you made it possible. Step out of the truck, Heather."

She rolled the window up a few inches. "Come out where I can see you first."

"Is that an order?" Faceless, his laughter sounded sinister. "You've got guts, I'll say that much for you. *Toniga.* What you guys lack in sense you try to make up for with brass."

"Or maybe cold steel. Maybe I've got a gun."

"Maybe not. I'm a bettin' man, and I think I'll bet not."

"What do you mean, 'guys'? What guys?"

"You're right. If you were a white *guy*, I might bet differently. You people."

"I'm not you people. I'm . . ." Her voice dropped when his silhouette finally appeared in the headlights. "I'm not getting out of this vehicle. Once you get out, you're dead meat."

"No. Once you get *into* the vehicle, you're dead meat. You're a live one is what you are. But foolish." The tall, lean silhouette moved a step closer. "Now, get out of the truck."

"The doors are locked."

"So I can't get you? What makes you think I want you? You had your chance, lady."

"And I'm sure I'll always wonder about the road not taken."

"Which one is that? You don't even know which one you took."

"If you'll just let me pass—"

"I won't hurt you," he promised quietly as he approached. "People who do things backwards get special consideration in Indian country. But we only let them go so far, and you've reached your limit, so you might as well jump out."

"And go where?"

"Guess we're down to my place. That's what you're lookin' for, isn't it?"

"Well, yes," she admitted as she stepped down from the sporty vehicle. She was trapped. She was going to have to brazen her way through this showdown. "I thought I might stop in during business hours and buy a flute."

"You don't need a flute, honey. You're blowin' sunshine up my ass just fine." He grabbed the door before she could close it behind her. "I can tell you're going to be a great source of entertainment for me."

"I don't think so."

"I'm easily entertained. Been living in the woods a long time. Remember that crazy redneck bastard in *Deliverance*? I think I've become the redskin version," he said as he scanned the interior of her vehicle. "I prefer women, though, so I'd be inclined to let Burt Reynolds and the boys float right on by." He punched off the headlights, turned off the engine, and took her keys. "Maybe you're related to Burt. I understand he's part Cherokee, too."

"Would it get me any points?"

"No more than the Cherokee thing gets you."

"You're saying I'm pointless." Not to mention brainless for not taking the keys herself.

"Not at all. You've put a few points on your side of the board." He chuckled as he pocketed her keys. "Hell, you showed up. A woman walks into the Cheap Shot alone, she scores without even batting an eye."

"I'm not much of a batter."

"That's good. You don't wanna blink during this next round."

"Don't you mean inning? If you start mixing your metaphors, you're liable to strike out."

"You're forgetting my home field advantage. I get to make up the rules as we go along. You could be in for some serious trouble."

"Yes, I guess I could be." She gauged the distance to his pickup, which he'd left running.

"You play nice—tell me who you really are, who you're working for, and what you want from me—and maybe in a couple of days I'll send you back to your relatives, relatively unharmed."

"You said you wouldn't hurt me."

"I did, didn't I?" He reached into her vehicle again, muttering something about hurt, like everything else, being relative.

As was stupidity, she thought wildly as she bolted for his pickup. He tackled her from behind as she sprinted headlong into the headlight beam, toppling her onto the hood. She was pinned under his body.

"This is like playing with a mouse," he whispered close to her ear. "What are you up to, little mouse? Who'd be dropping a pretty little white mouse down the back of my shirt?"

"Nobody dropped me," she insisted, straining to keep her face off the pickup hood. "Let me get my purse. I'll show you."

He let her up. She squared her shoulders and marched back to the Explorer, quickly retrieving her big leather purse from under the front seat. She shoved her wallet at him first, as though he were holding her up at gunpoint, then supplied him with a penlight, which she took back and clicked on for him.

"I told you who I really am, and I told you what I want. I work for myself." She speared a finger at her New York driver's license, her National Press Women's Society membership card, her platinum

Visa and gold American Express cards, all in the name of Heather Reardon. "Satisfied?"

"Not hardly. You white girls all look alike to me, especially in the dark." He shoved her wallet into her hands as he reached into the car for something else that might answer his questions—her tape recorder. He rewound the tape a bit, then played her travel notes back to her.

"I wanted to make sure I could find my way back."

"After you located my place?"

She nodded. "I'm doing a travel piece. I'm interested in your work. I met a man who has three of your flutes when I was doing a story on Native theater. Donald Yellow Earring?"

"No points for that name, either. We don't *all* know each other, you know."

"He talked like he knew you. Said you were the best—"

"People order my flutes through an agent. I don't know who they are, and they don't know me."

She folded her arms around her purse. "Lena Murphy handles the orders."

He slammed the Explorer door. "Shit."

"But she didn't tell me how to find you. I figured that out for myself."

"Are you a cop?" he demanded, grabbing her arm.

"Without a gun? Not hardly," she said, echoing him. "I'm not even a reporter. I'm just a freelance journalist."

"No matter what you're calling yourself, you smell like trouble to me."

"I showered this morning."

"Trouble's a scent that don't wash off, lady. I've been wearing it all my life." He leaned down, dipped his nose close to her hair, and inhaled audibly. "But I've got a feeling you know all about that, having followed your freelance nose all the way to God's country."

"I thought this was Indian country."

"One and the same. 'Bout all the country God's got left. The rest is all covered with cement."

"Oh, that's right." She tipped her head back and smiled. "Is that an original quote?"

"You tell me."

"I think it's been attributed to Barry Wilson, the act—"

"I know who Barry Wilson is," he told her as he opened the Explorer door again and hit the automatic lock. "Guess I must've stole it, then."

"What are you doing?"

"You don't wanna leave the thing unlocked. Makes it just as easy to steal as words and twice as tempting." He stepped back, eyeing the fancy vehicle. "Course it might get stripped. I hope you took the insurance option on the rental contract."

"I nev—what are you doing?" *Besides walking away with her keys?*

"I'm going home."

"You're not going to leave me out here!"

"That wouldn't be very nice, would it?" He became a silhouette in the headlight again as he turned to her. "Tailing people isn't very nice, either."

"No, but I . . ."

He was already climbing into his pickup. The slamming of the door echoed down the road. The engine roared, missing on one spark plug until he put it in gear and the pickup crawled forward. Heather backed up against the door of the locked Explorer. The pickup's passenger side door swung open. It was the only invitation she was going to get.

She took it.

2

Kole neither spoke
to her nor glanced her way as he drove
them down the gravel road, deep down
into a dark tunnel of trees. Heather had
given up counting turns. She was already
lost when she climbed into his pickup
truck. Taking his cue, she kept her eyes on
the road ahead and told herself it might be
time to start worrying. *Be afraid,* she and
Savannah used to whisper to each other
after a clumsy come-on from some guy. *Be
very afraid.*

But it was hard to fear any man
Heather's best friend had vouched for as
unstintingly as she had Kole Kills Crow.
Before becoming a leader in the American

Indian Movement—rabble-rouser to some, champion to others—he'd been Savannah's childhood hero. But she'd known him personally. Heather had only known *of* him. He was a man who championed his people, who believed in a cause. In a country full of causes, his was one that had touched Heather's idealistic soul as far back as she could remember.

And she had a memory that, present predicament notwithstanding, rarely failed. Her father had taken her to a powwow in Oklahoma when she was about five years old, and she remembered the bold, swirling colors, the enticing smell of deep-fried yeast dough, and the throbbing music, the night's pulse beat. But mostly she remembered her father's rare attention.

Her mother had stayed home, uninterested in watching the Indians dance, and Heather alone had been her father's companion. As young as she was, she had sensed a special bond with her father that night, something that made her more like him. Something that made him like her more. Whatever it was, it ran deep and true, and it was rooted in that night.

She had not shared another time with her father that was as memorable as that Oklahoma powwow. She would have to admit that her mother had truly raised her, but her father's absence had not been his fault. He was a military man. Her mother often said—sometimes angrily, other times wistfully or enviously or even lovingly—that Heather favored him.

Heather didn't know about that. There was the obvious physical resemblance, but in the end, she hadn't known her father very well, and she doubted that her mother had known him much better. She only knew that she wished he could see how far she had come and how close she was to achieving something of importance. A story.

Her father had been a storyteller. She was a story seeker. She also told them—wrote and published them—but for a journalist, the trick was finding the story that would mean something to people.

And her friend Savannah's infamous friend, Kole, meant something to his own people. It was Heather's intention to see that he—and, by extension, the cause of his people—would come to mean something to a broader community. To a journalist, injustice that had once been denied, then forgotten, was like an heirloom discovered in the closet. Unless Heather was uncharacteristically mistaken, the time for Kole Kills Crow's message had come. Savannah would be pleased for the man. Heather was pleased for the message.

Nearly a dozen years ago Heather had met Savannah Stephens in Manhattan, the mecca for hungry writers and hopeful models. The timing was perfect. They were both struggling with tight budgets, loneliness, and the tired feet and sore knuckles that came from knocking on too many doors.

Heather had been a reporter for a small newspaper in Virginia and a stringer for a couple of women's magazines when she was in college, but she always had her sights set on starting out in New York. She'd landed a job as a copy editor for the *Daily News* and with it the chance to fulfill her dream, which might have been cut short by high rent and slave wages had she not met Savannah, a sister dreamer. They'd first shared a cab, then an apartment, then peanut butter sandwiches, subway tokens, stockings, and secrets.

Heather had assumed the lead. She was, after all, the one with the more serious aspirations. Savannah was too beautiful to be taken seriously, and she'd grown up in the back of beyond. "Is that the way they do things in Wyoming?" Heather would tease, eliciting Savannah's mystical, slightly vulnerable smile. She'd mocked that western drawl, even though Savannah soon learned to turn it on and off to suit the occasion. Heather came to realize that Savannah's "smarts" were different from her own, oddly more down-to-earth, more practical.

Savannah knew exactly who she was, where she was going, what she wanted to be. In her business, appearances meant everything, and eventually she became a familiar face and figure—if not a household name—on the pages of Lady Elizabeth's Dreamwear Catalog.

It seemed a good balance after a time. Savannah's face was her calling card, while Heather traded and built on her name, her "people skills," her instinct for getting to the heart of the story, her talent for telling it well. Oddly—at least it seemed odd to Heather—Savannah was more the realist. Heather would not have guessed they shared a hero. The first time Savannah had shrieked his name when she'd seen Kole in a news clip—God, he looked good in handcuffs—Heather had asked enviously, "You *know* him?"

After he and his sidekick, Barry Wilson, were arrested in South Dakota and charged with every criminal act known to man, Savannah and Heather had subscribed to the Rapid City *Journal* so they could follow the trial.

"He'll beat this," Savannah had said. But Heather knew it didn't look good from the moment the change of venue was denied. Vigils, protests, and counterdemonstrations were held outside the courthouse. Savannah had just landed her first print ad job and couldn't get away, so Heather had taken the bus to South Dakota. Night after night she'd stood in the crowd of mostly Indian people and held her candle for the two men who were, she believed, simply trying to reclaim what rightfully belonged to their people. She hadn't been surprised when Kills Crow was convicted. But Wilson was acquitted, and that was the shocker.

Heather stole a glance at the man behind the wheel of the rattletrap pickup truck. Not only did her most trusted friend once know him well, but she was also raising his child. Being privy to that secret was Heather's ace in the hole. She figured it made her the next best thing to family. And Indians, from what she'd seen and heard, were big on family. She was plunging deep into the woods with a man who'd been arrested so often he'd once coached his arresting officer—

a rookie made nervous by the news cameras—on the proper procedure.

But Heather was no rookie. She knew a hero from a hard case con.
She knew how to get a great story out of either one, and she had the
National Press Awards to prove it. She would have been totally on
top of the story at hand—and getting the Kills Crow story would be
such a coup—which she, too, could count if she could check her
files—if only she had some idea where the hell she was.

Not to worry, she told herself. If she could find her way to Kole Kills
Crow's world, she could find her way back out when the time came.

The headlights suddenly illuminated a small cabin. A head popped
up from the scraggly grass, a pair of feral eyes glowing back at them.
"A wolf," Heather whispered, leaning forward to get a better look
before the animal ran away. Surprisingly, it bounded into the headlights.

"Part wolf. We're a pair of mixed-bloods." Kole cut the lights, then
the engine. The pale gray animal greeted him as soon as he opened
the pickup door. "Yeah, yeah, I brought you something to chew on."

Heather hoped it wasn't her leg. She believed in keeping only
small pets and viewing wildlife from behind a fence, but she couldn't
view much of anything until her eyes adjusted to the darkness.

"C'mon out." Kole gestured to her with one hand while the other
stroked the animal's pale fur. "He doesn't eat until I give him the
word. I'm the alpha male."

"I suppose I'm chopped liver," Heather grumbled as she slid gin-
gerly off the high seat on the driver's side, hanging on to the steering
wheel until her feet touched the ground.

"What do you say, boy?" Kole asked as the dog nosed Heather's
palm. She flinched when the animal barked, but he immediately
wagged his tail in truce and licked her fingers.

She hesitated to close the pickup door quite yet, even though the
dog seemed friendly enough. "What's his name?"

"He just told you. Woof."

"Wolf?"

"Woof. His tongue doesn't do *L*'s."

"Woof, then." She patted the dog's head, gave a small laugh. "I was afraid he was saying 'Good' and thinking *chicken*."

"If he smelled chicken, he'd let me know." He grabbed a small cardboard box out of the back of the pickup. "Let's go inside."

"And do what?"

"I'd say 'get to know each other better,' but you're obviously way ahead of me. So I figure we'll spend our first night together kinda evening things up. I'm gonna get to know you."

"You wouldn't hurt me."

"You're sure?"

"Absolutely. I'm not afraid of you."

"Then let's go inside." He tucked the box under one arm, laid a hand on her shoulder, and directed her toward the cabin.

"And you don't have to be afraid of me, either." She spoke with more enthusiasm than her dragging heels implied. "Because I would never hurt you. You have my word."

"What if I want you to hurt me? You know, a little pain for starters. You wanna start with your word, fine." He leaned close to her ear as he reached around her to open the door. "Lie to me, baby."

Oddly his warm breath gave her a shiver. She stiffened her whole body against it. "I'm a journalist. Truth is my stock-in-trade."

"Yeah, right." The door creaked when he pushed it open. "Watch your step."

"Yeah, right," she echoed softly in the dark as she used fingers and feet to find doorjamb and threshold. "Is this your lake cabin or something? I've heard that all Minnesotans have lake cabins."

"Like I said, I ain't from around here." He set the box down somewhere in the dark. "This is my hideout."

"It certainly is a good one," she said cheerfully, anchoring herself to the doorjamb. The door was still open, but the dog was stationed on the step. Heather tried to imagine leaping over him and taking off into the woods.

In the dark she heard a ripping sound.

"Come and get it, pal."

Woof trotted past her and claimed his prize from a piece of butcher paper. "Better than bird's legs," Kole told the dog, who brushed against the legs of Heather's jeans as he headed for the great outdoors.

"I don't have bird's legs."

"Who said anything about you?"A match flared, briefly illuminating his angular face, full lips hinting at a smirk. He lit a kerosene lamp, which cast a yellow glow when he fit the glass chimney in place. Beside it on a small wooden table was the box he'd brought in, sprouting the paper he'd ripped, a loaf of French bread, bottled water.

Sustenance for his prisoner, she decided.

He pulled a ladderback chair away from the table. "Have a seat."

"So . . . so this is where you live?" Wide-eyed in the dim light, she found the seat by feel as she surveyed the rustic cabin, taking in the stone fireplace, the woodstove, the iron bedstead in the corner. She folded her arms around herself against the chill, tucking her hands inside her camel-hair blazer. "Year round?"

"I don't get out much in the winter." He pulled two pieces of firewood from a box on the hearth and started laying a fire. "Or summer, for that matter. Is this the kind of ambiance you had in mind?"

"I would never have found this on my own. You could take me back to the bar, and I certainly wouldn't be able to find my way here again. Never. I wouldn't even try."

"Is that so?" He eyed her over his shoulder. "You seem pretty resourceful to me."

"I probably seem pretty reckless to you, too, but I'm really not. I was just trying to locate your, um . . ."

"Hideout," he supplied again.

"Studio. Shop, or whatever. I thought I had all the bases covered, and I didn't intend to—"

"I don't play games, Heather."

"You don't play baseball. Basketball was your game. Probably still is. I'll bet you have a hoop out here somewhere."

He sat back on his haunches, eyed her for a moment. Slowly he reached for another piece of firewood. "Yeah, us Indians are real big on hoops and baskets."

"I don't know about us, but—yikes!"

An orange cat had dropped from the rafters into her lap.

Kole laughed as he tucked the butcher paper into the firewood and set it aflame.

"How many animals do you have here?"

"Just the three of us." He brushed his hands on the legs of his jeans as he stood. "And the reporter makes four."

"I'm not a reporter."

He turned from the fire to stare through her, implacably showing her how little her protests impressed him. She stroked his cat and met his gaze, letting him see how little his doubts disturbed her. She had her own upper hand. Knowledge was power.

"The privy's out back," he told her finally. "And there's plenty of water, but no electricity. Whatever your story is, this is the perfect setting, right? Too bad you left your camera behind."

She smiled down at the purring cat. "Maybe we'll get it later, after we talk and you realize that I'm not really that bad."

"I can see that you're not half bad." He stripped off his denim jacket and dropped it over the arm of a tattered recliner near the hearth. "We don't have to talk. After you tell me what it is you want from me, the less you say, the better. All it takes is one lie to set the mood." He wagged a finger at her. "But make it a good one, worth saving up for. I've been holed up so long I've started eyeing the cat."

"I have a feeling you wouldn't hurt her, either."

"I can't get her to lie to me. She's too damn honest to please me." He dragged another chair across the plank floor—this one a kitchen chair with vinyl back and seat—spun it on one leg, and straddled it, leaning over the back, his face inches from hers. "So, who are you, Heather Reardon? That is your real name, isn't it?"

"Yes."

"I thought so. Doesn't do a thing for me, so it must be truth. What do you want from me?"

"A story."

"Mmm, a little tingle." Smiling, he rubbed his chest, caressing the shoe logo on his T-shirt. "Half-truth mostly leaves me cold, but there's promise in the omission." He leaned closer. "Come on, honey, do me one better. Who sent you?"

"No one. I came on my own. I've been looking for you for a long time."

"Why?"

"Because you don't want to be found, and that makes your story even more interesting—the fact that you're not dying to tell it." She offered a sympathetic smile. "I know who you are, Kole."

"*Kola.*"

"Kole."

He lifted one eyebrow, his dark eyes establishing his distance. "You haven't done your homework as well as you think. I'm already disappointed, Heather."

"*Kola* means friend."

"Yeah, well, that's me. So how about a little exposure?" He pinned her to her seat with a cold stare as he rose to his feet, still straddling his chair. Quickly he unbuckled his belt, unbuttoned his jeans, and peeled them over his right hip. She glanced down. *Kola* was tattooed over the ridge of his hipbone. "In case they find my body in a ditch somewhere, they won't have any excuse for cutting off my hands."

She met his challenge with her eyes. His mother, a founding member of the Indian movement, had supposedly died of exposure somewhere out on the Plains. Claims that the authorities had robbed the body of hands were widely denied, then muddied with counterclaims. The general public had paid little attention, but Heather knew about the incident from her research. Clearly he assumed that she knew, which also clearly made her suspect. Anyone who knew about him and wasn't with him was surely against him. He assumed he knew all his friends.

How different he was from his former partner in protest, the now semifamous Barry Wilson. How contrary were their circumstances. She had to be careful how she presented herself, for Kole had every reason to suspect anyone who had any interest in the man he had been ten years ago.

But he laughed as he buttoned his pants. "How long have you been in the news business, Heather? Seems like you've gone to a lot of trouble to track down a story that's missing the key elements of mass appeal. No corpse, no celebrity, no big money, and no sex." He sat down again, smiling. "Yet."

"You have a story, and I want to tell it."

"I don't think your world's going to be too interested in the story of a reclusive Indian flute maker, which is who I am. But go ahead and report on me. Debunk, demystify, and otherwise do me down and dirty. Whatever juices you up, lady."

"Kole Kills Crow has a story."

"Kole Kills Crow has been dead for years."

"And I'm not out to expose him or do anything to hurt him."

"I'm sure he'd be relieved to hear that. I'll send him a smoke signal, soon as you tell me exactly who it is he wouldn't have to worry about if he was still in a position to give a damn."

She gave a tight smile. "So you know him."

"*Knew* him," he amended as he pushed himself off the chair. A step back gave him refuge in shadows. "Knew him as well as anybody knew him. I was with him at the end."

"When his wife died?" Her question only gave him slight pause as he turned his attention to a wall shelf. She dropped her tone a notch. "Or when he gave his baby away."

"Both. I was there both times." He came away from the shelf with a carving knife, eyed her for a moment, then snatched the loaf of French bread from the box on the table. "What do you know about the baby?"

She drew a deep breath as the cat leaped from her lap to the table. Her connection to Savannah was her calling card, but it had to be the closest possible connection. It had to be above reproach.

"She's a beautiful little girl," Heather said. "Almost seven years old. The man she calls Daddy is really her uncle Clay, Savannah's new husband." She looked for some change in his expression, but he seemed completely intent on slicing bread. Quietly she added, "She looks just like her real daddy."

He flashed her a smile as the cat crept close to investigate another butcher paper package in the grocery box. "I hope you like it here, Heather. You might be stuck here for a while."

"How long is a while?"

"How long does it take for a seven-year-old to grow up? I promised Kole I'd never let anyone bother that little girl." He took out the package that interested the cat, tore into it, let the cat sniff the chunk of yellow cheese. "You want some of this, you little sneak?"

"I'm her godmother."

"What the hell is a *god*mother?" He sliced into the cheese, gave the cat a piece, then shooed it off the table. "God gave her a mother, and then He took her mother away. So I gave her a different mother."

"A wonderful—"

"I gave her a mother who was so far removed from my world that no one would ever link her back to Kole Kills Crow. I gave her to a woman I trusted."

"I know. She's—"

He wagged his head as he continued with his slicing. "I can't believe she'd tell somebody like you."

"What do you mean, 'somebody like me'? You don't know anything about me. And you're not going to know anything as long as you refuse to listen."

"I'm listening." He set the knife on the far side of the table, reclaimed his seat, looked her in the eye. "The part of me that isn't eyes and nose is all ears."

"Claudia is my godchild. Savannah is my best friend."

"Then obviously she's no longer my friend."

"She didn't tell me where you are." When the stony look in his eyes didn't waver, she pleaded, "How could she? She doesn't know. And if she did know, she would never tell me. She would never tell anyone. You know that's true."

"Because you say so?"

"You trusted her with a life you value more than your own."

"That ain't sayin' much, though, is it? I have no life."

"Then let me tell your story posthumously."

Even his smile had turned cold. "Make it a novel. Then you can say anything you want."

"I'm a journalist," she insisted. "I don't write fiction."

"Beautiful. Perfectly deadpan. You'll do well in Indian country with that kind of humor." He snapped his fingers. "Damn. I'll bet you left your paper and pencil behind in the car."

"I brought a laptop, along with an extra battery."

"That sounds kinky. Like I said, whatever turns you on. You keep pushing the right buttons, honey, I'll give you plenty to write about."

He lifted one corner of his mouth, his eyes suddenly flashing unexpected delight. "The kind of stuff that really sells."

"I believe in the truth."

"I'll just bet you do." He slapped a slice of cheese on a slice of bread. "Help yourself here. I believe in sharing. How did you find me?"

"I followed a trail you didn't know you left. Savannah had very little to do with it. The clues she gave were given unwittingly."

"Because she trusted you?" he asked, eyeing her as he brought the food to his mouth.

"I didn't exactly . . ." She hadn't asked about Kole straight out, but she'd noticed a postmark on an envelope that had come to Savannah through the art dealer who handled Kola's work. "She trusts me because she knows me well. And I didn't track you down on a whim. I've been interested in you for a long time. Since before you went to prison."

"You must've been about twelve then."

"I'm older than Savannah," she claimed, but his dubious look prompted her to add, "a little bit. But I was interested in you before I met her. I've always been fascinated with the American Indian Movement and all its offshoots." She watched him tear off a hearty bite of crusty bread. "And so little has been written about it."

"What are you talkin' about?" He had to chew a bit before he could go on, gesticulating with his free hand. "People like you keep getting the scoop from the ones who've suddenly developed a need to run bare-assed through every bookstore in the country. I'm waiting for Wilson to take a shot at it."

"I've already interviewed Barry Wilson." Oh yes, she had the upper hand, but the captive could ill afford to sound too smug. She tried for an artless shrug. "Interesting man."

"He is that."

"He talks about Kole Kills Crow the same way you do. As though he were dead."

"Must be true, then." He swallowed hard. "When did you talk to him?"

"I flew out to California a couple of weeks ago. He's got a part in a new movie with Mel Gibson, so I got to go on the set." She smiled as she eyed the bread and cheese he'd sliced, but she kept her hands tucked in at her sides. "I interviewed Mel, too. Very nice man. Very funny."

"Good actor, too, just like my buddy Barry." He reached for more bread. "You need something to wash this down with?"

Heather had still made no move toward the food, and now the cat had jumped back into her lap. She stroked her new ally into settling down and showing Kole how likable his guest was.

"I didn't tell Wilson this, but you're the real reason I interviewed him. I'm very good at finding a worthwhile story and then getting to the heart of it. You're the heart of this story. What makes it exciting to me is that very few people know that." She smiled. He was reaching for the bottled water, looking at her as though she'd just turned down steak in favor of hamburger. "Maybe nobody else knows."

"Maybe nobody else gives a damn."

"Maybe not. Which gives me a purpose, doesn't it? It's up to me to write the story in a way that persuades people to give a damn."

He lifted the bottle in salute to her. "Baby, you were born too late."

"I don't think so. I've made quite a name for myself writing stories that speak to the American social conscience. Granted, it's not as easy a sell as celebrity crime, but that just doesn't—how did you put it? Juice me up?" She watched his Adam's apple bob as he drained half the bottle in long, slow gulps. "By the way, I don't answer to 'baby.' "

He tried to swallow reaction and water at once and nearly choked. His eyes blamed her for it as he wiped his mouth with the back of his hand. "You will if you get hungry enough," he said after his throat was clear. "You sure you don't want any of this? You never know when you might get fed around here."

"Your cat looks pretty well fed," she said, stroking affectionately.

"She's an excellent hunter."

"So am I." Heather looked up from her ardent stroking to find Kole leaning over the back of his chair, his face closer to hers than she'd anticipated. "I found you, didn't I?" She hadn't meant to whisper, but that was how it came out.

"Let the feeding frenzy begin," he whispered back as he braced his left elbow on the back of the chair and cupped her face in his right hand.

His eyes were hard, hungry, resolute. She saw his kiss coming, but those eyes mesmerized her. She didn't close hers until his lips covered her mouth, stealing her breath along with her senses. Good Lord, he was as demanding and as deft and as delicious as she'd imagined when she was a green girl watching him make news. His tongue tasted of beer and bread, but better, bolder, spiced with the zest of his masculinity. She sampled it with wonder, even as she stanched the urge to reach for him and take more than a sample. She kept her hands on the cat.

Kole came up smiling. "Your lyin' lips taste very sweet."

"I haven't lied to you," she said in a voice that was remarkably steady, considering she didn't know where her next breath would be coming from.

"You said you weren't hungry."

"You're misquoting me." She met his amused gaze. "Something I promise never to do to you."

"Promises don't faze me, honey. I inherited a pretty good immunity to promises."

"And I'm allergic to 'honey.' "

He drew back with a laugh. "Reporters always did bring out the smart-ass in me."

"Not always," she recalled. "But that was the role you generally played, wasn't it? You were the tough guy. Wilson was the philosopher. Still, you let your guard down once in a while, and so did he. When that happened, it was pretty clear that you believed in the cause, while Barry Wilson believed in Barry Wilson."

"How'd you come up with that?"

"Short of checking in men's drawers, I really *do* do my homework."

"Good girl. If I had a red pencil, I'd give you an A." He pushed himself off the chair and turned to clean up the bread and cheese. "But you won't be taking your report card home for a while."

"I've been looking for you for a long time. Why would I want to go home now?" She reached for a slice of cheese, again politely shaking off his added offer of bread. "I wouldn't mind going back to the lodge, though. I don't see an extra bed here."

"What you see is exactly what I've got. Do you prefer one side over the other?"

"I prefer, um . . ." She shared her cheese with the cat as she glanced from the bed to the recliner to the door.

"Exactly what I've got."

She assessed him with a frank look. "If I decide to leave, you're not going to stop me."

"Who says?"

"I know you. Savannah and I were roommates for several years. We followed you in the news. That time you took over the post office, she said there was nothing to worry about because you would not harm those people."

He twirled the bread in its plastic sack, tied off the end, then speared it into the box and walked away from her, putting his back between her and the stone hearth. Hands low on his hips, he watched the crackling fire. When he finally spoke, she had to strain to hear him.

"We occupied a store. Just because they had a few mailboxes and sold stamps, they call it a post office."

"But you let the people go."

"Yeah, well, we held them for a while."

"That's not what most of them said," she recalled. "In their initial statements they said they were free to go, but they were more afraid of the police outside than the protesters inside. Later one of them changed her story."

"Terrorists." He grabbed an iron poker and used it to reposition the burning logs. "The governor of South Dakota called us terrorists. I think that's the preferred term nowadays."

"Misapplied in this instance." Drawn to the fire, the cat bounded to the floor. Heather felt the same pull, but she remained in the chair, a soft, sympathetic voice in the shadows. "The woman only changed her story after hours of questioning."

"Poor, simple Verna was in the wrong place at the wrong time."

"Were the hostages volunteers?"

He gave a dry chuckle, glancing over his shoulder before he set the poker aside. "Is that what you are? A volunteer?"

"I'm not afraid of you. According to Savannah, you wouldn't hurt a fly."

"See, now that's how much she knows about me," he said lightly as he added more wood to the fire. "I know exactly how long it takes to smother a fly under a cup. I know how many appendages you can rip off a fly before it dies. You spend some time behind bars, you learn these things." He stepped to one side, rubbing his hands over the side seams of his jeans. Firelight burnished his strong profile, flames dancing in his eye. "Savannah remembers a boy she knew once," he reflected absently.

"What about your brother, Clay?"

"My half brother." He retraced his steps, boot heels scraping the plank floor, then he straddled the other chair and confronted her across its tattered back, nose to nose. "What about him? You were roommates with him, too?"

"No, but I've met him. He's another one who thinks you're innocent."

"I pled not guilty. I never said I was innocent." Gripping the backrest he started out of the chair, then sat back down again, suddenly agitated. "When did you last see Clay?"

"A couple of months ago." She smiled. "They're all fine. Clay and Savannah and little Claudia—they're all doing just fine."

"I didn't ask."

"For the record, you didn't ask. Not with words, anyway."

"You know what? Sometimes when I trap a fly, the buzzing starts to annoy me. Then I'm liable to squash the damn thing."

"Okay, so you're a big fly killer."

"They say that's not all."

She met his challenging gaze with a nod. "Did you know him? The man who was killed in prison?"

"Sure, I knew him. First thing you learn is there's some security in numbers, and you mainly stick with your own kind."

"He was Absaroka."

"Very good," he acknowledged with a nod. "More popularly known as Crow, enemy of the Sioux. Nice little piece of irony there."

"That your name is Kills Crow," she said. "No one really believes you killed him."

"Really." He smiled as though he were indulging a roseate child. "Outside Indian country or the state of South Dakota, you can probably count on one hand the number of people who've formed any kind of opinion on the matter."

"You only had a few months left to serve," she reminded him. "Your escape is what they point to as proof of your guilt."

"I was standing two feet away from Daryl when they did him. They never found the gun, but they know damn well he wasn't shot at close range. There were plenty of witnesses, but they're all cons." He lifted one shoulder. "They hit the wrong man. That was the scuttle-butt."

"Someone was trying to kill you?"

The answer in his haunted eyes chilled her.

"Why?" she asked.

"Who the hell knows?" Abruptly he quit the chair. "Are you sure you're not hungry? I don't want you saying I made you go to bed hungry."

It seemed foolish to think she could hurt his feelings by refusing his food, but it was a sweet notion all the same. She reached into the grocery box. "Do you have any butter for the bread?"

He laughed. "I would have to kidnap a fussy eater."

He found her a jar of peanut butter. She slathered it on the bread, remarking that it reminded her of late-night snacks in the dorm kitchen in college. "My personal favorite was peanut butter and jelly on Ritz crackers."

He folded his arms and watched her eat. She had the feeling she wasn't supposed to waste anything.

"Your mother was involved with the movement, too, wasn't she?"

His bemused look turned into a hard glare.

"Okay, you start. What would you like to talk about?" She sucked peanut butter from her thumb. "It's just the two of us in this little cabin. We have to talk about something."

"You can give me a small break anytime now."

She noticed another table, tucked in the corner between a window and the fireplace. His workbench. "How about your flutes?" She moved toward the table as she finished off her bread. "Flute making. I'd love to know what goes into the making of such a beautiful . . ." Four of the wooden instruments lay side by side in a cloth-lined tray. She touched the open beak of the one that was carved in the shape of a long, slender bird. "May I?"

He nodded, watching her closely as she fit the wooden tube to her lips. It took her several tries to get a sound out of it. "So I skipped a lot of music lessons when I was a kid," she confessed as she experimented with finger placements on the holes.

"What did you play?"

"Violin. I wanted to play the drums, but according to my mother, real ladies don't drum."

"She's right," he said, moving behind her. "Drumming is a man thing."

She caught his eye over her shoulder as his arms came around her. "Do ladies play the flute?"

"I don't know much about ladies. I know *you* don't play the flute." He placed the index and middle fingers of her left hand over the first two holes. "Flute playing is a man thing, too, but women have gotten pushy with it, like everything else." He covered her right hand with his, placing three fingers on the remaining three holes, then lifting the middle one. "Now blow."

She lipped the bullet-shaped mouthpiece as though she planned to suck on it.

"Whoa, let's try a little subtlety, woman. This is sensitive equipment. Curl your lips back a little bit, like you've never done it before and you're not sure you want to. Look at me." He demonstrated, drawing his lips around his teeth. "Only not that much. Like maybe you'd sip through a straw."

"Do I have to swallow?"

"Damn, you're sassy." Delight danced in his eyes. "You can't slobber too much. This one's already sold. We're just breakin' it in gently. Try it now."

He lifted her fingers, pressed them down, and she blew until she thought she was probably blue in the face. She managed to produce a dolorous tweedle.

"You're trying too hard." He laughed when she gave up, gasping. "You're allowed to breathe."

She turned the instrument over to him for a real demonstration. "What do women get to play?"

"Heartstrings."

"Can I quote you?"

"Hell, no, you'll ruin my business. I sell these to women all the time. I figure they're buying them as gifts. Or hints." He played a quick scale. "They're used for courting. The music is seductive."

He played a slow, soft, drifting melody that reminded her of a birdsong in a canyon, a warm breeze, the taste of an unexpected kiss. When he was finished, the music lingered. She could barely move, barely breathe, even though she was allowed. She dreaded breaking the spell, hesitated to lift her gaze from the magic fingers, which were still now, blunt tips resting lightly over the five holes. The lower hand stirred, stroked the length of the instrument from its stops to its carved head.

He smiled when she finally looked up. "You hear that sound around the camp at night, you know there's some guy out there who's feeling a little horny."

"It's a haunting sound."

"It's a haunted feeling."

Slow down, she told her galloping heart as she stepped away, looking for something safe, anything innocent. Seizing upon the peanut butter, she spun the cap off, scooped, licked her finger. She'd taken some foolish chances before, but emotionally she always, *always* had the upper hand. She could feel him watching her, sense his amusement.

"What are you going to do with me now? I mean, you can't just . . ." She shrugged, took another casual lick. "You really should take me back to the lodge. I'm sorry for following you. It was foolish. It was downright rude." Another lick, a sheepish smile. "I didn't come here to make trouble for you. You really should let me go."

"There's the door."

"And the darkness beyond, and the woods, and the unmarked trails that pass for roads. Wolves, bears, snakes." She stood her ground as he approached her, a wolfish gleam in his eyes. "But am I any safer with you?"

"You know me. I wouldn't hurt a fly." He closed his hand around hers, drew her buttery finger into his mouth and slowly sucked it clean. His breath cooled her wet finger as he finished off the underside with his tongue. She knew then what a flute must feel like on the inside as his electrifying breath rushed through it, end to end.

He smiled into her eyes. "But neither would I let one go when she's such a great source of entertainment."

"I'm not going to sleep with you," she blurted out.

His laughter hit her in the face, the backwash of her own foolishness. He walked away. "I'm not going to stay awake with you," he told her as he flipped open the lid of an old steamer trunk. "I generally sleep in the middle, but I'm willing to compromise since you're more or less a guest."

"I'll take the chair."

"Suit yourself." He tossed her an army blanket. "You wanna go outside first, or should I?"

"Outside?" She caught the flashlight he tossed her. "Oh, that's right, outside. Is the wolf, um, dog—"

"Interested in your ass? I don't think so." He caught her scowl, pitched her a grin. "You need help?"

She pushed the door open, stepped outside, then stuck her head back in. "Is it directly behind . . . ?"

"*Directly* behind."

"Well, it's dark out here."

"You're a big girl, now, you'll find it. Just reach back."

She slammed the door. It wasn't so much the dark that worried her as the wildlife. She'd run into a rattlesnake in a gas station restroom in Arizona and a black bear in Glacier. She had a healthy respect for a wild animal's survival instincts.

She nearly jumped out of her skin when her light flashed on a pair of glowing eyes.

"W-woof?"

The dog answered. Relief. Nice dog. Good dog. It wasn't every dog that could say his own name. He escorted her to the privy, stood guard while she used it, then shepherded her back again. Very considerate dog.

At the cabin door she called out, "Can Woof come inside?"

"You wanna clean up after him?"

"Sorry, boy," she whispered. "You're such a gentleman, I naturally assumed . . ."

Kole appeared at the door. "The advantage to an outhouse is that people don't usually take so long," he grumbled as they crossed paths over the threshold.

"Well, excuse me, but I couldn't see my watch."

It surprised her to discover a basin of clean water, a towel, and soap on the table where moments ago the grocery box had been. Put there for her use, she decided. Even more surprising, the water was warm. She looked up to find a cast iron kettle on the hearth and something white draped over the back of the recliner. A nightgown? He had put out a nightgown for her?

Close. It was a long thermal shirt, which was preferable to sleeping in her clothes. She changed quickly and made her bed in the chair in front of the fire, which would have been fine if it actually reclined. All it did was tip back a little. The seat sagged. The springs were sprung.

"You gonna be all right there?" Kole asked when he returned.

"Fine, yes."

She watched the fire and listened to the water trickle into the basin, the boots fall to the floor, followed by the belt buckle. The light dimmed, and still she stared at the fire. Her feet were cold. Sleep would not come easily in this lumpy chair. She wondered if her breathing sounded as loud as his did. She wondered if he snored.

She wondered if *she* snored.

It was a small cabin, and he wasn't far away. Hissing. No, that was the fire. Grinding his teeth. No, that was outside, probably the dog.

The fire popped. Her feet were getting hot.

The chair groaned with the slightest shift of her body, as though she weighed a ton. The bed squealed. The chair squawked. The two pieces of furniture carried on this conversation until Kole threw off his blankets.

"You take the bed. You're making so damn much noise, I can't get to sleep."

Heather jackknifed in the chair. "I haven't made a peep, not one peep, even though it's impossible to get comfortable in this chair."

"*Peep* is about the only sound you haven't made. I'm gonna call you Wheezie." He started up. "Get over here."

"Stay there," she ordered as she padded across the floor, dragging her blanket like a three-year-old. "I'll share the bed with you. It's not that I'm being prudish or anything. I'm used to having a bed to myself, and I toss and turn a lot, and I just don't want to punch you in my sleep."

"Damn right you don't, because I'm liable to retaliate in *my* sleep." He gave her his only pillow as they tucked themselves in quite separately, back to back. "You shut up, settle down, stay on your side. I'll stay on mine, and we'll get along fine."

"In our *sleep*." She speared her arm beneath the pillow, plumped it up, and rested her head. She had the fireside view. That was nice. So was his bare chest, she recalled. Strong, smooth, firm. Was that a bare butt just behind hers? Behind her behind? She smiled in the dark.

He'd given her his pillow. He wasn't half as tough as he made out. She was going to get her story for sure.

She sighed. "What are we going to do tomorrow?"

He vaulted out of bed. She went still, thinking he'd be back momentarily. When that didn't happen, she sat up. He'd thrown a shirt on, and he was already pulling on his boots. And his butt was not bare. Before she could form a question, he was out the door. By the time her feet hit the floor, he was revving up his truck. When she got to the door, the headlights arced across her face.

"Was it something I said?" she called out to his red taillights. "Don't leave me alone out here in the middle of . . ."

The engine's roar dwindled to a distant hum.

She looked down to find Woof sitting at her feet. ". . . God's country."

3

Do you want to come in?" Heather asked Woof.

The dog declined. The cat deserted her, too, scooting past her bare legs to escape into the woods before she could get the door closed.

"Will you guys stay close by?" she called out to the darkness. She was pretty sure she heard the dog rustling around out there, but it could have been a bear for all she really knew. She couldn't find any way to lock the door, so she stuck her head outside again. "Woof? You can have the whole bed if you want. I'll take the floor."

The dog trotted around the corner carrying his bone and settled next to the planking that served as a front step.

"Thank you," she breathed. "You're my new hero. You have my permission to kill anything that moves."

She returned to Kole's bed and wrapped herself in his blankets with the warmth and the scent of his body. Curiously comforting, familiar. Maybe not so curious, since it was all she had of human company there in the middle of unbounded and unfamiliar woods. But since she'd never seen the man in the flesh before tonight, it felt slightly smutty and sneaky to be taking comfort from the smell of his skin. She liked it. Through the smoke, sweat, and soap, those pheromones were hitting the mark. And that *was* curious. Yes, she had her fantasies, but in practice she'd always been fairly sensible, maybe even a little cynical about physical attraction and pheromones. But something sure was working on her.

Now what? A sensible woman ought to be terrified. She'd written a story about a woman who had been kidnapped, hidden away in the desert, and left alone for days at a time. Your mind plays wild tricks on you, the woman had said.

Indeed. Heather's tricky imagination was telling her she'd been captured and deserted by the object of her own obsession. A crazy woman's dream come true. Bye-bye to good sense. After all, she was the stalker here. *She* had followed *him*. She'd gotten herself lost. She'd threatened his security. She'd tracked him down, blown her chance at the story like some overeager neophyte, and she'd driven the man out of his home, all in one night.

He wouldn't be gone long. He was trying to make a point with this stunt. She could have the pillow, but there would be no pillow talk.

Point taken, Kole. You can come back anytime now.

In the meantime she might as well try to forget where she was and get some sleep. He wasn't about to go off and forget about her. She felt as though she'd known him for years, and in many ways, she had.

She had actually known more than Savannah did about his mother's involvement with the American Indian activists who had gained attention for a segment of the population largely forgotten by mainstream America until the 1960s and '70s. Indians had been both demonized and romanticized in twentieth-century American lore, but it had taken the protest culture of the '60s to bring them to the fore as a group of Americans who had long been denied their land, their heritage, and their basic civil rights.

She knew that Kole's mother, Lana Kills Crow, had become a martyr to the Native American cause after the FBI had written off her death as an accident. Savannah had said that Kole wouldn't talk about it, and it was not right to speculate about personal things, but Heather always did her homework. She knew all about his mother's political activities with regard to Indian rights, her disputes with everyone from the Army Corps of Engineers to the rural electric company, her disappearance, the shoddy investigation when the body was found, the incredible theory that the victim had died of exposure when her skull had been shattered like the windshield of a car.

Kole had been living with his white father's family in Wyoming at the time of his mother's death. He'd done a hitch in the army before heading off to the University of Minnesota, where he'd hooked up with Barry Wilson, a charismatic college teacher whose roots in the urban American Indian community had blossomed into a full-blown movement.

Students like Kole, born on an impoverished reservation beyond even the fringe of mainstream American society, found themselves at the center of a cause. The main focus of their argument with government at all levels had been treaty rights. Among their assertions was the view that claims of eminent domain could not rightfully be applied on Indian reservations.

The American social conscience had waxed and waned from Lana Kills Crow's time through Kole's, but Heather firmly believed that people were just as hungry for heroes as they ever had been, and there was something intrinsically noble about the modern American Indian warrior.

Okay, maybe that was her college paper—"Arthurian Legend and Lakota Sioux Myth"—coming into play. She had to admit, she'd had to do some fancy academic tap-dancing to make that connection, but it had seemed pretty clever at the time. Journalism had been her forte, not literature. But she'd always been less interested in the events in the news than in the people behind them, and she'd been known to go well out of her way to get the story.

Somewhere beyond what she hoped were strong cabin walls, an owl reminded her how far out of everyone's way she was now. Everyone but Woof. She could still hear those canine teeth working on that bone.

She had a friend.

◆　◆　◆

Kole returned at daybreak.

It felt strange to be stepping over the dog and sneaking into the house, trying not to awaken a sleeping woman. It had been a long time since he'd come home to a woman, and he shouldn't be doing it now. He should not have brought her there. He should never have spoken to her at all—didn't know what he was thinking, dancing her around the Cheap Shot like some redneck showoff. Kissing her had been pure insanity. And now here he was, creeping up on a lump in his bed with a lump in his pants, noticing the rich luster of silky, light brown hair spilled across his pillow and letting his imagination tunnel into his blankets.

Damn, he should have just left her in the woods with her rental car, put a good scare into her. He could have sent somebody to collect her this morning, and he'd never have to see her again.

He shouldn't be seeing her now.

But she was a link. She was a hand reaching through the fog, a connection to people and places he was missing pretty badly of late, missing because he'd loosened his grip on obscurity. Losing his grip kinda left a guy with a free hand, and then here came this woman's hand, popping out of that fog. So what was a guy to do but grab her and haul her in for the night?

And then take off running when she got so close he couldn't breathe without drawing her under his skin, where no one was safe. Including him. Damn fool move. Had he forgotten that there was no place left to run? First off, he'd advise the woman to shut up about Savannah and Clay and the baby. Talk about anything else, but not them. He needed to find out what she was really up to, but he didn't need to open up *that* closet. If she got near the door, he'd just have to chase her away, even though she'd been with them recently and knew what they were doing and how they looked and what the baby was like now.

Damn his hide, if he kept this woman around, sooner or later he'd lose his grip in the worst way possible and beg her to tell him everything she knew. Awash in wishes, he'd go under unless he focused on something else.

Like the uncomplicated fact that a good-looking woman had crawled into his bed.

The cat had scampered in behind him, so he put some chow in a dish to keep her from spoiling the near-silence with her mewling. Then he carefully added wood to the firebox to chase away the morning chill.

He still hadn't figured out what he was going to do with his unexpected guest. He sat down in the willow chair close to the bed. He was thinking that just watching her sleep the morning away would be a novel pleasure. When she woke up, she'd probably start talking again. She sure liked to talk. Maybe he'd try feeding her. Then he could hike her down to the lake and let her paddle a canoe until she was too tired to think, and then he'd take another shot at discovering the real reason she'd gone to considerable trouble to dig him up.

He found it a little disconcerting to watch her open her eyes, unguarded and unperturbed, as though she were accustomed to seeing his face first thing in the morning. Her sleepy smile disturbed him deep down in his gut, as did her easy greeting.

"I knew you'd be back."

He managed to shrug off her complacency. "This is where I live."

"Exactly." Her pale arms emerged from his blankets for a languorous stretch. "Where else would you go? I wasn't a bit worried."

"I could tell that from the way you were snoring."

"Do I snore?" She propped herself up on one elbow and plowed her profusion of hair back with her fingers. "I don't, do I?"

"Haven't you ever wondered why you can't keep a boyfriend?" He rose from the chair. "Hungry?"

"Are you kidding? This early?" She tossed the blankets back and sat up, swinging her legs over the side of the bed as she glanced toward the window, looking for light. There wasn't much. "It is morning, isn't it?"

"This is what the forest people call morning." And her short but shapely legs were what he would call not half bad.

"Not exactly light," she observed. "More like, less dark than it was last night. I guess I'm not much of a forest person. I like mountains and beaches a lot."

"You came to the wrong place for mountains and beaches."

"Is it the right place for coffee? Coffee brightens me up no matter how dark it is outside. Coffee and . . ." She adjusted his shirt over her hips and tugged at the hem. "I suppose a bath is out of the question."

"Not completely. There's a washstand outside, right next to the rain barrel. You could probably squeeze your whole butt in, let your legs dangle over the side. Soap's out there, too." He handed her a towel, frayed but clean. "Call me if you get stuck. I'll make coffee, and then we'll scare up some breakfast."

"How does one 'scare up' breakfast?"

"There's a mirror right next to the soap."

She made a face. For the first time since he'd met her at the Cheap Shot Saloon, he caught himself truly feeling his own smile as he watched her grab her pants and head outside to use his facilities. She wasn't going to win any beauty contest, but she was damn cute. The kind Wilson used to call "a button." Never failed, Wilson's next line was always, "Where there's a button, there's a hole."

How plentiful—and willing—the women had been in those days. The loosely organized group of revolutionaries had been living on the edge, pushing the limits to make their stand, defying laws and boundaries in the name of justice, which, for their people, had become an obscure, even an obscene concept in the last hundred years.

But they were warriors again, reclaiming their pride with their freedom. They'd lived from day to day, liberated by their fatalism. Somehow one-night stands with nameless female followers—beauties, buttons, bovines, bitches, depending on the humor of the beholder— had become the norm. Being a renegade had had its privileges and its poisons, and he'd eventually choked on both. A woman had saved him, but salvation hadn't come without a price. Her love for him had been her undoing.

That was his story, and it was personal. The best way a guy could guard his privacy these days was by letting the public have its fantasies. Barry Wilson was a minor celebrity, and Kole Kills Crow was as dead as the movement they'd once championed. Being dead was one way to survive. The chicken-shit way, maybe, but at least it didn't drag anybody else down.

So now what? He dipped water into the speckled blue coffeepot. What was he going to do with this wayward woman hell-bent for raising the dead?

Enjoy her, maybe? She came in the door wearing his shirt and her pants, her face all scrubbed and shiny and framed with bits of wet hair, and he thought, hell, back in the old days there would have been no question. That gleam in her eyes was an invitation, whether she knew it or not.

"Keep an eye on the pot," he grumbled as he caught the door before she could close it. He went outside and dunked his whole head in the cold water, hoping it would wake him up with a clear answer to that nagging question: *So now what?*

It didn't.

When he went back inside, there she was again, handing him his own favorite cup full of the coffee he'd made. Just like she'd been invited over. Or worse, like it was something she did every morning. Where the hell did she get off? She didn't know him, didn't even know where she was. Didn't she realize that her rental car was not parked outside waiting to take her back where she came from?

"You make good coffee, Doris," she said. He raised a challenging eyebrow. She shrugged. "Just an expression. I don't even know who Doris is."

"Barry Wilson used to say that. I don't know who Doris is, either." Nor did he care. Probably somebody else who'd done Wilson's bidding. "Did he have you making the coffee, too?"

"I had coffee with him at a restaurant. I don't think the expression originated with Barry Wilson. It's not even much of an expression." She slipped into the recliner, rested both elbows on one tattered arm, and sipped her coffee. "What do you think of that last movie he was in? The one where he was the hero's New Age shaman sidekick."

"I don't see many movies."

"Have you seen any of *his* movies?"

"Saw the first one. Almost didn't recognize him, but you could really tell it was him by the way he walked."

"The way he swaggered?"

"Every man has his own swagger. Barry's is showy, kinda like a courting grouse. You see some traditional dancers strut like that, but that's the way Barry walks whenever he thinks anybody's watching. Got me into a fight once. Somebody called him a *winkte*." He gave a dry laugh as he pulled a chair close to the woodstove. "I guess they're really watching now."

"What's a *winkte*?"

"A guy who acts womanish."

"Does that offend you?"

"Nearly got my nose broken defending his honor." He studied his coffee. "Truth is, I always admired his style, the way he carried himself. He never looked down."

"He did look back, though."

"Hell, he taught history. You have to look back once in a while or you can't tell where you are. Or where you came from, or *who* you came from."

"You met him when you were a student at the University of Minnesota."

Kole nodded. "Barry was a teaching assistant. I thought he'd go back to it when he was acquitted of all the, uh . . . well, the charges stemming from our infamous last stand in South Dakota." He chuckled as he glanced away. He knew damn well that behind those grass-green eyes was some kind of estrogen-powered recording device, sucking in every word he said. But somehow it didn't bother him. "I was sorry to see him go Hollywood," he mused absently. "Barry Wilson was a hell of a teacher."

"You think he sold out?"

"Sold *me* out? No." Not that he hadn't thought about it during the 854 days he'd spent within prison walls, but he shook his head. "No, he tried to talk me out of it."

"Out of what? Taking the whole rap?"

"That sounds pretty dramatic." The seriousness in her eyes made him laugh. " 'Taking the rap.' You write for the movies, too?"

"I've written a couple of TV scripts."

"No shit? Cops-and-robbers stuff?"

She leaned across the arm of her chair, toward him. Her eyes widened. "Heroic idealist takes the rap for his self-serving partner."

"Only in the movies."

"What I meant was, do you think Wilson sold the movement out by going Hollywood?"

He lifted one shoulder. "I'm sure it pays better than teaching. I heard he got some kind of benefit program going for Indian kids. He's hanging out with the kind of people who know how to raise money for a good cause."

"That's not what your cause was about."

"*Is* about," he said automatically, which gave her cause to toss him a knowing smile. "Okay, you're right. It isn't about charity. Wasn't."

"Warriors don't beg."

"They stand their ground." He chuckled. "Yep, you've been talking to the quotable Mr. Wilson, all right."

"You went to prison so that he would be free to fight the good fight. But he sold out."

"Naw. Barry always had stars in his eyes. When they offer him a place in the night sky, you can't expect him to turn it down. Even if you can't see him with the naked eye, he still gets us some attention once in a while."

"But no real changes."

He shrugged. "That's entertainment."

"Entertainment can help bring about change, and entertainers can be very influential." She sipped her coffee. "Barry says he's moved on. What do you think that means?"

"Didn't you ask him?"

She gave him an innocent look.

"If you're trying for dueling interviews here, you're bound to come up short on this end," he told her. "I'm not Wilson's interpreter."

"Are you his friend, his admirer? Disciple, maybe, or his—"

"I'm not his anything."

"Have you moved on?"

"Does it look like it?" He pushed himself out of the chair and strode to the front window. Damn cat was creeping up the woodpile, stalking a downy woodpecker. "You know, I can already tell we'll get along a lot better if we don't talk much."

"Why?"

He turned from the window as the cat made her move. "Because all you know how to do is ask questions."

"I know how to listen. If I didn't, I wouldn't be able to do what I do."

"Which you're not invited to do here."

"All right, no more questions. Anything you say will be strictly off the record. Any little crumbs you decide to throw my way."

He smiled at the thought of her scrambling for crumbs. "Then you *are* hungry."

"I guess I am. Must be all this fresh air." She sprang from the recliner and surveyed the sideboard that served as his kitchen, the few groceries he'd brought home the previous night still there in the box. "Let the scaring up begin," she declared. "Tell me what to do."

"Take this," he said, handing her a net sack that might have once contained onions. "We're going hunting."

"What's in season?"

"No questions." He tossed her his denim jacket. He figured it would go well with his thermal shirt. "Just carry the sack."

She followed him outside. The sound of her shuffling along behind him in her little thin-soled shoes made him smile. He hoped she had some hiking boots packed in her luggage. If she didn't, she was a damn liar. Hell, even if she did, she was a damn liar. Certainly, backwoods recreation was not the reason she'd come here, and he had to keep reminding himself to be careful. He was beginning to like her a little too much.

He bent to pick up a long, sturdy stick. "It rained last week, so it's mushroom season."

"Some of them are poisonous, aren't they? Can you tell the difference?" She laughed when he gave her the stick and a sidelong glance. "Obviously you can, or we wouldn't be mushroom hunting. You're going to eat these, too, right? Do you depend heavily on wild food? Will we be hunting anything besides mushrooms?"

"That's five questions, and you didn't hardly take a breath." He found another stick and used it to lift a thatch of needles at the base of a tall pine. "Mushrooms might be the only prey you won't scare away."

"And they're easy pickin's," she surmised. "If you know your mushrooms."

He used his stick as a pointer. "Tell me what you think of these."

"Well, they're nice and fat," she judged eagerly as she squatted for a closer inspection. She looked up at him, all innocence. "Are they ripe and ready?"

"Not for a butt like yours, but perfect for a toad."

Her face fell. "Why don't you try one out, then?"

"Good one." He moved on, scratching at the ground like a blind man with a cane. "Here you go." He knelt in a fork of exposed tree roots and lifted a layer of leaf compost. "This is what we're looking for."

"Shall I pick them?" She squatted beside him on the balls of her feet, clutching her net sack. "How many will we need? I don't even know what we're making. I don't want to take too much."

"It's a small sack," he reminded her. He held out his hand for her first harvest. "Break it off higher. You leave some behind, there'll be more for next time."

She tried again, holding up the shorter stem for his inspection. He nodded, careful not to crack a smile. Her enthusiasm went to his head like goofy-gas.

"Are there berries or nuts we could gather, too?"

"Not in that sack." He had to laugh, couldn't help it. "The questions just keep pouring out. You can't help yourself. It's like a baby's drool."

"It's called healthy curiosity. Drooling is something else entirely. Would you like to see me drool?" She flashed him a flirtatious smile. "It'll take more than mushrooms."

"I've been living up here five years now. I can grow some pretty good stuff in the dark." He traded come-on looks with her as he reached for a mushroom. "And I've got better sacks."

"Spare me." She stood up.

He followed suit, towering over her. "Don't tell me you've run out of questions."

"Never. I don't mind sucking on a dry tit, but after a while my jaw gets sore." She plopped the mushroom sack in his hands. "And that's when I give it a rest."

"*Tuale*," he drawled, a Lakota catchall expression. "Nothing gets the blood pumpin' first thing in the morning like a sharp-tongued woman."

Impulsively, she stuck hers out at him.

"And when it's forked like that, it promises twice the tickle." With a jerk of his head, he invited her to follow him back to the cabin. "You wanna see my canoe?"

"Is this one of those things you grow in the dark?"

"Damn, you're a hoot. I'm growing this one in the backyard, honey, in front of God and everybody."

♦ ♦ ♦

They made omelets using the mushrooms and some wild rice he'd gathered and parched himself. Heather had never "fired up" or cooked on a woodstove, so Kole demonstrated the art of making flat-bread in a skillet and turning a perfect fold in an omelet without any sticking or scorching. She seemed impressed. The skillet bread was heavy and filling, but he explained that filling the belly was the point.

"Indian soul food," he called it, and he wondered—silently, for voicing such a question would be rude—whether she'd ever experienced a truly empty belly. If not, she was to be pitied, his mother would say. A person who'd never known real hunger couldn't fully appreciate food.

Not that he would wish hunger on this small woman. His shirt nearly swallowed her up. "Would you like to go down to the lake?" he asked.

"I'd love to." She looked up from her plate. "After you take me back to my car."

"That's right, you need your laptop out of the trunk."

"I'd like to get my clothes, too."

"Are they in the blue suitcase?" He smiled at her puzzled face. "Your stuff's out in the pickup."

"I don't want to leave the car out there on the road, Kole. It's a rental."

"It's on its way back as we speak. You're all checked out of the lodge, too. Express checkout. Credit cards make life so much easier, don't they?"

She swallowed a mouthful of egg, looked around for her purse.

"I haven't taken anything from you except the car, and that's going back to its owner." He shrugged. "And your freedom. I'm not sure just what I'm gonna do about that."

"I'm not worried. You can't keep me here forever."

"I don't know much about *forever*. What I do know is that being with me is likely to be hazardous to your health."

"Do I look scared?"

He considered her face for a moment, the bravado in the set of her jaw, the ridiculous trust in her eyes. Where had she come up with that?

"Do you know what happened to my wife?"

"She was killed in an explosion. The furnace blew up in your house, and she was the only one home," she recited, albeit gently. "There was no evidence of any foul play."

"So they say." He shook his head and gave a sorry smile. "Do you use words like that in your TV scripts? Foul play?" His shoulders quivered. "Sends shivers up my spine to hear you use words like that."

"I don't see how a faulty furnace in a house you lived in—what, six or seven years ago—could be a threat to my health."

"Not only yours but my daughter's. Do you think I gave her away for my sake?" His fork clattered against the tin plate as he shoved his breakfast aside. The memory of putting his crying baby in the arms of their mutual friend burned in his brain. "I didn't think Savannah would ever go back to Wyoming. I thought she'd stay in New York in a fancy penthouse and keep my kid far away from me and anybody connected with me."

"I offered them a place to stay, but she needed to go home. Have you called her since she married—"

"Yeah. Once. She let me know where they were and that my kid was doing good. That's it. That's all I care about."

"Did you talk to—"

"*Nobody else.*" The legs of his chair scraped against the floor as he abruptly pushed back from the table. "I'm a fugitive. Forever is how long I've been on the run. I was beginning to think they'd forgotten about me, that maybe it would be okay if I tried to live like a normal person. Maybe nobody would notice. And then out of the clear blue, here comes a reporter who knows all about me. And she knows where my baby lives." He eyed her speculatively. "Even if you're not *with* them, I don't know if it's them you've been talking to."

"Who?" She met his gaze without flinching, rising slowly from her seat. "Tell me who they are, and I'll tell you if I've spoken with them."

"That's what I'm hoping to find out from you. Who wants me dead?"

"You're a fugitive mainly because you escaped from prison."

"When Daryl Two Horn was killed, I knew I was gonna be next. One way or another I was lookin' at a death sentence, not the five years max the judge gave me. I decided not to hang around." He glanced away. "But I should've kept to myself. I should have left Linda alone."

"Have there been any attempts . . . since your wife was killed?"

He drilled her with another look. "You think I'm bullshittin', don't you? Maybe a little paranoid?"

"Make up your mind, Kole. Either I think it's all in your head, or I'm in on it with *them*." She wagged a finger at him as she stepped around her chair. "Or—try this one out—I came looking for you because I actually admire you. I think you got a bad rap, and I want to help you. What's so funny?"

" 'Bad rap.' " He couldn't help it. She cracked him up. "It's hard to believe anybody who would say that could be too devious. Plus, you're kinda cute for a Hollywood reporter."

"I'm not a Hollywood reporter." She shrugged, even blushed a little. "I hate being called 'cute,' and haven't actually sold any of my screenplays."

"Oh, yeah? Well, maybe *I* can help *you*." He draped an arm over her shoulders. "Most stories are written from the good guy's side. But what if you had a con for a consultant instead of a cop? You could maybe get something interesting going on that laptop of yours."

"You weren't in prison that long."

"Not long enough to suit the state, but it was long enough to get the routine down, believe me."

She nodded, absently claiming a scrap of skillet bread from his plate and taking a nibble. "This was delicious. I don't usually eat much breakfast."

"Around here we eat good twice a day, usually. Nobody skips meals, and I don't get any complaints about the cooking. I hope you like fish." Self-consciously he withdrew his arm. "You'll eat fish, like it or not."

"I love fish." She busied herself with gathering their plates. "You're a pretty gracious host for a kidnapper."

"You've been kidnapped before, have you?"

She smiled. "I'm an easy keeper."

"What do you do to earn your keep?" He stepped closer, trapping her gaze as he touched the corner of her smile with one finger and made it vanish. "What are you good for, Heather? Besides making up stories."

"They're good stories. You'll like them."

"If I don't . . ." He drew his finger down to the crease in her neck, then traced it slowly from one side of her neck to the other as he lowered his head to bestow an unplanned, unwise, uncontested kiss.

◆ ◆ ◆

Before they struck out for the lake, he unloaded her belongings from the pickup and brought them inside—suitcase, briefcase, even the damn computer. He figured any self-respecting kidnapper would probably make the captive do the carting, but he was hardly self-respecting at this point. He'd gone off the deep end, judgment-wise.

Might as well go fishing.

He liked having her follow him through the woods. She had put on a fancy pair of tennis shoes, so he got a kick out of lengthening his stride and listening to her scramble to keep up. Like the moss carpet and the dense vegetation, her struggle kept her quiet. Temporarily.

"The thing is," she said suddenly between a huff and a puff, "I think you were absolutely right to protest that waste dump deal. And then the claim to the land that—"

"What thing?" He glanced back, unable to squelch his amusement. "Where did that come from?"

"We were talking about . . . back at the house, you were saying . . ." She ducked a pine branch, skidded down a needle-sown slope and caught herself on a lichen-decked rock, missing no more than a beat or two in her chatter. "I guess I was just thinking about it. The reason you ultimately destroyed all that government equipment that you . . ."

He paused, turned, waiting. He'd thought about ways the past might catch up with him again, the sound of it, the scent, what shape it would take. There would be sirens and shouting, guns and hand-cuffs, the stink of sweat and the taste of blood.

Surely it would not wear a woman's face.

"Barry Wilson says you really were acting on your own," she was saying. "He called you a *renegade* renegade, but he asked me not to quote him on that." She chuckled. "Of course, he fully expects me to."

"We're going fishing," he said woodenly. They'd reached the lake. He pushed a low spruce branch, holding the door open between yellow-green woods and the lake that mirrored its changing colors. "And I fully expect you to fish."

"That's . . . sort of what I'm doing."

"You can't bait me." He turned on her. "I don't give a good god-damn what Wilson called me. You got that?"

"Yes. I understand that."

"Good."

"I understand completely. You've protected him so long and so—"

"Listen, Heather." He grabbed her skinny arm. "Either you drop this now, or I'm going to tie you to this tree and leave you here to commune with nature all you want while I go fishing. Would you like that?"

"You didn't bring any—"

"I don't make idle threats. And you're not gonna wear me down, so give it up. I really want to like you."

"But you don't want to become *overly* fond of me. That's not good policy for a kidnapper."

"I'm making up the policies as we go along."

She smiled. "I really want to like you, too."

"Well, here's your chance. I'm at my best when nobody's talking."

"Does it scare the wild critters away?" she whispered. "It's so quiet here. Where are all the birds?"

"Gone south." Despite his policy, he kept talking while he plowed into the willow thicket, where he'd stashed his canoe. "You want noise, you oughta hear this place in May and June. Big birds, baby birds." He chuckled. "Buzzing bees, biting bugs . . ." Turning in the parted brush, he caught her eye. "Bears, bats . . ."

"Bass?"

"Bingo." He lifted the green fiberglass canoe, bottom up, from its makeshift rack. "Did you bring any bass bait?"

She giggled. "What do bass bite?"

"Bread and butter."

She plunged her hands into her pants pockets. "Bubble gum!" she proclaimed, but all he could see was a bit of pink paper. "Button! Hook!"

"Hook?"

Gleefully she displayed a paper clip. "And you've got a boat with a complete bottom to boot. Does it get any better than this when you're at your best?"

"You'd better believe it, baby."

He told her to take the front seat before he pushed the canoe off shore. He kept two fishing poles racked in the canoe, and he'd brought bait. Heather took to her paddle eagerly. They fished the shallows for fall-spawning lake trout. Kole enjoyed Heather's excitement over her first catch. He was almost sorry to have to tell her the fish was too small to keep. She was quite happy to return it to the water when he assured her that it would not be shunned for having been touched by human hands. The two fish they chose to keep for supper had both taken Kole's bait, which was fine with Heather. She said she liked the release part the best.

He'd given her his baseball cap to wear—partly to keep the sun out of her eyes, mostly because it helped him think of her as a fishing buddy instead of a reporter—which left his dark hair to soak up the warmth of the autumn sun. She shed her sweater. They put their fishing poles aside and drifted in still, sparkling water, saying nothing to spoil the serenity. At last she seemed to understand the beauty of saying nothing. They paid little heed to the dark clouds, popping out of the blue and multiplying like mushrooms. The first drops of rain on Kole's face were cold and rude.

"We'd better get back."

She was disappointed. "Maybe it'll quit."

"Or maybe we'll be bailing water," he warned as he pulled their string of two fish from the water, then took to his paddle.

They learned a new rhythm as she responded to his lead and their paddling became synchronized. She didn't have to be told when to switch sides, and she felt like a natural, as though she might be getting the hang of it instinctively. She sat up proudly and took the rain full in her face. She was Earth Woman.

At her back he was wishing he'd stolen all the bras from her luggage before he'd turned it over to her earlier. Her white shirt had turned transparent in the rain. He glanced at the sweater she'd pulled off under the sun and stuffed under her butt for a seat cushion, which was the only thing it was good for now, wet as it was. Wet as she was, as they both were. One of the fish flipped its tail against the bottom of the canoe, welcoming the rain. But it was Heather's tail that interested Kole.

No, it was her back, long and sleek and fine, a moving sculpture. There was no prettier sight than a woman's back. It had been a while since he'd found himself in a position to appreciate that beauty.

Linda had had strong shoulders and sweet, slim hips. He'd been so persistent about backing away from memories of his dead wife that they surprised him now, sitting easily with him as he watched Heather's back muscles undulate. He smiled. She would feel those muscles tonight.

She would be sleeping in his bed tonight, and she wouldn't be alone. He wasn't going over to Jack's place again. He'd taken enough razzing.

She wasn't even his type. Not that he had a type, but if he did, she sure as hell wasn't it. Christ, she was *white*.

She was wet. White didn't matter much when he was looking at her through the rain, watching her put her back into the effort, *their* effort. Colors darkened and ran together. Motion turned fluid, and rhythm claimed command. She obviously felt it. She slipped right in and started doing his dance, no questions asked.

He decided he liked her wet.

They upended the canoe and stowed it on the makeshift rack Kole had built in the thicket. With two swipes of his knife he cleaned their fish before they trekked back to the cabin. Rain rattled the yellowing birch leaves overhead, collecting in dollops to bombard their backs. Heather laughed and redoubled her pace when she spotted his pickup through the trees. "First dibs on the bathroom."

"Have at it," he said. "I'll get a fire going."

"Can Woof come in?"

"Hell, no. He's wet."

"So am I."

"You smell good wet. He doesn't."

They crossed paths in silence when she came inside, although he spared her a quick nod for the pail of water Heather carried. She was picking up on the routine. He used the toilet, washed up, gathered an armload of firewood, filled another bucket with water from the overflowing rain barrel, then headed for the door. But he stopped dead in his tracks in front of the window. He stood there, drenched with rain and gray shadows in the depths of late afternoon, and he watched what he should have ignored, for his own sake more than for hers.

Nearly nude, her back to the window, his guest was spongebathing from a tin basin. She turned slightly as she lifted her arm, the curve of her breast burnished by the fire he'd made in the fireplace. She'd pinned most of her damp hair up, but loose bits curled at her nape and temple, feathers that might tickle his nose if he were to sneak up behind her and plant a kiss somewhere. Her smooth shoulder, maybe, or the back of her neck, which she was washing, or the channel her spine made for the runnel she'd squeezed from the sponge. He imagined catching those few drops of water with his tongue before they trickled into her bikini panties. Pure water, straight from the heavens, salted by her skin—God, he could actually taste it, taste her.

Suddenly tortured by thirst, he dropped his head back and opened his mouth to the rain. Chickens had been known to drown themselves this way. He'd never seen it happen, but he thought it must be true. He couldn't drink, couldn't catch a breath, couldn't think straight.

He was horny as hell. He ought to drop the wood and water on the porch, drop his jeans on the floor, drop the woman on his bed and screw her brains out. She was putting on a damn show, and she had to know she was killing him with it. What was he doing, standing outside his own window and looking in, like some deprived kid?

He was using his head, staying out of trouble. She was a *wasicu*, for God's sake. If he'd been willing to get involved with a white woman, he could have had a real beauty. Why would he settle for the best friend?

But as he watched Heather step into her jeans, he couldn't remember what exactly was so beautiful about Savannah. Heather could sell those panties she was wearing, easy. Hell, he'd pay top dollar right now. She zipped her jeans and turned to reach for the sweatshirt she'd laid on the back of the recliner, presenting him with a nice view of her breasts. Nice breasts. It would feel so fine to lay his face between them. Ah, risky pleasure, the kind he'd long since restricted to his fantasies. It was that hardship that had him all tied up in knots, not this bold and foolish woman. Not Heather.

Heather. Perfect name for a female Wasp. Perfect agent for stinging a male 'Skin.

Heather. Perfect sweet-melon breasts, delicate waspish waist.

Woof nuzzled Kole's hand. He looked down at the big, glowing eyes that could see into his mind, and he chuckled. He had some nerve, applying the term *foolish* to Heather when he was the one standing outside in the rain, letting it stream down his face like tears.

◆ ◆ ◆

She was dressed when he came inside. She greeted him with a smile. He returned a quick, hot glance as he dumped the wood on the hearth and set the water near the stove. He peeled off his wet denim jacket and tossed it over a wall hook, then jerked a chair away from the table, spun it on one leg, and sat with his back to her to pull off his boots.

"It's really coming down out there now, isn't it?" she said, feigning innocence. She knew he'd seen her dressing. She'd felt his eyes burning her skin. She hadn't meant for him to, exactly, but she had no place to hide. Neither did he. They were going to have to show each other a little courtesy.

"Do you want me to start the fish?"

He peeled off his wet T-shirt.

She squatted next to the woodstove and opened the squeaky firebox door. "Still warm. Should I use . . ."

Heavy, sodden fabric flopped over the back of the chair. His jeans. Bare feet padded across the plank floor. *Should I use what?* She couldn't remember. She sneaked a peek at his bare butt. Two tight knots at the bottom of a long, sleek, brown satin back.

Courtesy.

"Wood." He caught her with a quick, canny glance over his shoulder. "It's a woodstove."

"Kindling?"

"How do you usually get a fire going?" He turned away.

"Matches."

He muttered something that sounded like "rubber stick," which she repeated as a question.

He laughed as he zipped his jeans. "*Rub* a *stick.* Like, to start a fire?"

"It takes two sticks." She shoved a log into the firebox.

"Not in this house," he said, then added, "Wait a minute. Stand up and drop those jeans. Maybe I missed something."

"I doubt it."

"You didn't either, did you?"

"Sticks and stones." And one more log, but it was a tight fit.

"I'll do an encore if you will."

"Will break my bones," she muttered as she struck a match.

"That's not gonna happen. I won't be jumpin' on your bones." He clucked. "Can't even joke with you."

"When was I supposed to laugh?"

"See, that's just it. We don't even have the same sense of humor."

She brushed her hands on her thighs as she stood up, admiring her flickering handiwork. "But we're both hungry, and we both like fish."

"Oh, yeah." He sauntered over, from bed-space to kitchen-space, wearing only his jeans. "Hungry enough to eat it raw." Her admonishing look made him laugh as he reached for the skillet. "I can't help it, honey. You keep feedin' me all the right cues."

"That is *so* not funny."

"Hey, you're black and white; I'm red all over. Right about now it's either painfully funny or just plain painful." The skillet hit the stovetop with a clunk. "You want it poached or fried?"

"How do you like it?"

His eyes trapped hers in a heated stare-down. "You look so damn . . ." The way he forced the words between his teeth almost scared her. The weight of his arm on her shoulders almost sank her. The way his kiss pressed her neck into the crook of his elbow and tipped her head back over his arm almost hurt her, and the heat and hunger of his mouth almost undid her. "Don't ask," he whispered when he took his lips away. "Just tell."

"You're the expert," she managed to say. "What's the best way?"

"Slow-cooked." Slow slide of his arm and his foot, one step of separation. Slow grin. "You keep this up, you're gonna have more trouble than you know what to do with, lady, so let's just cool it."

"I'm not here to make trouble, Kole."

"Then shut up and open up a can of something to go with the fish."

"The best way to shut me up is tell me stories. Tell me about your—"

He grabbed her chin and kissed her again, even harder this time, nipping her lower lip, then touching, soothing with the tip of his tongue. "I know all the best ways to shut you up, and the best ways to open you up, and the best ways to make you . . ." The look in his eyes made her quiver as he rubbed his finger over her lip. "But I don't wanna go there, and neither do you."

He was wrong on both counts, and they both knew it. They could hardly look at each other for fear of admitting it, so they ate their supper in silence. They cleaned up their dishes without saying much, and when she asked for a place to put her belongings, he snapped at her. She understood his need to take a little anger to bed with him so that she would turn from him and he could turn from her.

But sleep was elusive.

The sound of rain falling on the roof had slowed, softened. Heather lay still when Kole moved, afraid that he would touch her, disappointed when he did not. She held her tongue when he left the bed, the tongue that had tasted his and would have called him back if she had allowed herself to utter words. She didn't move, hardly breathed, kept her eyes closed and attuned her ears to his quiet movement. She imagined, weighed, decided. When he came back, if he spoke or touched her in any way, she would open her arms to him.

But he'd left the bed and soon left the cabin. His soft order for the dog to stay behind was followed by the quiet closing of the cabin door. Heather rolled on her back and touched the place he'd left warm.

The pickup door opened and closed. With eyes shut tight, she waited to hear the leaving sound of the engine so that she could say to herself, *gone. Good. Now I can sleep.*

But there was no engine. Instead, the haunting strains of a Native flute taught Heather's heartstrings to play along with its melancholy song.

4

The distant rumble of an engine drew Heather to the window. Woof hopped off the front step and wagged his tail, giving the master's-home sign well before the vehicle came barreling through the trees. "Why aren't we sunning ourselves by the lake?" Heather whispered to the cat as she crushed her cigarette out in a jar lid—the first smoke she'd had since the bar—and went back to scraping eggs off the bottom of the skillet on the stove. Plenty for two, just to show she had him figured, right down to the minute.

"Breakfast, anyone?" she offered without looking up.

"I've got work to do," he grumbled, whacking the door shut behind him. "I don't know about you, but I can't afford to be playing around all day."

"What don't you know about me? I'm not asking you to play with me. I'm inviting you to eat." She handed him a plate of eggs. "Good morning to you, too."

"Inviting me to my own table?"

"To eat your own food, but I did the cooking this time. What do you need to know?"

"I need to know who . . ." He sent the plate sliding toward the middle of the table and turned on her, his dark eyes piercing the aura of her innocence. "I need to know what kind of an invitation that was last night."

"You were the one playing the flute."

He grabbed her shoulders. "You want me to play with you, Heather?"

"I'm offering eggs this morning," she said, meeting the challenge in his eyes with quiet reason.

"You tell me how you found me and who put you up to it, and then we'll play. You do me scrambled, I'll do you over easy."

"Kole, I—"

"Two pretty, white eggs." He slid his hands over her shoulders to her upper arms, squeezed and lifted her to her toes, smiling as her shirt drooped below the swell of breasts pressed between her arms. "You bathed them right in front of that window for me."

She raised her brow.

"Oh, yeah, honey, you had me drooling." Chuckling, he let her heels sink back to the floor. "I had a dream last night that I got laid by a beautiful pair of eggs."

"You were peeking in the window?"

"I was on my way into the house." His hands let her go. His eyes did not. "This is my house, Heather. You came looking for me. Remember? So you tell me your story, and then we'll play house."

"I don't have a story. I want to tell yours."

"That's bullshit. Nobody in her right mind would go to all this trouble just to write a story about me." He glanced away. "To shut me up, maybe. Somebody's gone to a lot of trouble over the years to shut me up. If I thought I could trust you, I'd send you back where you came from so you could tell them I got nothing to say anymore."

"I'm not—"

"I got nothing to say, nothing left for them to take. *Nothing*." Again he nailed her with a sharp look. "So what do you want from me, Heather?"

"Your story."

"Is that all?"

No, that was not all, and he knew it, and she ought to say it, as a matter of simple fact. But that hard gleam in his eyes made her feel as shy as she'd been as a young girl when her wants had been unattainable, needs unmentionable and unseemly. It was a stupid feeling. She was mad at herself for being the one to look away.

"Is that all, Heather?" he implored, softly this time.

The unexpected tremor in his voice drew her back. "I . . . really want you to play the flute for me."

"That was for you last night." He stepped so close she could feel his heat, lifted his hand and curved it to her cheek so delicately that she was aware of the fine fuzz that grew on her face and the warm dew of his palm. "That was me aching all over for you last night," he told her, and she could almost feel a soreness lingering in his throat.

"I ached for you, too."

"I know," he whispered, taking her into his arms. "The flute never fails." He kissed her, a teasing, nibbling, tip-of-the-tongue, testing kiss. "But I do," he confessed. "I fail badly. I meant to share the ache," he whispered against her neck. "I didn't mean to come back for more."

She shivered from the warmth of his breath. "You were going to disappear again?"

"I thought about it. You scare the hell out of me, woman."

"Well, you don't scare me at all." To prove it, she laughed. "In fact, when I finally went to sleep, I dreamed of you."

"You're either very foolish or very cold-blooded." He leaned back, as if he could tell by looking at her.

"Judge for yourself," she said. "I seem to be rushing in."

"Just try to rush me." He was backing her toward the bed, stripping off his shirt, his eyes as wolfish as his dog's. "If I go back to jail over you, I'm takin' all your secrets with me." He pulled her hips to his, took hold of the bottom of her sweatshirt. "You gotta be real slow and careful about collecting a woman's special secrets."

She met his gaze, drew a long, breast-lifting breath, and slowly raised her arms.

He peeled the generous garment up, up, exposing her bare breasts, covering her face, smiling when she could see him again. She started to lower her arms, but he tightened the sweatshirt around her wrists and backed her up one more step, to the edge of the bed.

She sat. What else could she do? Her hands were tied. When she looked up, she found him waiting for just that cue, the trust in her eyes.

He laid her back, pinning her hands above her head with the tangled sweatshirt. Deliciously frightening. Oh God, when had she last shaved under her arms? He kissed her neck, nipped her collarbone, made her forget about razors and armpits.

"Scared yet, my little rush-in fool?"

"Irish," she gasped. The fingers of his free hand had become a spider, stealing over her breast, one appendage at a time.

"Yeah, I know what you wish." His nose traced a serpentine trail over her other breast. He worried her with pad of thumb and tip of tongue, tugging lips and abrading teeth, suckling, suckling . . .

"Oh my Lord, I really need my hands."

Deep, dark chuckle. "What for, my lady?"

"I want—" What? With him breathing over her wet, taut, tingling nipple, she wanted what? "—to do my share."

"You are. I touch, you feel." He tended to her other breast, took what was left of her breath away. "I have never let a hostage go . . ." he told her solemnly as he undid her jeans, ". . . unsatisfied."

"I'm not . . ."

"Shh." He blew his warm breath into the valley between her breasts. "Cool patience."

"Not a hostage," she insisted, her eyes drifting closed, arms relaxing, giving in to his hold as the sweet breeze from his mouth swept down her middle. "I'm, ah . . . volunteer."

"Ahh, yesss, volunteer." He dipped his tongue into her belly button. "My favorite hostage flavor."

"You're nuts."

"They come with dessert." He loosened his hold on her sweatshirt.

Her hands slipped free as he rose over her. She tucked them into the front of his waistband, flipped open his snap.

He smiled down at her, scooting her toward his pillows. "They're volunteers, too."

"I'll be kind."

And she was, but he was kinder. She had never known such exquisite attention to her most sensitive places, such care of the secrets she was most sensitive about. He played her body as though he had carved it himself for making sweet music, sharing in her pleasure, bumping her high notes up with his own.

And when they came down, the music echoed, so mellow, so pure and fine that neither spoke. They merely touched. Simply, gently touched soft places still quaking.

Finally he leaned close to her ear and whispered, "Do you want to see my canoe?" He smiled innocently in the midday shadows. "The one I'm making by hand."

"Really." Her merriment blazed in her eyes. "I think I pretty much got the hang of the way it functions. What are the dimensions, exactly?"

He laughed. "Oh, it's longer than most."

"But is it wide enough?"

"Plenty wide for a little thing like you." He pulled her into his arms. "You're a naughty lady, you know that? And you struck me as such a classy chick when I first saw you." Then he confided, "And you're very tiny."

"Can't I be both naughty and classy?" She drew back, looked up, puzzled. "I could have sworn I didn't strike you at all when you first saw me."

"Sure you did. And I proceeded to strike out."

"That first approach was just a little too direct."

"That's the only kind I make these days." He sighed, stroked her hair. "I don't know what to do with you now, Heather. I just gave you all I've got to give. You know that, don't you?" He glanced askance. "And don't start that story crap again. We're past that."

"How did we get past it?" She turned in his arms, braced herself on her elbow. What was happening between them was separate, yes, but it didn't cancel out her purpose. She hadn't sought him out for sex, but for a story, and she never got past the story until she had it down on paper.

"I'm a good writer, Kole. I've written about a lot of fascinating people. I'm less interested in the events that make the news than I am in the people involved. I want to know who they are and what they think and what brought them to this moment in their lives. I want to know why they touch so many other lives and how they touch them and what difference it makes."

"I've made no difference," he told her flatly. "Nothing I've done has changed anything for the better."

"I don't think that's true."

"You callin' me a liar?"

"No, I'm just saying . . ." She shook her head, drew a deep breath. It was her turn to sigh. "You've called attention to some important issues, Kole, and I think you underestimate—"

"How the hell would you know?" He eyed her playfully. Too playfully. "How much time have you spent on a reservation?"

"Actually, I have spent . . ." She wanted him to take her seriously in this matter, and he didn't. His eyes were full of dare-you, doubt-you. "I've researched several stories on a number of reservations. I did one not long ago about what's happening with traditional medicine among some of the Plains Indian people, interviewed some fascinating people. And, of course, that ties in with the Indian Health Care System, so I reported on how difficult it is for people to get anything but essential services, especially surgery. The condition has to be life-threatening."

"And what's changed since you published your story?"

"I . . . I don't really know. I'd have to do a follow-up."

"Or maybe a postmortem."

"Maybe. You're right, it's too important to go away and forget about it. I *will* follow up. But my interest, as I said, is more in the people behind the story, the people who . . ." She laid her head back down in the crook of his shoulder. "You had the right idea, Kole. You did what you had to do to bring attention to our Indian reservations."

"*Our* Indian reservations?"

"Okay. Okay, you're right, that sounds patronizing. But your people didn't create them. Mine did."

He flicked a finger against her arm. "Damn Cherokee."

"No, the people who . . ." She flicked him back. "I *do* have a little Cherokee in me."

"No kidding," he said with a chuckle. "Does his father have a little oil well?"

She smiled, feeling full of herself, her wit and her sexuality all of a piece and blooming simultaneously. "Maybe his oil well is bigger than your canoe."

"Ah, but if you're interested in native ambiance, a canoe has a more authentic . . ." He drew her hand down to his penis, coaxing her to pump him up a bit. ". . . feel to it."

"Especially if it's hand-hewn."

"Oh, yeah, hew away, naughty lady."

"I think our humor is very complementary."

He sucked a quick breath through his teeth. "This ain't funny, honey."

"It's fun, though."

"It's the most fun I've had in a long time." He reclaimed her hand and brought it to his lips as he turned to his side to face her. "Am I sleeping with the enemy, Heather?"

"Me? You haven't actually slept with me yet."

"Yet?" He propped himself up on his elbow. "How long can I keep you?"

"How long can you make your story?"

He glanced down pointedly. "Is that the story you want? That's as long as it gets, but I can tell it over and over. You might get yourself stuck in a rut."

"I think that's where you are. Maybe I can help you get out of it, Kole."

"By writing about me?"

"It's happened before. If you didn't believe in the power of the written word, you wouldn't waste your time on that column you write for Jack's newspaper. The power of public opinion."

"You know how much of the general John Q. Public reads *Native Drums*?"

"Now, that's where I come in. Do you know how much of the public reads Heather Reardon? You have a story to tell, and I have publishing credentials up the wahzoo."

"Show me." He grabbed her hips and rolled her toward him. "Come on, now. Where's you're wahzoo? Is that where you keep your little Cherokee, too?"

"You're impossible!" She flicked him again, snapping a fingernail against his biceps as she pillowed her head on his forearm and nuzzled the crook of his elbow, "You keep saying you don't know what to do with me, and I'm telling you what to do with me. *Use me.*"

He laughed. "Hell of an offer. Where have you been all my life?"

"Use me to get you the attention your story deserves."

"Why?" He anticipated her answer and cut her off. "No, why *me?*"

"I'll admit to having some fantasies about you over the years, thanks to our mutual friend, Savannah. We were both pretty starry-eyed about a lot of things when we moved in together. We shared a tiny walk-up flat. It was a nice neighborhood, but such a far cry from home for both of us."

"Where are you from?"

"I was born in a military hospital in Maryland. My mother's from Virginia, and that's where she lives now. I have an apartment in Manhattan. So I'm from a lot of places." She lifted her shoulder, then tucked her chin and confided, "Not from anywhere, really."

"Maybe you're from all those places."

"I don't think so. I don't feel as though I am. I don't know what it feels like to be *from* somewhere. My mother does, though. She's very much a Virginian. They go way back on my mother's side." She smiled gently. "Just like yours. Do you feel like you're really *from* South Dakota?"

"Oh, yeah. My bone marrow's made of gumbo."

"Isn't that Cajun?"

"South Dakota mud." Hovering over her as she lay against his arm, he combed his fingers through her hair until he could cup them around the back of her head. He traced circles on her temple with his thumb. "You're takin' notes, aren't you? Bet you've got a tape recorder between your ears. Where'd you get the green eyes? Mom or Dad?"

"My mother's are hazel." She rolled her eyes, casting back for the images time had left in her head. "My father's were, too, if I remember correctly. My parents split up when I was about six, but they never divorced. My father was in the army, and my mother didn't like moving around. He'd send us lovely gifts from exotic places, but his visits were rare. He died when I was seventeen."

"You miss him?"

"No." She shook her head, shrugged, finally admitted, "Sometimes. That's where the little Cherokee comes from. He told me about it once. When I asked my mother about it, she said he didn't have any family history, so I should just ignore him."

"Where was he from?"

"Oklahoma, I think. Originally, anyway. We were there for a little while, and he seemed to be particularly . . ." At home? Rooted? He was never particularly either, but it was one of the few times he seemed to belong to her, to allow her be part of his real life. Otherwise he'd been a transitory figure, a guest bearing wonderful stories and gifts. "His family was military, too," she said, realizing that both terms, for her, were synonymous with *remote.*

"It's probably true, then. Everybody from Oklahoma is part Cherokee, seems like."

"But that doesn't really make me part Indian."

"I don't know. Who am I to say? Talk about your Irish, my father was a white rancher."

"But you were raised by your mother. I think it has a lot to do with the way a person's raised, don't you?"

"She sent me away when I was thirteen. Didn't really *send* me, I guess. She took me herself and dropped me off. Said I had to live with my father. Little town called Sunbonnet, Wyoming. About as far away from Indian country as you can get."

"I've been there," she told him eagerly. "There's a huge reservation just down the road. Shoshone, I think. I mean, I know you're Lakota, but Indian country includes all tribes, doesn't it?"

"Yes, it does. But it doesn't include white towns, even if they're right on the reservation. There was one other Indian kid in my class in high school, and he transferred out."

"From what Savannah said, you were quite a hero in high school."

"Whose hero? Hers?" He laughed. "I ain't complainin'. I did okay. I had friends."

"Girlfriends?"

"One or two."

"According to a reliable source, you were very popular with the girls."

"Sounds like you and your roommate already have your story half written."

"With considerable input from your former, what, mentor? Comrade-in-arms? What would you call Barry Wilson?" She studied him for a moment. "Partner in crime?" No response. "How about *traitor*?"

"I don't call him; he don't call me."

"He says you—"

"I don't wanna talk about Wilson. Let's rewind." Smiling, he drew quick circles on her temple, winding a hank of her hair around his forefinger. "Back to where you were tellin' me about your little Cherokee. Your dad claimed it and your mom denies it?"

"She said he never told *her* about any Indian ancestry. Like that meant there wasn't any, and he just came up with a story because he knew I was interested in Native American culture and history," she said. He was grinning. "American Indian?"

"Which term do you prefer? As a little Cherokee?"

She sighed. "I wish I'd never mentioned it."

"Too late." He touched a finger to her lips. "So your mom thinks it's bullshit."

" 'Bullshit' is not part of my mother's vocabulary. She's a very classy southern lady, my mother. Soft-spoken, gracious, always smells like jasmine. To look at her, you'd think she spent her afternoons playing bridge and sipping iced tea, but she's actually quite a businesswoman. She deals in real estate."

"I don't know what jasmine smells like." He dipped his head to nuzzle her hair. "You smell like wood smoke and morning pleasure."

"Is that different from evening pleasure?"

"We'll see."

They looked frankly at each other. The pillow talk came too easily. There was no *we*. Beyond his bed, they made no sense. Between morning and evening pleasure there was only the absurdity of her presence.

"What would you do if I went out the door and kept walking?" she asked quietly.

He shook his head.

"Would you stop me? Would you drag me back?"

"We won't know unless it happens."

"I know you don't take me seriously, but I have a reason for being here, a good one."

He brushed her hair back with careful fingertips. "This wasn't good?"

"It was, but it doesn't have anything to do with what I want from you and what I can do for you." She squeezed his arm once, twice in response to his dubious look. "I can bring attention to your cause. I can show people the injustices."

"Injustice done to Indians is old news. People know about it, and they regret it, but, you know, it all happened a long time ago, so what can you do? Most people are quite happy to feel sorry for us." He laughed humorlessly. "I hate that. I really do."

"I feel sorry for *us*, frankly."

"What, you've got the oil, you've got . . ." He scowled. "Don't you little Cherokees have any casinos?"

"Give me a break, huh? Us *white guys*. The sins of the fathers are to be visited on the children. That's what the Bible says; that's what we say we believe. But so far all we do is apologize and come up with stuff like casinos as a consolation prize. It's like, you know, the big question in *Macbeth*. Can you expect to be forgiven and still keep what you gained by committing the sin?"

"You're gettin' heavy."

"No, really—"

"Yes, really. My arm's goin' to sleep."

"I thought we were fitting together quite nicely."

"Parts of us do." He slid his arm all the way under her head as he lay back down beside her. "But when you started gettin' all philosophical on me just now, your weight about doubled."

She laughed.

"So let's just keep it simple," he said. "I don't have a cause, and the last thing I need is attention."

"Then I'll have to try walking away, just to see what happens."

"Should keep things interesting."

"I wish you had a VCR," she said after a quiet moment had passed.

"Bored?" He *tsk*ed with mock sympathy. "I guess it might be a good time to try to make a break for it."

"What fun would it be if you were expecting it?"

"Might not be any fun at all. Except the part where the door hits you in the ass on the way out." She flicked him again, and he added, "Or the part where the bears fight over your wishbone."

"Intimidation is a sure sign that you care. No, the reason is that I have a videotape that I'd love to show you."

He chuckled. "I'm not really into that kind of stuff. Sex and lies are good enough for me."

"You're on the tape. So is Barry Wilson," she said. He groaned, but she went on with her explanation. "It's a collection of news clips and interviews from the days when you were more newsworthy. I think it'll help you understand why I'm so interested, why I've been interested for a long time."

"I do understand why you're interested. You've got your jasmine, I've got my Indian mystique. If I could figure out how to bottle it, we wouldn't need casinos."

"It has nothing to do with—" She laughed. Maybe it was too easy with him. Too much fun, surely. A deceptively fine fit. "It's my mother's jasmine."

"But it comes in a bottle, right? I'd call mine 'Noble Warrior' or 'Savage Surrender,' something like that. I know I could make some serious money."

"You sound like Wilson now. I always thought you were angrier but fundamentally more sincere."

"He did most of the talking."

"But you did just enough. And you were willing to put your life on the line. He never really did that." Then, softly, "You went to prison for him, Kole."

"Hell, I said I wasn't guilty, but they had me cold on wrecking their bulldozer. The kidnapping was a crock anyway. Typical FBI overkill. If you were a big Indian instead of a little Cherokee you'd know these things. They needed to get somebody so they could shut down the resistance, and there was no need for both of us to do the time."

"That's an amazing sacrifice."

"It's nothing. My *mother's* sacrifice was amazing. My wife's was . . ." He drew a deep breath, blew it out slowly, and in that moment she glimpsed his cherished sorrow. It pinched her somehow. "My wife's was needless. A terrible waste."

"Who stood to gain from her death? Or yours?"

"I don't know. We weren't bothering anybody. All we wanted . . ." The look he gave her turned menacing. "As long as they leave my daughter alone. Who I am, what I've done, none of it touches her. You got that?"

"I understand," she said, dauntlessly meeting his gaze. "Believe me, Kole, I would never jeopardize Claudia's safety."

"She's all I've got." It was a quiet, desperate admission, one she knew had slipped out of his mouth before he could contain it. Too late, he pressed his lips together, closed his eyes for a moment, and when he opened them she caught his sheepish glance, his chagrin, as though he had no right. "No, you're right, I don't even have her."

"I didn't say that. You have her in a good place. She's well cared for, well loved."

"I never thought she'd end up in Sunbonnet. That's the last place I would have sent her. Sometimes I think about trying to get her back." He smiled sadly. "I just *think* about it, all right?"

"Savannah adopted her. She's her mother now. And your brother—"

He sat up suddenly, swinging his feet to the floor. With his back to her, arms braced as though he was ready to push off the bed, he barked, "What about this videotape you wanna show me? What am I supposed to see on it?"

"Maybe a little bit of what I see." She clutched the sheet to her breast and scooted across the bed to the edge, where she sat with her feet tucked under her bottom. "Maybe you'll understand why I think it's so important for you to tell your side of the story."

"Who says we've got sides?"

"Everyone has sides. That's what makes life interesting."

"We could go over to Jack's. He's got TV, VCR, electricity, gadgets up the *ozeki*." He turned to her, his eyes bright for her once again. "That's a Lakota wahzoo."

"Is Jack Lakota?"

"No, but they're made pretty much the same, except a Chippewa's *ozeki's* soft and flat." He reached over and patted her own soft rump. "We got the horse, they got the sofa in front of the TV."

"I've got the chair in front of the computer," she said, swinging her legs over the side of the bed. "I'll get the tape."

He eyed her meaningfully, then quietly offered her an out. "You wanna take the rest of your stuff along?"

"Not today."

5

Kole was quite proud of his canoe.

He'd been working on it all summer, and it pleased him that he knew every inch of it intimately, the way a man comes to know his woman. The sound of Heather's footsteps made him smile. The snapping twigs and rustling leaves proved that little Cherokees weren't very stealthy. But they knew how to follow just fine.

Her footsteps enchanted his ears, as did the lovely echoes of her quickening breath, her desperate demand, her soft entreaty, the sweet urgency when she'd called his name. He had forgotten the way it felt to come home to a woman he wanted, to be welcomed, to be wanted in return. He hardly knew her, but he knew that she had one mole on the underside of her left breast and another low on the soft, small pillow of her belly. He had kissed them both. And she had kissed the tattoo on his right hip four times, a kiss for each letter of his real name. *Kola.* The name his mother had given him.

He'd started calling himself Kole when he was in school. Kids had begun teasing him about being named for a soft drink. He'd had a dream once that he was looking up from the bottom of a glass at the ugly freckled face of Richard Klein, who was threatening to drink him. Waking up in a fevered sweat, he'd decided, no more Kola.

But he'd come full circle. He was Kola again. Kola, the guest in the land of a traditional enemy of his people. Kola, the reclusive artisan, the eccentric Indian flute maker. Kola, the mysterious writer of a column that appeared somewhat erratically in an obscure weekly newspaper that was circulated mostly by mail. Kola, the friend.

Whose friend? And who were his friends? Did he really have any?

He'd lost track of most of his old friends. He counted Jack Laurent among the few friends he trusted, the few who could put who he was together with where he was. And now, this woman, who not only knew who he was and where he was—which could be changed quickly enough—but knew who his child was and where she lived. And those things could not be changed. Claudia knew nothing of him, but he would always know her. He'd done all he could to protect her identity, to give her a secure and loving home. Those things *must* not be changed.

And now this woman.

It was too late to wonder whether she could be trusted with his most sacred secret. The question was, how would she use it? What did she want?

"A rare experience," she was saying to his back. He turned to her, puzzled. She offered that bright-eyed, chipper smile of hers. "A ride in a hand-hewn canoe would be so exciting, especially the maiden voyage."

"You'd do it?" He laughed when she nodded eagerly. "There it is, Woof. We've got our maiden."

The dog was more interested in the chipmunk that had just taken refuge in a rotting deadfall.

But Heather was fascinated the moment she saw the framework of what would one day be a birchbark canoe. She had all kinds of questions, of course, and Kole admitted that he couldn't answer them all. He told her he was learning the craft the Indian way—step by step from an old guy who just showed up once in a while to lead him through another step. Kole wouldn't be able to finish the thing unless the old guy kept showing up. But so far, with the hand-hewn ribs carefully soaked and shaped and tempered by the coals of a reverently tended fire, the boat was a work of art.

"So, are you still willing to be the guinea—er, maiden?"

"You know as well as I do that I can't truly claim to be a maiden. But she is." She patted one of the frame's lithe wooden ribs admiringly. "And I'd love to help you try her out when she's ready."

"A threesome?" He wagged his head. "I don't know about you little Cherokees."

"Well, I know all about you," she warned as she flicked her finger against his square chin. She'd sure picked that gesture up in a hurry. "I know you're impossibly cocky."

"Now there's a word that'll sell." The spark of humor faded from his eyes. "Is that part of your story?"

"No." She gave him a warm smile. "That part's my secret."

♦　♦　♦

They passed the Cheap Shot Saloon on their way into the little town of Blue Fish, on the reservation of the same name. It was one of four businesses—gas station, general store, six-room lodge—that appeared to be thriving. There was a "Burger Palace" with plywood windows and padlocked doors. The bait shop was closed for the season, and the Native Crafts shop was closed, according to Kole, for lack of interest.

"Where's the casino?" Heather asked. "Don't all reservations have casinos?"

"And aren't all Indians getting rich off them?" Kole spared her a glance as he backed the pickup into a curb space in front of a white frame building with a small sign in the window identifying it as the office of *Native Drums*, the most renowned and widely read Native American newspaper in the country. "What kind of research did you say you've done?"

"I know most Indians aren't pocketing any profits unless it's a paycheck for working there, but I haven't visited a reservation yet that doesn't have some kind of casino."

"Blue Fish is no exception, but the operation is farther south, where they can get some traffic. They cut a deal with a community off the reservation, which means if you want a casino job, you move. And that means it's even quieter here than it was before, which suits a retired renegade like me just fine." With a hand on the driver's-side door handle, he lifted an eyebrow. This was it. Once they got out of the pickup she was free to walk away whenever she chose. "Got your video?"

She nodded. "But that defeats the purpose, doesn't it?"

"*Now* what's your purpose?"

"Building the casino off the reservation. I thought it had to be on reservation land to avoid some of the state restrictions. I thought the idea was to bring in business and jobs and—"

"Money. The idea is to get non-Indians to put some of their coins into our machines. Put their money on the table. How many non-Indians do you see around here?" His gesture encompassed a nearly deserted street, and Heather wasn't about to take inventory. He gave a nod of satisfaction. "In case you haven't noticed, most reservations can't exactly claim location, location, location."

"So . . ."

"So, no, I don't expect Indian gaming to bring about the rebirth of the Great Sioux Nation. But you already know that."

"I read your column religiously."

"Developed a taste for Kola, have you?" He smiled, reached across the seat, and touched her chin in a way that made her stomach flutter. "You're a cute little Cherokee, you know that?"

With a growl and a quick head move, she trapped his finger between her teeth.

"Hey, Kola!" Jack rapped on the pickup roof, startling them both. "Didn't I warn you not to get too close?" He laughed. "It's always the small ones that bite."

"Christ. I'm in for it now," Kole grumbled as he jerked on the door handle.

Jack backed out of the way, grinning. "Hey, how's your story coming?" he called out to Heather as she emerged from the pickup. "You think it'll bring us in some tourists?"

"I've run out of ways to entertain her," Kole said. "She wants to watch videos."

Jack slapped Kole's back and hooted. "Hell of a kidnapper."

"He didn't kidnap me," Heather protested as she followed the men to the door. "I was . . . I got lost. Now I'm sort of stranded without a car."

"I took it back to the airport." Jack opened the door to his newspaper office, which was also home, and held it for Heather as he reported, "Got it in just under the wire so you didn't have to pay for another day."

"Thank you." She stepped inside. The front room was obviously multipurpose—an office with two desks, computer, sofa, chair, TV, kitchen table cluttered with papers, boxes, soda cans, and chips and dip. "I'm *definitely* stranded without a car, but thank you for saving me the fifty-four dollars."

"Hey, no problem." The wiry young man cleared the newspapers off the sofa and offered her a seat. "So what's your big interest in our good friend?"

"I'm a good friend of a good friend. I've been interested in Kole—Kola's story for years." She sat on the edge of the sofa, knees pressed together and bridged by the videotape. Kole took the chair, and Jack sat down next to Heather as she went on explaining, "It seems to me that his work is unfinished and that he ought to be free to continue with it."

"The best way to keep a nation down is to silence their leadership," Jack said. He had a craggy, pitted face, eyes that bespoke keen interest and intelligence, scraggly hair he hadn't taken the time to wash lately. "That's been our problem for over a century. There's a reason why we're almost invisible, why we have so little voice."

"I hear *your* voice, Jack," Heather said persuasively, angling for an ally. "I read your newspaper."

"Is that what brought you here?"

"Sort of, when I figured out who 'Kola' was."

"We have regular contributors all over the country."

She glanced at Kole, whose eyes told her that he was just as interested in her answers as Jack was. "I followed the leads, Jack," she said, "just the way you do."

Jack leaned back, eyeing her suspiciously. "Who are you to write his story? You're from another world, for crissake. You know how many white guys come out here, spend a couple months, go home and write a book about us? You guys got more Indian experts than we got Indians."

"You guys?" She was beginning to resent having those words applied to her. "Which *guys*?"

"She's part Cherokee," Kole put in, giving her that infuriating deadpan look of his.

"That's not what I meant," she retorted. "Forget I ever said that, okay? I just meant, I'm not *you guys*. Whoever that is, I'm not that. I'm not an expert. I don't have any expertise, don't want to be an expert, won't ever *claim* to be an expert. When I write Kole's story, you'll hear his voice, not mine. Very little of mine. I'm really very good at what I do."

"So am I," Jack said. "Why should he be tellin' you stuff when I understand better and I'm a writer, too?"

"Because I'll reach more readers."

"White readers," Jack said.

"Among others, but mostly white, yes."

"So they won't read me, but they'll read you."

"No, that's not . . ." Heather threw her hands up, but she wasn't surrendering. "The thing is, I have a track record. My stories are regularly published in national magazines and some of the biggest newspapers in the country. I've published two national bestsellers. My book will be excerpted in major magazines, and it'll get lots of reviews. It'll make the *New York Times* bestseller list, partly because I'm well-established in the world I come from, and that's where the readers are."

"You ask me, Kola, this woman's pretty damned uppity. But I guess you're not askin' me." Jack turned back to Heather. "So, are you saying Indians don't read, or just that they don't buy enough books to get you on these fancy lists?"

"I'm not saying . . ." Heather sighed. She was doing very badly here. "Your world knows the story," Heather explained, changing her tack. "Mine doesn't. They think they do, and that's why they locked Kole up. But they don't."

"War of the Worlds: The Next Generation," Jack quipped.

Kole ignored him. "They locked me up because I was convicted of committing a crime, and I ain't bellyachin' over that. Technically I guess I took over a U.S. Post Office, even if I only meant to occupy a general store. I did run that 'dozer off a bluff, which was a pretty big piece of federal property, and I busted out of prison, called the President of the United States a lyin' weasel—I did it all. Except kill that kid. That I didn't do."

"You haven't been convicted of that," Heather reminded him.

"I woulda been if I'd hung around."

"Do you know—"

"When did this project become a book?" Kole's eyes chilled her as he eased forward in the chair. "Huh? I thought you wrote for some magazine or other. I thought you were just trying to squeeze some little magazine article out of this adventure of yours."

"You haven't even agreed to that much."

"That's right, I haven't."

"So what difference does it make? I won't publish anything without your permission."

"How do I know that? Obviously you don't have to worry about me taking you to court."

She met his icy stare without blinking. "Obviously I can't publish anything as long as I'm stranded in the woods with a renegade fugitive and his big, bad wolf."

"You got a point." He raised a warning finger. "But leave Woof out of it. He's completely innocent of all my crimes."

"Like Barry Wilson?"

His laugh surprised her. He shook his head. "Man, you're as persistent as a little terrier." He gave a quick chin jerk, pointing with pooched lips. "Let's see what you've got there. Show me your amazing video."

Jack popped the tape into his machine and turned on the TV. The cassette contained a montage of news clips, some culled from the archives of local news stations, some that Heather had managed to tape off the news herself. Kole was not as vocal as Wilson was, but when he spoke, there was no doubting his conviction.

"Jesus, when was I ever that young?" he mused, regarding an early clip of a student protest at the American Indian Center at the university. His long, dark, unbound hair showed no hint of gray. When the microphone was shoved in front of his young face, he spoke of promises made, an understanding reached, changes in the offing. "Or that naive?" he muttered as he watched.

"What were you asking for?" Jack wanted to know. "You said something about religious freedom."

"A couple of guys got thrown out of school for using peyote, and then they banned us from holding sweat lodge ceremonies. Said they couldn't be sure what we were doing in there."

Jack pressed the pause button on the remote control, turned to Kole, and stared for a moment, deadpan. "So, what *were* you doing in there?"

"If you'd stop wimping out every time we have a sweat, Laurent, you'd know."

Jack glanced at Heather, gave a sheepish shrug. "I've tried, but all that steam and all those sweaty bodies in that closed-in space, I can't take it. I'm claustrophobic."

"You're a poor excuse for an Indian is what you are. Now turn this thing back on and let's get it over with."

All eyes turned back to the TV set. They had become a team, Wilson and Kills Crow. In one news clip, Kole carried a rifle and rode a horse bareback to meet a convoy of National Guard. He laughed and said it was a good thing they'd only wanted to "parley."

"It's funny Wilson was the one who got into the movies," Jack said. "Looks like he was all talk and you were the action."

"Whose idea was that?" Heather asked, nodding toward the screen.

Kole spared her a glance. "What?"

"That appearance on the horse."

"It probably grew out of something Wilson said."

"His wish was your command?" She was baiting him, and they both knew it. "He told me that sometimes he would throw out some wild idea—more or less thinking aloud—and you would jump out there and start the ball rolling."

"So he forgot to say 'Just kidding'?" Kole laughed. "That Indian humor can turn around that quick and bite a guy in the ass."

"Even a guy who—"

"Hold it! Stop the tape." Kole held up a hand as he leaned forward, studying the screen.

Jack clicked the remote control and banished the picture.

"No, I mean, can't you freeze it on . . ." Kole gestured impatiently. "Lemme see that gadget."

Again all eyes turned to the screen as Kole rewound the tape and played the section that interested him, once— "Ho-lyy . . ."— twice—". . . shhee-it."

He slid off the chair as he rewound for the third time, knelt close to the screen, and played the tape again. Barry Wilson, surrounded presumably by friends, was giving an interview about being nominated for an award by the foreign press for a supporting role in a film that nobody in Hollywood had gotten too excited about.

Kole turned to Heather. "When was this filmed?"

"I have all the dates on that card in the box. Maybe a year ago?"

"What was this guy's name? Some kind of fish." Kole bowed his head and tapped the remote control against his forehead. "Damn, what . . . Numbers meant more than names."

"Numbers?"

"This guy . . ." He activated the pause button, then pressed his finger against a background face on the screen. "Seal! Tom Seal."

"That's no fish," Jack said. "Are seals fish?"

"An AIM member?" Heather asked quietly.

"Hell, no, he was an inmate." Kole pivoted from the screen, his eyes fairly glowing. "He was always trying to get next to me. I thought he was trying to hit on me at first. Little weasel, I never did trust that guy." He swung back toward the picture, studying. "What the hell is he doing with Wilson?"

"He works for him," Heather said.

"As what?"

"I never did figure that out. Gofer, maybe?"

"Good job for a weasel." He pressed the rewind button and paused on a slightly different angle. "I've always figured he had something to do with Daryl Two Horn."

"The man who was killed?"

"The man I'm supposed to have killed. We were in the yard when Daryl got hit. Seal offered me a cigarette, which was like . . . Nobody gives cigarettes away without a reason. So I'm lookin' at him, like, what's up with this, and there's this pop, and Daryl goes down not five feet away from us. They found the gun in the yard, and they were makin' out like it was somebody in the yard that did him. Hell, everybody knew it wasn't close range. We all heard it. But they were saying it was somebody in the yard."

"That was the report," Heather said.

"Yeah, well, I was there," he reminded her. "You think they're just gonna find that gun in the yard? When they questioned me, somehow they had a witness saying I was braggin' around I had a gun and that Daryl was supposed to be an FBI informant and all kinds of crazy shit. Daryl wasn't even a player. He was just a kid who had stolen a car."

"Why would anyone kill him?" Heather asked.

"Good question," Kole admitted softly as he studied the screen. "And why would Seal help me bust out during a transfer to a local jail? We were going to appear in court and . . ." He returned to his chair. "I always thought the escape was a little too easy. But, then, how smart are cops? A chance comes along, you take it. South Dakota's a death penalty state."

"Did you ever talk to this Seal about Wilson, or mention Wilson to Seal?" Jack asked.

Kole shook his head. "I haven't had any contact with Wilson since the trial. And one thing you learn about prison life pretty quick is not to trust your neighbors. I wasn't too chatty with anybody."

"But everybody associates you with Barry Wilson," Heather said.

"Most cons don't keep up with current events." Kole suddenly grinned at her. "Honey, you are gonna be so disappointed when you finally realize how unfamous I am. The only Indians most Americans can name are Sitting Bull and Geronimo."

"Most Americans can't name the last five presidents, either. That doesn't mean I can't sell your story."

"You'd be better off following Michael Jordan around. Or Michael Jackson."

"Overdone," she said. "I'm determined to do Kole Kills Crow."

"Then you'll go home happy?"

They exchanged loaded looks.

Jack cleared his throat. "You guys want me to wait outside?"

He laughed. She rolled her eyes.

"So, what about this Seal?" Jack asked Kole. "Is he Indian?"

"He never claimed to be."

"That's something he'd 've probably whispered in your ear when he was trying to—"

"If you're smart, you'll back away from that subject, Jack." Kole raised a cautionary finger. "And don't ever go there again."

"Just . . ." From the look in Kole's eyes, Jack could see that kidding was not an option. He hung his head. "Sorry, Kola." Back to the video. "If, uh . . . if this had been taken in South Dakota, maybe it could be a coincidence, them hooking up with each other. But in California?"

"Well, it's Hollyweird."

"But you have to wonder why you end up in prison while Barry Wilson gets a movie break."

"I don't see what one has to do with the other. He used to make fun of Hollywood Indians, but I always thought he'd make a good one." He pointed to his former fellow inmate on the screen. "It's this clown I have to wonder about. Why is he cozyin' up to Wilson?"

"Or vice versa. I'd say we need to find out who Tom Seal really is."

"He's an ex-con."

Jack scooted closer to the arm of the sofa, closer to Kole. "Can we even be sure of that?"

Kole shrugged. "Unless he was pretty damn hard up for a place to stay."

"Maybe somebody planted him."

"To kill Daryl Two Horn?" He shook his head slowly, considering. "Why?"

"He must've been gunnin' for you," Jack theorized eagerly.

"You know, this question just keeps on poppin' up." Kole glanced at Heather. "Why me?"

"Because you're not just any reclusive Indian flute maker," she said.

"Why don't we go find out *why you*?" Jack was so eager to get started, he was ready to fly off the sofa. "Kola, this could really be big."

"I'm not doing this cockamamie march of yours, Jack."

Heather straightened in her seat. "What march?"

"Look at the rabbit ears springin' up on this one," Kole said with a chuckle. "Nope, sorry. Those days are over for me. There is no way I'm going back to the pen."

"Nobody's going to—"

Kole turned on Jack. "They never charged anybody for Two Horn, but you know damn well who they'll try to charge. I got no chance of beating that rap. No chance in hell."

"We'd protect you, Kola. You know that. Nobody's gonna give you up. You'd be traveling incognito."

Kole's expression softened. "In what kinda tow?"

"In disguise," Heather said eagerly.

"And we'd lock her in a closet someplace until we got back," Jack said with a wink.

"No way! I'm going, too."

"You two have fun." Kole flopped back in the chair, grinning. "Jack's got a story. Maybe you wanna *do* each other." He laughed when Heather glared at him. "Well, you're both writers."

"More people would join if the man they know as Kola was with us," Jack said. "*Our* people. You've said it so many times in your column. If we could ever get together—all tribes, all nations—and speak with one voice, they'd have to listen. A growing caravan of Indians, heading for the coast to make their pitch—wouldn't that be a sight?"

"I fought for water rights, protested dumping toxic waste on Indian land, funding cuts for the Indian Health Service, the desecration of sacred sites. My mother fought for the Black Hills, for self-determination, for decent schools." He offered an open-handed gesture. "The learned editor of our most respected newspaper wants to protest the damn *movies*."

"That's all most people know about us," Jack explained, obviously for Heather's benefit. "What they see on film. The news is all about entertainment these days. You've gotta do some kind of a tie-in, you know? If you play your jokers right, they fall all over themselves to get the first interview and get you to their Oscar night parties."

"Christ, another Wilson," Kole grumbled.

"No, I'm serious," Jack insisted. "The American Indian hardly exists for most other Americans except in history—which Americans know about as good as they know their geography—*and* on film. So what we want is for Hollywood to stop showing some of those old western reruns on TV. We want them to hire more Indians and to ask us who we are and how we should be portrayed instead of some white anthropologist or historian."

"What about white journalists?" Heather asked pointedly.

"They need to pay their dues, do their research the right way." Jack turned to Kole. "By helping me get this guy interested in this idea, which I seriously think is a good one."

"It sounds exciting to me," Heather said.

"That's because you've got nothing to lose," Kole sneered.

"You're right. It's easy for me to say."

"You've got some fantasy about me." Kole jabbed a finger in the air. "Both of you. I ain't no hero material anymore. Hell, I never was. You wanna tell my story? All right. I'll answer your questions. Tell you the whole sorry tale, beginning to end. You got Wilson's version. You might as well have mine."

"Bobby Bear would let us use his camper," Jack mused, already cooking up a plan. "I could drive. You could ride in back. Nobody'd ever have to see you unless you wanted 'em to."

"I ain't ridin' with you, man, you're the worst driver I know," Kole said. "Anyway, what if we break down? You know how old that thing is? Bear's been running it all over the country to powwows every summer since the last treaty was signed."

"If it breaks down, we fix it. We'd look out for you, bro. I've already got it mapped out, hopscotching across the West, hitting a whole bunch of reservations along the way." Jack brandished a road map. "We'd carry you along like an egg in a basket."

"Ain't *that* damn delicate," Kole grumbled as he snatched the map to get it out from under his nose. "You're supposed to be such a smart guy, but the truth is, you're out of your so-called mind, Laurent."

Grinning, Jack glanced at Heather. "I got the idea from a TV documentary."

Kole snapped the map open and spread it across his knees, mumbling, "I thought you hated TV."

"I watch the History Channel, Discovery Channel, PBS," Jack claimed, but when Kole glanced up with his get-real look, he added, "Okay, music videos and basketball. Anyhow, I saw this documentary about the Bonus Marchers back in 1932. Twenty-five thousand World War I veterans descended on D.C. asking for the bonus money they'd been promised. They weren't supposed to get it until, like, '45, but, hell, it was the Depression, and they were starving.

"They started out from up in Washington State with just a few guys, but as they traveled across country, more and more guys joined them until they had this huge army of protesters. It was just shameful, you know? Here these guys had fought for their country, risked their lives, and ended up with no jobs, no way to support their families. There were a lot of Indians joined up in World War I."

"We love to fight, don't we?" Kole's tone dripped with irony.

"We do our share. Anyway, all these Bonus Marchers wanted was what they'd been promised."

"Did they get it?"

"No, they got run off by the U.S. Army. That was the most shameful part. Mounted cavalry charging down the street against our own war veterans, right there in the nation's capital."

"Did they fire on them?" Kole quizzed.

Jack nodded.

"Casualties?"

"A few."

"And that's where you got this idea for something for us to do?" Kole clucked, tongue in cheek. "I've already been there, Jack. You figure everybody can see that your cause is just. You figure they won't shoot. Even if they do, the cause is like a Ghost Dance shirt. It can repel the bullets. It's a holy thing, covers every part of you. You can do no wrong."

"Like a Crusader?" Heather asked. The men turned to her, surprised, as though the fly on the wall had spoken. "You know, back in the Middle Ages. When a knight pledged himself to crusade, his sins were covered in advance."

"By God?"

"Well, no, by the pope."

"My sins are between me and God," Kole said. "For right now I'll worry about covering my ass with more than just dreams and painted cloth."

"What about Linda?" Jack said.

Kole glared at him.

"A murdered wife is a pretty damn just cause, if you ask me," Jack said.

"I ain't askin' you."

"She'd want you to stand up for—"

"She'd have nothin' to do with this harebrained idea of yours."

"How do you know?" With a dramatic flourish Jack grabbed the remote and clicked the video back on, running the tape back and forth until the images of Barry Wilson and Tom Seal appeared in the same frame. "What are those two guys doing together, Kola?" He pressed a forefinger over Wilson's face on the TV screen. "You went to prison because of this one, bro, I don't care what you say. And then along comes this other guy."

"When I got sent up, Seal was already there."

"And he sets you up somehow."

"I don't know that for sure," Kole said quietly, shooting a hot stare across the room at the screen.

"And you bust out, and then you lay low for a while, and finally you hook up with Linda. You think maybe you're okay after a while, so you quietly get involved with a group trying to hold out against a dumping site on Indian land way the hell down in Arizona some-where. You think you'll just help out behind the scenes, nothing public—"

"And somebody blows up my house," Kole finished for him. He

shook his head, still intent on the screen. "Barry wasn't in on it. He'd never get his hands that dirty. Look at him. He's all show. All talk. He wouldn't let anyone hurt Linda. Hell, he . . ." He opened his hands, looked at Heather, who had spoken to Wilson recently, then Jack, who had never met the man. "He couldn't. Why would he?"

"I ain't sayin' he would or did or meant to—I don't know. All I'm sayin' is, what's this about?" Jack nodded toward the TV screen. "You gotta wonder."

"No, I don't." Kole snatched the remote from Jack's hand. "It's part of a show, a game. Walkin' on the wild side with an ex-con. It's just like Wilson. All the world's a stage."

But he couldn't take his eyes off the screen. He backed the tape up for one more icy look. "Too bad he can't act quite as good as he thinks he can."

6

When the dream started, Kole was able to tell himself it wasn't real. He could feel himself inside his own head, could see with his own eyes a road at the end of a shaft, could tell that he was the one driving some kind of vehicle, but he couldn't feel his hands on the wheel or his foot on the pedal. He could see that he was driving, though, because he was also outside himself looking on. It was that kind of a dream.

Just go along for the ride, he told himself. If you wake yourself up, you won't be able to go back to sleep. *It's only a dream, so just relax and play along.*

The woods were dark and quiet. Ah, a

silent dream in black and white, shadows and moonlight. Nice. He was driving a soundless glider truck. Either that or he was deaf. He could feel the cool wind in his face, but at first he heard nothing. Then someone turned the sound on. He tried to ignore it, but like a squealing mosquito, it crept up on him from behind. It worried his ear until he was able to identify it as the soft, thin, distant cry of a baby who had almost tired herself beyond the reach of the pain in her gut.

Driving her around sometimes soothed her, but not this time. Every time he turned the pickup toward home, she'd start in again. He knew why Linda's headaches were getting worse. His head hurt sometimes, too, but he knew it wasn't the same for his wife. She truly suffered. He didn't, not really. Once he got out of the house, he felt better.

He didn't mind driving the baby around late at night. He relished the freedom to go out and keep going, without ever running into a fence. He felt bad about the baby's pain, about his wife's pain, but fresh air and freedom were all he needed to take his own pain away. "Can't you feel it in your stomach?" he asked the baby. Linda had told him that air was causing all the trouble, but he didn't believe that. He figured his little one had inherited her father's gut-gnawing demon.

The night air and the motion of the pickup usually appeased the restless demon, but not tonight, not completely. The baby's wail was so melancholy, it nearly tore his heart out, infecting him with a strange feeling of desperation. Had to go home.

Couldn't go home.

Had to go home.

He was tumbling, stumbling, moving in circles as the wailing gained strength and grew more insistent. It wasn't just a baby anymore. It was a siren. The headlight became firelight. The light at the end of the tunnel, life's tunnel, death's light. Their house was on fire, and he was running for it, like a horse going back to a burning barn. Then he realized that he was carrying his baby—*their* baby. Frantically he searched for someone to take the baby off his hands, but there was no one. He was alone in the woods with the fire and the baby and the siren.

The light exploded in a kaleidoscope of color, hurling the pieces of their brief life together through the roof, like a scene from a macabre cartoon. Chair, table, broom, lamp . . . Linda. Arms and legs flailing, she catapulted into the night sky, headed for the stars.

The baby slipped away from him as he surged through the darkness after his wife, crying out to her.

She kicked back, crushing his balls. Glittering eyes peered at him through the gloom. Kole lifted a shaky hand, touched a cold, wet nose. Oh God, she'd gone to the sky and become a wolf.

A soothing hand slid up his bare back. "It's all right, Kole. You're—"

"Linda?"

"Heather," the voiced said softly. "Woof, get down. He's okay."

"Heather . . ." He drew a deep, tremulous breath as the ball-crusher retreated to the floor. "Sorry." He groaned. Really bad form, calling out the wrong name.

"Me, too." She stroked his back. Her warm, steady hand felt good against his clammy skin. "Not that I'm here," she whispered, "but that she can't be."

"Jesus." A cold shiver slithered through him, head to toe. "Goin' crazy again."

"You're all right." She put her hands on his face and tried to coddle him, treat him like her baby, babbling to him and petting him. "Lord, you're shaking. Let me hold you."

He wasn't her baby, wasn't her lord, wasn't even her man. What kind of a man dropped his baby on somebody else's doorstep? Damn his eyes, he'd dropped her, lost her, let her slip away.

He pushed the slender, cleaving arms off, away from his body. "I have to get up," he said, sounding gruffer than he intended as he swung his legs off the bed.

"Am I in your way?"

"It's not that. I don't want to sleep anymore." He paused, closed his eyes, and let the soft cry fill his head again. "That sound. I want to put that sound into a flute."

"What sound?"

"The baby." He was halfway across the room, feeling around the workbench in the dark until he found a flute. He could tell by the feel that it was the loon's head flute he'd just finished. "I wonder if I can get a flute to cry like that. Not like the usual wailing baby. More like a lament. It's like . . ."

He blew into the mouthpiece and tweedled in a minor key, then shook his head. "That's not it. I think I could get it, though, if I shorten up the . . ." He played another birdlike riff.

Heather scooted to the foot of the bed, clutching a quilt to her breast. "You look like a Greek god," she said. "Didn't Apollo play the flute in the nude?"

He watched her trail the quilt across the floor as she came to him. "Didn't those guys do everything in the nude? What's with the blanket?"

"This is Norse god weather, and *they* never did anything in the nude." She opened her arms and enclosed them both in the quilt. "Let's stoke up the fire and go back to bed. A fire is great for sending bad dreams up in smoke."

"Not this dream, honey." He slipped his arms around her, taking the flute in both hands and using it to pull her close. "This one gets its power from fire."

"Maybe talking about it would drive it away."

"Maybe I don't want to drive it away." He rested his chin in her hair. He was breaking his own rules simply by mentioning the two he'd lost. "It's the only way I can still have them. I know it's not right. You're supposed to release the spirits after a year."

"Claudia isn't a spirit. She's very much alive, much loved, very happy."

He nodded. He knew all that. He had done the best he could, and if he could believe this woman, his daughter was not only happy, but she was also safe. And no longer his daughter.

"Let me tell you about her," Heather urged.

He pulled away, sliding the smooth flute over her bare hip as he withdrew.

"Oh, Kole, she's so—"

He placed two fingers over her lips and whispered, "Don't."

She sighed. "Tell me about your dream, then."

"Nothing to tell. The baby's crying and the house is on fire. Ladybug, ladybug, fly fly away."

"But the baby . . . Claudia wasn't in the house, was she?"

"No, she was with me."

He tried another flute, which resonated at a higher pitch. *Wheee. Wheee.* Too cheery. "She was—what do you call it? Colicky."

"Which means . . ."

He smiled around the mouthpiece of a third flute—a private smile in the darkness—then played a few notes, a closer approximation of the sound he sought to duplicate. It amused him that the man in the room was familiar with colicky babies and the woman was not. He was one up on her. He'd once been a father.

"She'd start in crying just about the same time every evening," he explained. "The only thing that seemed to help was a ride in the pickup. Usually that would put her to sleep, but it didn't work so well that night. We couldn't go home as long as she kept on cryin'. Linda would get these bad headaches, and she couldn't stand noise or light. So my wife was the only one in the house when it went up. The baby was with me. Or I was with her. She saved my life, I guess."

"Savannah claims that Claudia saved her life, too. Did Savannah tell you that she had breast cancer?"

Breast cancer? Savannah? It took a moment for the concept to sink in. Savannah was just about the most physically perfect woman he'd ever met. "She said she moved back home because she'd been sick. She didn't say anything about cancer."

"She had a rough time. She says Claudia was her reason for living. You should see her, Kole. She's so—"

He cut her off with more flute song.

"It's not like most adoptions," she persisted when his music stopped. "They're your family. You really should see her."

"You really should keep your 'shoulds' to yourself," he suggested amiably as he switched flutes. He toodled a bit. "Close, but still not right. How's Savannah now? Did they get rid of the cancer all right?"

"So far, so good. She had a mastectomy, but you'd never know it. She's got it all together now, she and Clay. Claudia will be their only child, unless they decide to adopt again."

"Maybe I should get to work on it, huh? For a little wedding gift?" He hooked his arm around her blanket-draped shoulders. "How about it? You wanna go in on it with me? We should try for a boy so they have one of each."

"Maybe we should both keep our 'shoulds' to ourselves and get down to some 'woulds.' " She slipped the flute from his hand. "I would love to learn how to make one of these."

"Right now?"

"If you're going to work on it now. You said you wanted to get that sound out of a flute. Show me how you do that." She blew into the flute—one long, low, single note. "I want to hear what you heard in your dream."

"Believe me, you don't," he assured her as they moved toward the bed. "I let the baby go, but Linda . . ."

"Would it sound self-serving if I said you probably need to let her go, too?"

"Yeah, but who could blame you?"

He was joking, but since he didn't laugh, neither did she. He realized she didn't know quite how to take him sometimes. Still, sweet woman, she let him come. Come hard, come easy, come suspicious or scared. *Come as you are.* She was the first to witness his dreams. She was the first to touch him when he trembled, to hold him when he wanted to run. He got back into bed with her, just as she'd suggested, but without tending to the fire. He wanted to warm her himself.

"Maybe I'm not the one holding her here," he mused, stroking her hair. She'd brought the flute to bed with them, laid it on his chest, her head on his shoulder. "Maybe she can't leave, can't move on because . . ."

"Because you can't move on?"

"Because of the way she died. There was stuff blasted all over the place. Clothes hanging in the trees—the baby's little shirt with the snaps, Linda's T-shirt, the one she'd worn that day, it was blown out of the house and hanging there like wash on the line. But she was inside. She was in bed, trying to get rid of that headache. They found enough to identify her. But maybe it wasn't enough to take her into the next world. I mean, when the FBI investigated my mother's death, they cut off her hands and sent them to their lab in Washington. For identification, they said."

Her hand slid over his right hip to the tattoo he'd taunted her with, and he closed his eyes in the dark, enjoyed the feel of her rubbing the letters of his name, telling him she knew. She knew him. She knew who he was and what was in his heart.

"My grandmother was beside herself over that," he confided. "After we buried her, Unci—that means my grandmother—Unci sat me down and made me write a letter to the president, asking him to tell his men to send her daughter's hands back. 'How will she get along in the next life without her hands?' she told me to write. So I wrote what she said. But I never mailed it like I promised, 'cause I knew the president was never gonna see that letter, and whoever did would just get a big laugh out of an old woman asking the president to send her daughter's hands back."

Heather lay still against him for what felt like a long, heartfelt time.

Finally she cleared her throat, croaking a bit on her first couple of words. "But . . . but if you could've gotten the *New York Times* to print that letter, you can bet the president would have seen it. That's the power of the press, Kole. Public opinion is so—"

"The FBI would have said we were lying. We were mistaken. We were *misinformed*. That's the word they'd use in their official comment. It's one of their favorites.

"Then the conspiracy theory nuts would come to our defense, making it even easier to write us off as politically motivated or paranoid or just plain ignorant." He brushed his fingertips across her forehead, as though he might discover her thoughts by touch. "Do you believe me?"

"Yes."

"No hesitation. I like that." He rested his head back against the log wall and smiled secretly in the dark. "Why do you believe me? Because you've slept with me?"

"That has nothing to do with it."

"You sleep with guys who lie to you?"

"I don't just go around sleeping with *guys*. I don't . . ." She flicked a finger against his side. He knew he had it coming, so he rewarded her with a yelp. "You're lucky I didn't flog you with your own flute," she said. "I believe you because I've followed this story, I know the background, and I'm very intuitive about people. You're telling me the truth as you know it."

"The truth *as I know it.* You're saying I could still be paranoid."

"And politically motivated. But not crazy, and definitely not igno-rant."

"I'd feel pretty good about that assessment if it wasn't coming from a woman who'd thrown herself under my wheels, practically begged me to hold her hostage. If I'm crazy, you're a damn loony tune."

"I'm not exactly a hostage."

"You're not the first, either. I've had volunteer hostages before. Those women at the post office, they offered to let me tie them up, said I could do all the flute-flogging I wanted."

He knew she was smiling. He could feel it, which scared him some, being able to feel her humor without seeing or hearing the usual signs. This shouldn't be happening, and he knew it. She'd caught him at a bad time. Or he'd caught her. At this point he wasn't sure what was going on, or who'd started it or why. He had a pretty good idea how it would end, and he suddenly realized that he'd be sorry when it did.

Shit.

He took the flute from her hands as he shifted her in his arms and slid down in the bed. The rough-hewn wall was a lousy backrest. He had plans for putting a headboard on the bed, making it himself. But that was one of those plans that smacked too much of settling in per-manently, and this wasn't his place. Linda's father had offered it to Kola, said he could stay as long as he wanted to. But Kole Kills Crow had no place.

"You want me to tie you up?" he said, trying to change the subject in his own head.

"I can do you if you'd like."

He laughed. "I might take you up on that sometime when I'm feeling really crazy. Like when the voices start nagging at me, telling me it's time to drag a new woman back to my hideout for a little variety."

Propping herself up on one elbow, she took her weight off his shoulder. "Vy don't you make yourself comfortable on my leetle couch and tell me all about deese voices, Mr. Kills Crow." Her foreign accent was strictly Hollywood.

"You're not messin' with my voices, lady. They're good company."

"Not tonight they weren't."

"Yeah, well . . . I did get a little crazy for a while. After I'd given the baby up and I knew she was safe with Savannah, I went off the deep end and holed up with a bottle and a bad case of the blues."

He didn't mention the gun. He'd wanted to kill somebody, and there was only one guilty party close at hand. Remembering all the shit that had gone through his head then made him feel a little queasy, even now.

"What turned you around?"

"It was a who, not a what. Jack, the yak-yak. Jack, the pest-hunting pest. He wears contacts most of the time, but when he puts on those big horn-rimmed glasses of his, he looks like a little owl." He chuckled. "It was good ol' Jack *whoooo* . . . dragged me out of my hole and pecked at me till I staggered to my feet."

"Skinny little Jack?"

"The only muscle he's developed in his whole body is the one inside his chest. Persistent as hell, that guy. He got me writing for his paper. It was his idea to sell the flutes through a dealer. Linda's grandfather taught me how to make them, but it was Jack who helped me make it profitable. He thinks I'm some kind of symbol of . . ." He tapped her on the head, as though blessing her with his flute. "But that's bullshit, and you're both full of it."

"Maybe." She laid her cool hand on his cheek. She smelled of the cinnamon and apples they'd baked for supper. "Maybe we know you better than you know yourself."

"Hell, you're both professional buttinskis." He turned his face to her palm and touched its center with the tip of his tongue, taking salt and sustenance from her hand. "I don't know why you've let me get this close to you."

"I've known you for a long, long time."

"Then why have I let you get this close to me?" He pressed a kiss into the wet hollow of her palm. "I don't know you at all."

"Yes, you do. It doesn't take much to get to know me. I'm not all that complicated."

"You gotta be. You're a woman." He blew a long, deep sigh. "You and Jack are two of a kind. I'm living the simple life, and you're both trying to tangle it all up."

"How far has he gotten in his plans for a protest march?"

He shook his head. "I guess he's gonna try it. I don't know how much support he has. I mean, who really cares about Hollywood's fairy tales?"

"Who really cares about water rights and toxic waste dumps?" she shot back. She sat up, turning to him and pulling her legs under her, the better to spring on him, like some soft, round-eyed rabbit.

He groaned. She was winding up to make her push.

"You know what it takes to shake people up, Kole. It's about grabbing attention, and in this day and age, you need some kind of a screen for that. You need a soundtrack and a headliner, an endorsement from a pretty face or a—"

"Or a stunt. What, a hostile uprising isn't enough of a stunt?"

"Well, it's just so seventies."

"So I'm a throwback."

Enthusiasm pushed her voice up an octave. "But I think real Indians marching across the real American West to meet the myth makers is a wonderful idea."

"I think you guys are right."

"You do?"

"About Seal and Wilson. I know damn well Seal was in on killing Daryl Two Horn. I don't know how or why, but I know in my gut he was in on it."

He paused, letting that much sink into his own psyche as more than a hunch. It was knowledge. It was a foundation, lying there waiting for someone who cared enough to start building on it.

Heather said nothing, but he could feel her excitement. In the dark her little nose for news was probably twitching like mad.

Foundation. In his mind's eye he saw himself reaching for a building block, and he knew damn well it would hurt to lift the thing. He braced himself with a deep breath and spoke quietly into the darkness.

"I don't know who killed my wife, but I'm thinking Seal knows. And I've gotta wonder about Wilson." He got a sick feeling, just saying it. But just saying it, hearing it, made it real. "Okay, I've gotta do more than wonder."

"I didn't say anything."

"No," he said softly, "but the voices did."

7

On the one oil-stained hand—his head stuck under the hood of prospective transportation—Kole felt like some chintzy farmer counting a gift horse's teeth. On the other hand—also oil-stained, and for no good reason, since he didn't know much about engines—he had his ass to protect. He knew the offer of the camper was a generous one, but he also knew how old the thing was. If he had to put this particular gift horse out of its misery along the way somewhere, he would be walking in deep shit.

"You really think this old heap of tin can make it to California?"

"Depends on who's driving," Bobby Bear

said. The big man with the beady black eyes, ample brown cheeks, and sparse goatee patted the silver camper's one good headlight affectionately. "She needs a couple of parts, but nothin' major. This ain't no ordinary heap of tin. You're lookin' at a genuine Silver Streak, man."

"Use your imagination, Kola." Jack gestured with an enthusiastic flourish. "It's a tipi on wheels."

"That's right," Bobby said proudly. "You just have to know how to take care of her." With the toe of his tennis shoe he tapped the side of a milk crate he'd hauled out and dropped on the ground next to the side door. "Right in here you got your complete emergency kit. You got your gas can, baling wire, duct tape, cardboard, siphon hose, can of STP." He pointed with his lips toward the open door. Kole could see a table surrounded on three sides by a booth with threadbare blue cushions. "Mostly everything works," Bobby said. "Except the refrigerator, air-conditioning, tape player. Radio pulls in both AM and FM. You don't wanna use the toilet too much, but the shower works good."

"An indoor shower," Heather marveled.

Kole shot her a warning glance. He'd asked her to let him be the judge of whether the camper was roadworthy. She was to be seen but not heard, like a good little white kid. He'd forgotten that good little white kids were also taught to agree to any terms just to get their way. In her head Heather was already on her way to Hollywood with a crazy bunch of Indians.

"I'm mainly concerned about the motor and the tires," he told Bobby.

"It's all there. She's got some miles on her, so she uses oil. But all you have to do is carry some along and watch the dipstick. Don't let her overheat." Bobby brushed some dried mud off the side mirror. "Make sure she has water before you fire her up. She drinks a lot, but

I don't hold it against her." He chuckled. "You take care of her, she'll take care of you. Guaranteed."

If there was one thing Bobby Bear knew, it was automotive engines. Kole surveyed the acre lot full of old heaps Bobby had salvaged. He'd made a pretty good living buying and selling junkers and parts. He wasn't much of a body man, but he could get almost any wreck to run.

Bobby kicked a front tire on the camper. "Hell, you got at least an eighth of an inch of tread on most of the tires. You're set, man. Drive to Australia if you want."

A rejection of the camper would be a rejection of Bobby. The image of the generous helper saying "take my horse" came to mind. *Damn movies.*

Kole laughed. "If we get to the West Coast, we'll get Wilson to part the waters for us."

"Hey, did you see him on *Baywatch*?" Bobby asked. "I forgot, no TV. How about you, Jack?"

"I must've missed that episode," Jack said. He was sitting on the trunk of an old blue Camaro. "Did he get pulled from the water by one of those babes in the little red swimsuits?"

"Playing an Indian, you know he didn't get no girls. Not on that show. It's all blue-eyed blondes. But you gotta admire the way they run across the beach in slow motion, long blond semaphores waving in back, buoys bouncing up front." Bobby cupped his hands in front of his own ample chest and demonstrated the motion in the universal language of ogling males. "But our brother Barry didn't even have to get his feet wet for his mouth-to-mouth scene."

"I saw it." Heather was laughing now, too. She'd let the boobs gesture slide past. "You're gonna love this," she promised Kole.

"Damn, don't tell me he gets to make a pass at the girl."

Jack hopped down off the Camaro. "Wait, was that Wilson? He's this old Indian guy who's come home to die. Somewhere along the way his tribe lost their land to the *Baywatch* babes. I *did* see that."

"I'd rather see the babes on that beach than ol' Barry," Kole said.

"Hey, they wrinkled him up real good, made him look like he was at least a hundred and ten," Bobby said, using his hands to add dimension to the scene. "So he's sittin' there on the beach, smokin' his pipe in front of the campfire. It really reminded me of the old days, the way he was surrounded by his young followers, everybody waitin' on him to make a move. *Baywatch* gave him this real foxy granddaughter to speak up for him. In his old age, see, he can only speak Lakota."

"Lakota?" Kole shook his head, laughing. "First of all, the only Lakota Barry Wilson can speak is what I taught him. And second, I never heard of any Sioux claim to any beachfront property."

"You sure?" Jack tossed Kole a red bandanna he'd pulled out of his pocket. "You guys claim everything else. But we all know you lost your lake property when we ran you out at spear-point."

"You didn't run us out. We got tired of eating rabbits and slapping mosquitoes." Kole wiped his fingers on the bandanna, which was already thoroughly stained, probably with ink. "But I don't think any of our cousins strayed that far west."

"It's true," Heather attested. "Even I recognized that he was speaking Lakota."

"All Hollywood Indians speak Lakota." Jack was watching Kole wipe the oil off his hands. "I don't know why you guys get to be the big stars all the time, like there's only one kind of Indian."

"Because John Wayne wouldn't look too good chasing after a bunch of rabbit hunters." Kole shoved the bandanna into the breast pocket on Jack's denim jacket. "How many wagon trains did you Chippewa knock off, huh?"

"Ojibwe," Jack corrected.

"Whatever. You're fishermen."

"So are you," Heather teased, turning to Bobby. "That's all he serves his guests."

"He better remember, he's a guest, too. We can always run his Lakota ass out a second time."

Kole eyed the Silver Streak. "Looks to me like you're already workin' on it."

"You can stay behind if you want, Kola. Guard the fort." Jack sidled up to Heather. "You must've studied their history, right? What was the expression Crazy Horse used for the Sioux who hung around the fort waiting for handouts? Weren't they something like 'Laramie loafers'?"

"That's what I read."

"That's cold, Laurent." Kole glanced back and forth between Jack and Heather. This was a lightweight conspiracy, but a conspiracy nonetheless. "Tipi on wheels," he mused, staring at the battered camper. He'd already decided to head west and look Wilson up. He wasn't sure this was the best way to get there. He didn't want to risk any hide but his own.

Glancing at Heather, he knew damn well he was looking at the best way. Surely the most pleasant. He took his risks, she took hers. They might as well do it together—a red man and a white woman going down the yellow brick road in an old Silver Streak. He smiled. Bring on the Technicolor.

She returned an over-the-rainbow smile, but he knew they weren't smiling for the same reason. She was thinking about him, all right, but in black and white. She had no idea what lay ahead, but she had her story all mapped out on paper. She'd already decided who the hero was and who was the villain. All she needed were the facts to prove that her instincts were right, that Kole Kills Crow was another Martin Luther King, Jr.

Try again.

Kole was no orator. He hadn't been exactly nonviolent. But he didn't know the history of the civil rights movement well enough to come up with a better comparison. That was Heather's job. Maybe she'd suggest that he was the reincarnation of Sitting Bull or Geronimo, the last of the renegades.

Which didn't bode particularly well for the end of his own story.

But he'd been giving her bits and pieces, and he knew now that he was ready to give her more. The whole nine yards on his side of the fence. On the face of it, he didn't look much like a hero. After all, he was still a fugitive. Good guys didn't run. A real hero wouldn't ditch his kid and hide out like a mole. But there was, as Heather kept saying, more to it than that. Maybe it was time to get it down and put it in print.

Maybe he really did care what the people outside Indian country thought. He'd been hiding out so long, he'd begun to feel invisible. Once in a while he would take a chance and leave the reservation to take in a movie or see a friend, but he lived like a shadow. He was there, but no one really saw him.

Except Heather. She'd known who he was right away, as though there was still something inside him that glowed in the dark, still some fire in his belly. Maybe that was why he'd taken her in, taken to her, taken her. When she looked at him, she saw Kole Kills Crow. She knew him. She appreciated him. And that felt surprisingly good to him.

God, yes, he wanted somebody to know his side, *his* truth. He wanted his family to know him, finally.

And he wanted his life back.

* * *

"Will we be going anywhere that might have an office supply store?" Heather loaded her laptop and her small suitcase through the camper's side door. She ought to be thinking about buying a few clothes—she hadn't brought much—but first things first. "I'd like to buy one of those old-fashioned writing tools that you don't have to plug in. The manual kind."

"Hammer and chisel?" Kole tossed in two duffel bags. The second one clattered when it landed. "I'm taking mine along. I've got work to do, too."

"Not *that* manual." She punctuated the word with a finger flick against his chest. "I'll tell you what, though, a manual typewriter seems almost as archaic as carving on tablets. I have an electric one somewhere. No, I guess I gave it to my mother. Where would you even find a manual typewriter? I've never used one."

"Never? Was this your first outhouse experience, too?"

"Of course not. I'm a woman of the world. But *you*—how long did it take you to get used to not having a phone or any electricity?"

"Not as long as it took to get used to going without sex."

She glanced away, feeling oddly self-conscious. "How long did that take?"

"I was almost there, and then you came along." He grasped her hips and pulled her to him, his cocky smile touching his eyes. "Now I gotta start all over."

"Yeah, well, life without a phone is one thing, but life without e-mail?" She shook her head, but she returned his playful smile, enjoying the ease and the familiarity of his gesture. "Weird."

"You should talk, honey. By the way, you can't do e-mail on a type-writer."

"No, but I've heard some people still use them to write. All you get is hard copy, but it's something."

"You'd have a real hard copy if you used a chisel."

"It would be good to take a cell phone along, don't you think?" She plunged her hand into the leather purse she'd stashed behind the passenger's seat and pulled out her Nokia.

"You've had that all along?"

The wide-eyed expression on his face was almost laughable. She'd actually surprised him. "It doesn't work up here."

"You already tried?"

"Wouldn't you?" She smiled knowingly. "I'll have to recharge the battery somewhere," she said as she turned to put the phone back in her purse.

"That's not goin' with us."

"Why not? As a safety measure."

He grabbed her arm. "Whose safety?"

"Kole, you have to trust me. You can't do this with me unless you trust me."

"You're doing this with me. You're goin' along for the ride *with me*. You're an observer, a guest." He took the phone from her hand. "I don't know much about trusting people, Heather. I trust that dog."

They both glanced at Woof, who lay close by, watching, listening, waiting to see who was going, who was staying, and what part he might play.

"I know what he's gonna do, when he's gonna do it. I know if I call him, he'll come to me any way he can. He won't change except to get old and die. But people's wants and needs and plans change like the wind." Kole's dark eyes plumbed the depths of hers. "What's to trust?"

"You trusted Savannah," she reminded him quietly.

"It wasn't about trust. I did what I had to do. I made a choice I never want to have to make again."

"But you must have trusted her."

"*Trust me*, honey, I don't know anything about trust. What I know about is doing what you have to do when you're boxed in so tight you have to fight for every breath. I've got plenty of experience there." He slid his arms around her again, rubbed the butt of her leather-encased cell phone up and down her spine like a massage tool. "I like being with you, Heather. I'll do what I can to please you while we're together. But don't ask me for trust."

She stood up to the unyielding look he was giving her. Couldn't he tell by now? She was *worthy* of trust. Everyone knew that—everyone who knew her. She kept confidences. She treated people with respect.

She kept her word. She had a reputation for being trustworthy. "Trust me" was easily said, it was true. What woman hadn't heard those words bandied about and thought, *Easy for you to say?* But she of all people had earned the right to say them. She had proven herself to be trustworthy. She had high standards, sterling ideals. That was why she was there.

You have to trust me, damn it. I'm trusting you.

Didn't he realize that? They'd come so far in such a short time, she thought. How difficult could it be to take the next step? Trust. It was a fragile gift, certainly. He made it sound both perfidious and precious when he said the word. A rare treasure.

She would get it from him somehow.

◆ ◆ ◆

Before sunup the following morning at least two dozen would-be marchers gathered at the Cheap Shot. Jack had done his public relations job well, and if the march were to be made on foot, no problem. But they were a few vehicles short of anything resembling a caravan.

"Too many riders and not enough ponies," bartender Mario observed. He'd made his feelings about the scheme pretty clear. He wasn't going, and he hated to see some of his best customers getting ready to leave town. He'd already announced that tap beer was going to be half price for the next week. Bobby Bear said he'd take one, but Mario reminded him that the bar didn't open until noon.

Even after several people admitted to being less than totally committed to making the trip, there were still more riders than passenger seats.

"Who's riding with you, Kola?" Toby Dogskin wanted to know.

Kole nodded at Heather.

"Is that all? And you've got Bear's camper? Hell, I'll jump in with you."

"Take my pickup," Kole offered.

But Jack piped up with, "You gave me your pickup."

"Well, you take Toby, then."

"I'd rather ride in the camper," Toby said. "If it's just you and her, you got plenty of room."

"We're working on something, me and her," Kole said. In response to Toby's suggestive smirk, he added, "*Writing* something together. She's a writer, and we're writing a story together. You can't have a bunch of people around you when you're writing."

Heather nearly crowed aloud. She knew he was trying to avoid making eye contact with her, but she stared at his profile so hard he finally gave in to a quick glance. She beamed. The glance became a lingering gaze. He finally rolled his eyes to cover up the self-conscious smile she detected tugging at the corners of his mouth.

"Hey, Kola," Toby called out as he laid claim to the passenger seat in Kole's pickup. Kole turned. Toby flashed him a wide grin. "You be sure and practice safe writing."

✦ ✦ ✦

Kole took the wheel for the first leg of the journey on roads that snaked through the woods and skirted shoreline after shoreline in the Land of Ten Thousand Lakes. There was no such thing as a straight shot in the North Country. They were all back roads, bending in conformance with the lay of the land and the water's dominant claim. This was country that retained vestiges of wildness, even though more and more sportsmen were insisting on invading it with their motorized toys.

Kole explained that he had taken refuge in the North Country much the way his wife's ancestors had, driven from the arable land in the south by armed invaders. Eventually the invaders saw something they wanted in this territory, too. Not fish for food, but fish for sport.

Not living, breathing trees, but timber. Not earth, but minerals. It was a clash of values.

"That's why we're writing our story," she said with a smile. "I liked the way you put that, by the way. *We're* working on something."

"I have a feeling Toby caught my drift better than you did."

"I'm taking you at your word," she said happily. "I think people in this country are gradually, oh-so-gradually waking up, Kole. Value systems don't change overnight, and European Americans or whatever we want to call that part of ourselves—it's part of you, too—they've lived and died by feudalism, mercantilism, capitalism, the gold standard and possession being nine-tenths of the law for so long—"

"You make it sound like a religion. 'Lived and died by.' "

"Religion is part of it," she said. "The Church has always been part of it. We've always sort of denigrated any kind of spirituality that ties in to the natural world, from the Celts and Druids to Native Americans. The Church called it witchcraft, satanism, idolatry, or just plain superstition. But Christians are as superstitious as anyone else, and Satan is a Christian image, not Celtic, not Native American. Christianity is unique in its belief that there exists a pure and perfect evil, namely the Devil."

"Really?"

She offered an apologetic smile. "Sorry. I didn't mean to lecture."

"Aren't you a Christian?"

"Yes, I am. I was brought up that way, and I believe in God, so I worship as a Christian. But the Church—you know, the political institution in all its earthly power and glory—well, you have to be realistic about the role it plays, especially when you talk about property and people's values."

"Property values and religion?" He laughed and shook his head. "Honey, I don't know how you mix those two."

"Change 'values' to 'respect.' Respect for property and property claims, property rights. The claim to the land in the name of the queen or king was blessed by God. But you talk about respect for the land, the earth itself, the animals and plants that live and grow here naturally, blessed by God, that's more—"

"My speed," he finished for her.

"Exactly. But we're coming around, I think. People are coming around." She shrugged as she flipped open the Minnesota road map. "I hope it's not too late. If we don't come around soon, I personally think we're sunk. I thought we were going to be hop-skipping around from reservation to reservation. Why are we stopping in Minneapolis?"

"There are more Indians in Minneapolis than on most reservations."

"More cops, too. Isn't it dangerous?"

"Have you committed a crime?"

She gave him an innocent look.

"Are you planning to?"

She shook her head.

"Then you have nothing to worry about, do you?"

"*You* do."

"Well, that's because I've done wrong."

"You've broken the law."

"Isn't that wrong?"

She flipped the armrest out of the way and turned as far as she could in her chair. The map slipped to the floor. "In this case, it's not quite that cut-and-dried, is it?"

"If you say so."

"What do you say?"

He shrugged. "I knew I was breaking the law, and I know damn well the law wasn't made to be broken."

"But you didn't do it for your own gain."

"I didn't?" It was his turn to flash the innocent look. "What'd I do it for?"

"You took over that store and held people inside because you were trying to make a point about the fact that the store, which was being sold, was sitting on land that, by the existing treaty—in other words *by law*—was supposed to be turned back over to the tribe if the trading post—which eventually became a general store—"

"And a U.S. Post Office," he reminded her.

"*And* a post office—if that was ever relocated, the tribe was supposed to get the land back."

"So I broke the law of the land to get the land back from the law?"

"To make a point about 'taken land'—any land taken by the government is supposed to revert back when it's no longer needed for the government's original purpose. Like the land claimed by the Corps of Engineers for water projects like the Oahe Dam in South Dakota, river bottom land which they now say they no longer need, which is the *real* point, isn't it?" She snatched up the map and started folding it as she spoke. "That land should, by long-standing agreement, revert back to tribal ownership."

"If you say so."

"*You* said so. I have it on tape," she said, shaking the map at him. "You pointed out that *they* were the ones who allotted the land and declared your people the owners, and then *they* reneged on it, but they had this one small loophole in *their* law, and you were—"

"You sure it wasn't Wilson?" he asked placidly. "We look a lot alike."

"You do not."

"Sound alike, then."

"You do not."

He laughed. "If you say so."

"I want to know what *you* have to say about what you said back then."

"Nothing."

"I mean, knowing what you know now, after all that's happened—"

"Nothing's happened," he insisted. "Nothing's changed. I don't know any more now than I did then, and you've got such a good story goin' already, you sure as hell don't want me to screw it up. So you tell me. Did I make a point, and if I did, who got it, do you think?"

"Well, I certainly think—"

He startled her by suddenly reaching across the space between them and putting his upended fist within an inch of her mouth. She flinched.

He chuckled. "Talk into the microphone, please, Miss Reardon."

"You, Mr. Kills Crow . . ." Slowly, subtly, she released the breath she'd caught for a moment ". . . are not an easy interview."

"Yeah, but you are." His eyes sparkled knowingly. "Which is hardly a big surprise."

"Considering what an easy lay—"

"Considering what an easy person you are to get to know." He withdrew his "microphone" and gave a reassuring nod. "To be with."

"Really?"

"Really. You're just plain easy, lady." He whistled a few bars of "Lay, Lady, Lay" until she punched him in the arm. He laughed. He was doing that a lot more lately—laughing. "Hell, you know you're not gonna be able to go through with this interview thing now. You haven't committed any crimes, but you've crossed over the line. You've done the big *D* with your subject. You're too close."

"What's the big *D*?

"Dirty," he whispered, his eyebrows bobbing.

"It was not dirty."

"Close, though. More than close. You got the cigar."

"No way! I got the canoe, was what I got." And now she was laughing. Doing it more lately. Laughing. "I don't do cigars."

"Canoes are much more wholesome."

"Much. This book is going to be about more than one person, even though the focus will be on you. I want the reader to be able to examine a lot of issues for himself, but do it through your eyes, through your experiences. Walk a mile in your moccasins, so to speak."

"You don't wanna use that line. It's *way* old." He flashed her a raised eyebrow. "So to speak."

"But the concept isn't."

"I don't know about that. Nowadays it's more like, walk a mile in my Web site." He slid her a naughty look, a wink. "Feel my virtual reality."

"Well, well," she chirped. "The reclusive Indian flute maker turns out to be surprisingly well versed in cyber-lingo."

"Jack is all hooked into this stuff." He shrugged it off. "So Kola has his own Web site and an e-mail address. But it's not like he gets a ton of mail."

"*He?*"

"My other self. Which one of us are you writing about?"

"Both," she said. "But I'm still trying to figure out how to tell them apart."

"Easy. One of us is pretty schizy and the other is in denial."

"I don't see that at all. Now, back to my original concern. Isn't it dangerous for you to go to Minneapolis?"

"I don't know." He lifted his hand off the steering wheel and snapped his fingers. "Hey, maybe nobody wants me anymore. Wouldn't that be a kick in the gut? Hidin' out all this time like I'm some big catch for somebody, and the cops are sayin', 'He killed what? A crow? Hell, don't call us—call PETA.' "

"Can't you ever give a friend a straight answer? I'm not asking as a journalist. I'm asking as a friend."

"You got a little identity crisis goin' on, too?" He gave a teasing *tsk*, shook his head. "You and my good friend Jack, the pest, you were both all hot on this idea. Now last night he says, 'Okay, maybe we oughta fly you out there in a private plane or something.' " He laughed. "Like he's got a private plane."

"I'll bet the Mille Lacs people have a plane. They've got quite a nice casino."

"Chippewas can't fly. If they offer me a ride in a boat, I'm there, but I ain't takin' off in a plane with no Chippewa pilot."

"*Ojibwe.*"

"Whatever." He reached with a loose fist to give her a playful clip on the chin. This time she didn't flinch. "See, now, a little Cherokee, that's different. Don't you guys make planes?"

"I don't think the plane is related to—"

"You sure? Whoever started making that plane could be part Cherokee. Could be related to your dad."

"I don't think so."

"We're all related," he reminded her, quoting an old Lakota saying. "Do you believe that?"

"Is that anything like, 'We all look alike'?"

"It's more like, all of us. We're all relatives. You, me, Woof, Cat." He nodded toward the back of the camper, where both animals slept, then glanced at a half-finished project that lay on the floor between driver and passenger. "The tree this flute comes from. The rock that got crushed to make this path we're driving on." His eyes met hers. "You believe that?"

"I do." She lifted one shoulder. "Sort of."

"It sounds good, though, doesn't it?"

She nodded.

"Put that in your book then," he teased, mimicking a character from *Dances with Wolves*, a movie they'd agreed—during one of their many recent conversations about movies—was, for all its inaccuracies, a cut above the rest because of the Indian actors.

She laughed. His imitation was perfect.

"The answer is, yeah, it's a little risky, me going to the Cities, but I've snuck in and out a few times before. If I get caught, I'm out of the game, which could happen anywhere along the way. In that case, we'll see what team you're really playing for."

"I'm not on a team. I'm the chronicler."

He nodded, said nothing.

"*Sneaked*," she said quietly.

He questioned her with a look.

"In my book the past tense of 'sneak' is 'sneaked.' " She lifted one slight shoulder. "Just . . . one writer to another."

"One Indian to another, you little Cherokees probably sneaked, but us Lakota, we snuck. And we were always real good at it." Noting her quick smile, he amended, "I said we *snuck*, not suck."

8

THE MILLE LACS BAND OF OJIBWE
WELCOMES YOU

It was a big sign, a good sign that Kole
would be safe during their first stop. Beautiful Lake Mille Lacs had been at the center of intermittent, sometimes bitter
controversy between the Ojibwe and the
rest of the world. First it was the Sioux,
who finally moved south and west to
become horse masters, hunters, lords of
the High Plains. Then came the waves
of white immigrants—the trappers and
traders, the farmers, the loggers. But there
had been no opponent more powerful and
persistent than the sport fisherman. Like

so many other natives, the Ojibwe had been willing to share, but not to vacate. They wanted to remain in their ancestral home and live as Ojibwe, changing with the times, yes, but on their own terms, just as the immigrants' relatives did in their native lands, from Norway to Germany to China to Somalia.

"We don't go to their homelands and tell them how to take fish or how to conserve them. There was an abundance when they came here, so I guess we must have known something about conservation of natural resources," said Carl Shinny, the self-appointed chairman of the unofficial community meeting that Jack had prompted by spreading the word that "different ones" were gathering in the school cafeteria to plan a protest rally.

There were as many assumptions about what would be protested as there were people who showed up. Carl started the conversation with fishing rights. "So these complaints about the resorts not making any money last summer because the Indians are taking too many walleye is bullshit."

It was a dispute that Heather had heard before, or one exactly like it except for the type of fish. In one case after another, the courts had recently been deciding in favor of the American Indian. As in several other states, non-Indian Minnesotans had learned the meaning of a term most of them had, until lately, had little reason to know anything about: treaty rights. Much to many people's surprise, the Supreme Court had recently upheld the terms of treaties between Native people and the federal government dating back more than a century. Their ancestors had tried to protect whatever they could in those agreements, and the right to hunt and fish was one of the things they managed to hold on to.

"We probably don't need any lessons on the value of the rainforest and the prairie sod, the beaver and the wolf," Carl said. "We coulda told them if they had any ears. But they gotta chop it all down, plow it all up, dam every river and drain every slough."

Jack picked up the ball with a flourish of gestures. "Now they're like, wait a minute. What's wrong with the water? What's up with the wildlife? They got plenty of habitat. You set aside your national parks, your wilderness areas, your Indian reservations, you got all your wildlife covered."

"We need the rest to build on," Carl mocked, spearing the air with his finger. "We're builders."

"But—" Jack wagged his finger as the takeoff became a dialogue. "Remember, if we want to save the planet, we gotta save the rainforest."

"That's right," Carl agreed eagerly. "The *world's* rainforest. Ours, we already cut ours down, but that was ours. What we gotta do is we gotta keep those Africans and those South Americans from screwing up the *world's* rainforests."

"Plus, we can't let those damn Chippewas be throwing their spears and nets around our walleye," another man put in.

"It ain't civilized."

"Civilized, hell, it just ain't sportin'."

Kole had been sitting quietly, but the banter finally made him smile. "You a sportin' man, Carl?"

"Yeah, I'm a good sport. About some things, anyway. If I lose a bet or miss a shot of some kind, I don't cry around about it. But a deal's a deal, and a treaty's a treaty. I ain't such a good sport about getting screwed out of what little we were supposed to get out of it. I think we oughta be marching on Washington."

"Naw, people do that all the time," Jack said. "Nobody hardly notices anymore."

"Not unless you got a million marchers," said a buxom woman wearing a Green Bay Packers sweatshirt.

"Maybe we could make it look like a million if we bring in some heavyweights. They don't take an exact head count, you know. They go by how much space you take up." Jack turned to the man who was taking his turn at the coffee urn. "Boo Boo, you count for at least three."

"That's always been the complaint," Kole said. "We take up too much space."

"But we can't come up with no million 'Skins, so we gotta use our imagination," big Boo Boo allowed. "You want me to do my part, you'll have to feed me up some, Laurent. Triple helpings."

"Yeah, talk about using your imagination," Jack said with a chuckle. "Seriously, that's what we're doing. Hollywood or bust. You can bet *Entertainment Tonight* gets better ratings than the *Nightly News.*"

"Yeah, but what are we gonna do when we get there?" Carl wanted to know. "What are we marching on? We gotta take something over, right? Stake a claim."

"Baywatch Beach," Jack said. Boo Boo whistled. "Those chicks are deadly in the water, but I hear they're helpless on land. You see them running in place on the beach?" Jack pumped his skinny arms and demonstrated in slow motion. "So we take our signal mirrors, see. They can't resist a mirror. 'C'mon, girl.' " He whistled, then demonstrated his technique by running backward, baiting his prey with an imaginary mirror. "Circle 'em up just like stampeding cows, surround them and claim their beach. We'll make all kinda headlines."

"Then what?" the Packers fan challenged.

"Then we explain that since for ninety percent of the population we only exist on film, we demand accuracy," Jack said. "We want people, not caricatures. We want them to be honest about the past and to admit that we still exist in the present."

"We want more Graham Greenes," another woman said.

"More parts for Graham Greene," echoed another.

"And after we make Graham Greene rich, what then?" the Packers fan wanted to know. "What do the rest of us get besides a long trip and thirty seconds of fame?"

Carl laughed. "We get to tell about the time we cooled our heels in a Tinseltown jail."

"We get some answers," Kole said quietly. "I get some answers."

"You get yourself free, Kola," Jack said. "Those answers are the keys to your freedom."

"Maybe. At least it'll be settled." Kole glanced at Heather, who was an observer, strictly a bystander. He lifted one shoulder. "My daughter will be safe, and the spirits can rest easy."

"We don't want you stickin' your neck out around your enemies, Kola." Carl offered Kole a piece of frybread from a cardboard box that was sitting on the table next to the coffee urn. "Just your friends."

Kole reached into the box. "It'll be interesting to see who they are, won't it?"

♦ ♦ ♦

The caravan left Mille Lacs four vehicles longer than it was when it arrived. They were up to ten.

Heather had taken over the driving when they reached a state highway. The camper was like a peak in the middle of the line of mostly cars, a couple of pickups. All she had to do was follow the taillights. Kole laughed when she expressed her appreciation for the willingness to devote time and energy to a cause on such short notice.

He mistook her tone for sarcasm. "Getting on the road is the only cause we need," he said. "Hallelujah, we're going somewhere." He blew into one of the stops on the flute he was carving and got it to squeal, a sound akin to delight.

"We're going to the big city," she mused. "I think we should skip this stop, Kole. Let Jack make his pitch to the city Indians. I'd feel safer if we drove on to the next reservation."

"You would?"

She shrugged, concentrating on the two-lane road ahead. There had to be good reason for the abundance of roadside deer warning signs. "I'd feel like you were safer."

"We don't want me getting arrested before you know enough of my secrets to fill a book."

"We don't want you getting arrested." She spared him a pointed glance. "Period."

"Weren't you right in there with Jack saying, 'Come on, Kole, show us how brave you are'?"

"*Us,* but not the rest of the world. Just the people who look to you for inspiration."

"Jesus Christ, Heather, I don't know where you get this—"

"The people who don't want you getting arrested," she insisted quietly. "You can show us."

She expected him to call her on her choice of a pronoun, her pre-sumptuousness in including herself. When did she become part of *us*? She was looking for inspiration now? What happened to the story? Where was her objectivity?

But he'd gone dreamy on her, staring off into the late-afternoon haze, the stubbly remnants of an alfalfa crop appearing to flow past the window. "I'd like to see the baby first," he said distantly.

First? she wanted to ask, but she didn't like the sound of it—like one of those before-I-die wishes—and she didn't want to hear it again.

So she argued instead. "She's not a baby."

"She is to me. Savannah's offered me pictures, but I turned them down. I know I'm asking for heartache, but I want to see her now."

"So you're going out there to get yourself caught," she said, flip-pantly playing the bully. "You think maybe somebody's trailing you?"

He shrugged. "I think maybe somebody'll sell me out, but it's not gonna happen before I come face to face with Wilson. I won't let it."

"You don't trust me?"

"Who said anything about you?"

She glanced at him under an arched eyebrow. "I'm the only non-Indian around."

"Who, you? My little Cherokee?" He chuckled. "Anyway, who said anything about non-Indians? That wouldn't be a sellout, would it?" He wagged his head, gave a humorless chuckle. "A sellout is a stab in the back from one of your own. If we could stop squabbling among ourselves and work together, we'd be dangerous. But various tribes have always had their differences. Even the bands and the clans within the tribes. We don't even remember why. We just know you can't trust those guys from across the river."

He tapped her knee with the mouthpiece end of the unfinished flute. "And you guys, you colonists, you've always known that, and you know how to use it."

"I'm not a colonist."

"Okay." He tapped again, as though he were testing for reflexes. "Using natives against natives is one of the best strategies you ever came up with, and you did it all over the world."

"And as soon as we move out, the fighting starts again," she returned.

"So you got yourselves an obligation now, not to mention a colonizing tradition to uphold, all the way back to the Roman emperors. Praise God for the purveyors of peace."

"*I'm* not a colonist. Some of my ancestors were Irish. The English took our land, for heaven's sake."

"So you took ours, for your own sake." He drew an arc in the air with the end of the flute. "Land, free for the taking. Just put up a soddy and start plowing. No matter how you look at it, you come from a long line of colonists, honey."

"Well, so do you. On your dad's side, anyway."

"I don't count that side."

It was her turn to chortle a little.

"Hey, I didn't know that side until I was thirteen. By that time your identity is set. I was Lakota in my head, Lakota in my heart. I didn't know anything else." He eyed her with a challenge. "Do you feel like you're Irish?"

"Not really."

"Cherokee?"

She stared ahead for a moment, recalling the time she'd attended the powwow with her father. Two wannabes. The music wasn't quite the same as the way she'd heard it in the movies. The costumes were much prettier, and the dance steps were far more exciting. She'd asked her father if they could dance, too, because other people seemed to be joining in. But he'd said he'd never been much of a dancer. "We'll just watch," he'd said. Soon his head was bobbing with the beat of the drum.

Two wannabes.

She wasn't sure what he'd wanted to be then. Whatever it was, she'd wanted it, too, for she'd most wanted to be his daughter.

She shook her head sheepishly.

"What are you, then? Besides a cute little colonist?"

"American." Her father would agree. He had worn the uniform with great pride. Never much of a dancer, never much of a family man, but always a patriot. There was nothing wrong with that, and no one would persuade Heather otherwise. "I'm American," she repeated, flashing him a cool, self-assured glance. "Aren't you?"

"I don't know. If we had a war with, say, Russia or China, I'd definitely be American. Or Grenada. I could really get into it with those Grenadians. Is that what they call themselves? United we stand against the Grenadian menace. But . . ." He ran the pads of his fingers over the wooden instrument, feeling for flaws. "I have a cousin who was in the National Guard when AIM took over Wounded Knee back in '73. He was a paratrooper. It looked like his unit was about to get called up, and his commander called him in and asked him whose side he was on. He said he'd belong to Uncle Sam as long as he was in the chopper, but as soon as he hit the ground, he was Lakota. He wasn't about to turn his weapon on his own people."

"But they're Americans, too."

"If we went to the war with the Irish, whose side would you be on?" he asked, and she laughed at the notion. "No," he insisted. "Say the IRA decided that the United Stated was to blame for the Irish troubles."

"I'm an American, but I'm not a colonist."

"Your ancestors did all the dirty work. You're benefiting more than they did."

"I don't even own a garden plot, for God's sake."

"See, that's what you all say. In the name of God, we claim this land."

"I thought it was in the name of King Ferdinand and Queen Isabella," she recalled. "And by the *grace* of God."

"Then you oughta have a garden plot, Heather Reardon. But don't come to me for it unless you wanna grow buffalo grass or prickly pear cactus. All I have is badlands and gumbo." He smiled. "Come to think of it, I heard the wildflower rustlers have been out there diggin' up purple coneflowers, so I guess there is something else out there suddenly worth stealing."

"For herbal echinacea," she supplied. She'd read about the latest excuse to rape western lands of a resource that, until recently, few people had thought of as anything but a weed. "I'll bet that's originally an American Indian remedy?"

"You think?"

His sarcasm stung. "I do, you know," she said calmly. "Once in a while."

He nodded, glanced out the window, and after a long moment quietly said, "I'm sorry."

"For what?"

"Being a smart-ass. When you said you'd feel safer if we didn't stop until we hit the next reservation, you were thinking of me. And that's nice. If I had any kind of manners, I'd be nice back." He sighed as he leaned back in his seat. "I used to have pretty good manners. Must've lost 'em along the trail somewhere."

He was forgiven. "Where do you think you lost them? In prison?"

"Maybe."

"What was it like there?"

"Not nice. Not something a man wants to describe to a woman— what it was like to have no liberty, no say, no power over your own destiny. You follow their schedule, their rules, you do what you're told and you watch your back." He turned his head on the headrest. She could feel him watching her, waiting for her to turn and connect, however briefly. And so she did. "Not something a guy wants his woman to hear about," he told her.

"His woman?"

He backed down with a lip-shrug. "Any woman."

"I'm not any woman. I'm a writer. I don't want to be spared any details."

"You got all you're gettin' on that score, at least from me."

"I should've asked Tom Seal."

He sat up slowly, looking at her as though she'd just confessed to some crime. "I don't want you talkin' to Seal. I don't want you any-where near Seal."

"Kole, you don't have anything to say about who I talk to. I'm actually very much my own woman."

"You're not gettin' around that ex-con unless it's over my dead body."

"*You're* an ex-con."

"I'm an escaped con. There's a difference."

"Armed and dangerous? You'd at least have to be more dangerous than an ex-con."

"You'd think so, wouldn't you? So don't cross me." He leaned closer. "Except in bed. You can cross me, boss me, toss me, do whatever you want to me between the sheets. Feel free to use your considerable imagination on me in bed."

She cocked her head toward the back of the camper, where Woof and Cat were curled up together like the lion and the lamb. "That little bed's not big enough for three," she said.

He cocked a quzzical eyebrow.

"You, me, and my freelance imagination."

⧫ ⧫ ⧫

The American Indian Center was a gathering place in South Minneapolis. Kole had been there often in the old days, but not at all lately, he told Heather as they entered through a back door. Jack had sent out word of their visit, and Kole was not as easy with it as he claimed. Without touching him, Heather could feel the tension in his body. He was less subtle than usual about taking inventory of every detail of his surroundings. Any odd sound turned his head.

But he greeted people in a friendly way, noticeably humbled by the turnout. Word of mouth had been the only means of advertisement, but people showed up in droves to hear him speak. "I didn't plan to get up and talk," he whispered to Jack as they took seats in folding chairs.

Jack brushed the concern off with a forget-about-it gesture.

"This is your fight, Laurent. I came along as backup."

"So back me up." Jack nodded toward the microphone somebody had just placed on a table in the front of what, with its basketball hoops and rack for folding tables, apparently served as an all-purpose room. "You know writers can't speak worth shit. Right, Heather?"

"I know I can't." Backup was a good role, she decided.

"I should walk right out that door," Kole muttered as he stood.

He hesitated, and for a moment Heather wondered which he would reach for—mike or door handle. She had been only speculating when she spoke of the people who looked to Kole for inspiration. She'd seen it years ago when she'd quietly taken part in the vigil outside a South Dakota jail, but she was only guessing that others remembered.

She'd guessed right. No name was announced, but the crowd applauded when he claimed the microphone. He started by thanking the cooks, saying that he had sampled the frybread that would be served with the feed that would follow the rally. "I know Indians," he said. "You guys'll listen to anybody spout off for food that good."

But the talk he gave was wondrous. It started with his enchanting flute music, which wrapped itself around each listener and drew them into his story about a brown-skinned boy who loved sitting in a dark movie theater and watching stories unfold before his eyes on a big screen. He wanted to be a cowboy. He liked to ride horses, and his uncle had a few cows he'd let the boy trail around the pasture. Whenever a western movie came to the theater, the boy was there, front row, center seat. He knew he'd be a cowboy himself someday if he could figure out how not to be an Indian.

Kole believed that stories had great power, and he reminded his audience that their ancestors had held the same belief. Reputations were built on stories. The life of the people was remembered in stories. But it was important to remember and to convey stories in their purest form, so that those who followed would know the nature and spirit of those who came before.

"For lies are butchers of the spirit," Kole said, his voice so deep and quiet and laden with long-stored passion that it drew his listeners' backs away from their chairs. "And the way we are too often portrayed by people who never bother to find out who we are distorts our lives and the lives of our fathers and grandfathers. These distortions butcher our spirits. Our white neighbors readily admit that they know little about us, and many of them are actually curious. Interested. But we've been fed so much of this mythology ourselves, we don't even know the truth about ourselves anymore.

"What will our grandchildren learn about their heritage, and who will teach them? Our children? They love television and movies as much as any kid does. If they continue to feed on these images, if the world feeds on these images, is that who we must become? Is that who we have already become? Are we as pathetic as so many people think we are?

"To hear them tell it, the best part of us rode over the hill and vanished into the sunset a long time ago. We're like the Old South, you know, we're gone with the wind. Doesn't matter if you screw with the history a little bit or have an Arapaho speaking Lakota. Who's gonna know the difference? They get us all wrong most times. They even get the drum wrong. This is their idea of an Indian drum." He bent close to the table and pounded with flat hands, saying, "*Dum* dum dum dum *dum* dum dum dum. Does that sound like our drum?"

He signaled for the three men sitting around a bass drum in the corner to take up their beaters, back him up with the true rhythm. Their soft drumming echoed Heather's pulse.

"Why can't they get that right?" Kole asked. "If they listened to their own hearts, they would know. They would know, but they don't, because they'd rather hear themselves talk. It's the heartbeat. Speed it up." The drummers picked up the pace. "It's the hoof beat of the buffalo, running, running. It's life. It's freedom. But who's gonna know, and who's gonna tell them except us?

"We're invisible to these people around here. My cousins, you all know that. Outside of this neighborhood, people know us by what they read in their school books, which was damn little, and what they've seen on film.

"So let's go out to Hollywood and make some noise with the film-makers. It's been a while since we've made any noise."

A woman in the audience piped up. "It's been a while since *you've* made any noise, Kola."

"I'm going along for the ride, mostly. In my case, invisible is a good thing. Only the believers can see me."

"Not every believer can be trusted," the woman said, a comment that prompted Heather to turn toward the voice of a striking Indian woman, tall and lean, dressed in red and black. Her words of warning seemed to come from experience.

"I know that, Marty. But you take the risk when the cause is important enough to you."

"I'll put up some gas money out of my casino income," an older woman offered.

"And I'll talk to my sister," said another. "She loves this kind of stuff. She was in on the Alcatraz occupation back in—was it '68, '69? Nine months later she had her first kid. Named her Rockie. Spells it the girl's way, you know, with an i-e. Boy or girl, my sister was gonna name that baby for The Rock."

Kole grinned broadly. "Tell your sister to come along. Bring the kids."

"Hell, she's got grandkids now. Whole bunch of little pebbles." The term drew a round of laughter. The woman raised her voice above it. "I'll tell her. She still talks about what a smart move that was. When the government abandons property like that, it's sup-posed to go back to the previous occupants, which would have been the natives. They had to do something once they evicted the protest-ers, so they started giving tours. Now everybody wants to go to Alca-traz."

"Wherever we go, it's bound to become the next place everybody wants to be." Kole looked at Heather. "You'd think we were just downright irresistible." He turned to the first woman to respond.

"What about you, Marty? You ready for another round?"

"Of what? Finger-pointing games with Uncle Sam?"

"Jack says I'm his backup. I want you to be my backup."

They exchanged looks that spoke of a shared past. The adventure he proposed would be similar to one they both remembered. Or more than one.

"Who's your *kola*, Kola?" Marty asked.

"This is my driver." Kole slid Heather a subtle wink. "Little Cherokee."

9

Y ou're so much better than Barry Wilson," Heather whispered, smiling in the shadows.

"Oh yeah?"

She'd been angling for a rise, but there was none in his voice. It was stony and still, like the hand that had been stroking her hip, and the joke was suddenly on her. "As a motivating force," she added quickly. "A rallier. You were wonderful."

His hand slid over her belly as he propped himself on one elbow, his angular profile silhouetted against the sheer white curtain that surrounded the camper's over-the-cab platform bed and softened the glow from a streetlight. "Rallied you pretty good, did I?"

She touched his smooth cheek. Little hair grew on his face, none on his chest. "I handed you that one on a platter."

"I like the way you express yourself during your rally." His middle fingertip traced the rim of her navel, as though he were creating a tiny cup out of clay. "Makes me want to keep motivating just as long and hard as I know how."

"And you do know how."

"And now everybody walking by the camper knows I know how."

"It's three in the morning. Nobody's walking by."

He chuckled. "New York isn't the only city that never sleeps."

"It's much quieter here," she whispered. "But not as quiet as your cabin. I was beginning to enjoy the difference between quiet and *peace* and quiet."

"It's not my cabin," he reminded her. "And peace is deceptive. I can't let myself forget that. Especially . . ." He slid his arm beneath her shoulders and pulled her close. "If I had decency at all, I would send you packin'. Drive you away with a stick if I had to."

"A stick would work."

"But I have no decency."

"Not a shred." She touched the silver streak of his hair that had caught a bit of light. "I can take care of myself, Kole. This story is important to me. This is a story I was born to write."

He laughed. "You are so full of it sometimes, you know that?"

"Full of myself? Did that sound pompous?" She apologized with a hug, tucking her head under his chin. "I've thought about it a lot since Jack took exception to the idea that I should be the one to write about you. I've asked myself who I think I am, and my answer is that I think I'm Heather Reardon." She looked up at him. "I *know* I am, and I know I have the skill and talent. And the motivation."

He squeezed her bottom as he pressed her against him, sandwiching his hard penis between their bellies.

"Don't be a smart-ass, now," she warned, torturing a groan from him with a sensuous belly roll. "I came into the picture with plenty of motivation that had nothing to do with sex."

"Mmm. I don't know, honey, looks to me like you've been gettin' off on pictures of me for some time."

"I have not."

"I've been mind-fucking you, and I didn't even know it. I feel a little cheated."

"You were married. You would have been the one cheating."

"I don't think it counts on my end."

"Your end always counts." She practiced her belly dancing again. He met her move with a teasing prod. Her laugh bubbled deep in her throat. "See, it's the penetrating end." She bucked against him. "And I prefer to think of it as mind-loving. You got into my head and got me all stirred up."

"Damn, you're easy."

"Not so," she claimed. "In fact, I have a reputation for being a bit cold, but you fired me up. You came on to me with mind-blowing passion, and you made me see things differently, feel things, *conceive* of things I—"

"Now, wait a minute, honey, you've just gone from fantasy to science fiction. Any conception you got out of all this is purely immaculate. For once I'm completely innocent. But you . . ." He brushed her hair back from her temple. His face was shadowed, but she could feel his eyes searching hers for a clue to the truth. "I've gotta wonder if you really know what you're doing."

"Of course I do."

"What's the attraction? Is it me or my cause?"

"Inseparable."

"Are you sure about that?"

"Absolutely."

He sighed and shook his head. "You don't need me to write this story, Cherokee. You had it all mapped out before you got lost in the woods." He rolled his shoulder back against the mattress and stared at the ceiling a couple of feet above their noses. "See, that was your problem. You packed the wrong map."

"That's not the way I write. Believe it or not."

"I'll believe it when I see it."

"If you don't see yourself in what I write . . ." It was her turn to prop herself up and lean over him. "If it isn't a mirror into your very soul, Kole Kills Crow, you can burn it yourself."

"While you make another copy?"

"No."

His laugh was decidedly cynical.

"I'm not promising you won't see things you don't like, but I can say it'll ring true. That's what I do best. I don't insert myself editorially. I reflect the subject of the work. And if I reflect *on* the subject at all, I make that clear."

"Don't you decide what to put in and what to leave out?"

"I have to."

"Well, there it is." He tucked his hands behind his neck, his arms hooked like chicken wings.

"Yes, but my judgment on that score is what makes—"

"Haven't I compromised all that?" He read her puzzlement and clarified quietly, "By inserting myself physically?"

"Absolutely not," she snapped, stressing each syllable. No one but Reardon could compromise a Reardon piece. She tempered her tone. "No, you haven't. I can still be objective."

"But won't you have to confess your bias? Won't you have to reflect on that?" He ran the pad of his thumb over her eyebrow and down to the outside corner of her eye. "Make it absolutely clear that you're looking into my soul through the eyes of a deeply and repeatedly and splendidly motivated woman?"

"You flatter yourself." The palm of her hand became a pad of paper. "I must make a note of that."

"Answer me," he demanded. "Won't you have to expose yourself, too?"

"You're making love to the woman, not the writer."

"Inseparable."

The sudden knock on the door of the camper canceled her search for a comeback. Woof leaped over the little kitchen table, furiously repeating his name.

"Minneapolis police," said a male voice. "Is this camper occupied?"

"Yes, it is, Officer." Heather pasted her fingers over Kole's lips as he flipped over and parted the curtain. "Just a minute," she called out. The man standing on the curb passed the first test. He was wearing a uniform. "I'm in bed. Let me get . . ." She gestured frantically for Kole to stay put as she slid into her jeans and dangled her legs off the bed. "Am I parked where I shouldn't be?"

Kole's arm came around her neck from behind, his warm breath tickling her ear. "I'll drive."

She shook her head. Woof's barking covered her whisper. "This thing can't outrun a squad car. Maybe you can sneak out the other side."

He nodded toward the door. "So he gets his buck before the season opens?"

She wrenched her shoulders and dropped through the ring his arm made, her bare feet shocked by the cold floor. Searching it for a top to put on, she came upon his jeans. She tossed them up, and he plucked them out of the air.

"Control your dog," the voice outside ordered.

"He's all bark." With the arm she'd just plunged into a bulky white sweater, she motioned for Kole to grab Woof.

"If he comes at me, he'll be all dead."

A flashlight nearly blinded her when she opened the door, but she shaded her eyes with her hand, keeping the man—or at least his outline—in sight. "I'd like to see some ID that doesn't fire any bullets," Heather said calmly, feeling with her foot for the shoes she thought she'd left near the door. "Preferably the badge of a *peace* officer."

"Heard some voices," the man said as he turned his flashlight on the card with his picture on it. "Just wanted to check things out, make sure nobody was trying to break in. Is this your outfit, ma'am?"

Woof continued to bark.

"It's okay, Woof. The policeman is our friend." Heather scooped Cat into her arms before she opened the screen door. A woman holding a cat had to look pretty nonthreatening. "That's what my mother used to say."

"Yes, ma'am, she was right."

"The camper is actually on loan." She stepped down to the curb. "From the owner, of course. I flew in from New York to, uh . . . write a travel piece about Minnesota, and I ran into this really interesting . . ." She gestured toward the Indian Center. "Well, this story just fell into my lap. Along with the camper."

"Is the owner around?"

"No, but I can give you his name and—"

"It's all right. I ran a check on the plates. I just wanted to make sure everything was all right. There was some kind of powwow going on at the Indian Center earlier, so we're just following up on—"

"I was there," she enthused, cuddling Cat against her breast. "As I said, I'm a writer. I'm looking for local color."

"You've come to the right neighborhood for that. I wouldn't spend the night on the street, though, if I were you."

"Am I breaking the law?"

"No, but being you're from out of town, you might not realize that you've picked a bad . . ." The policeman glanced past her, through the open door. "What kind of a dog is that?"

"Down," said a low voice behind her.

Woof plastered his belly to the floor on command.

"He's my dog," Kole said from the shadows.

Heather's pulse raced. What in the name of heaven and hell was he thinking, showing himself like this?

"He listens pretty good." The officer rested his hand on his holstered service revolver. "Are you the owner of the camper?"

"No. I'm just a passenger."

The policeman turned to Heather again. "Is everything all right, then?"

"It's all right with us if it's all right with you. We're . . ." The tentative way Kole reached from the dark interior to grip the door frame was curious, but the sound of his bare foot seemingly feeling for perch on the threshold quickly drew her attention. She looked up as he stepped into the light. He was wearing sunglasses.

She smiled. "We're fine."

Woof growled again.

"I could've sworn he was a wolf, but . . ." The officer questioned each of them first with a look. Then, "He's a guide dog?"

Kole said nothing.

"I . . . I didn't mean to be nosy. I was in canine up until a year ago, when my partner died. I haven't been able to replace him. I could tell your dog was special." He touched Kole's hand. "I'm sorry. Dan Rogers."

Kole accepted the handshake. "Kola."

"Ko . . . ?"

"Kola," he repeated, accenting the second syllable. "I'm a writer, too, and, uh . . . we're both writers. But she's doing all the driving. They won't give me a license in this state. Now, if we were in Alaska . . ."

"Is that where you're from?"

"I'm from a place that's even darker than that, Dan. Even darker than that." Using the doorframe as a guide, Kole sat down in the doorway.

"I understand." Dan glanced at Heather, then at the dog standing guard at Kole's shoulder. "You've got a real nice lookin' dog there."

"A dog's a dog, Dan. What I really want to know is . . ." Staring straight ahead, he asked, perfectly deadpan, "How does the woman look?"

"Great. She's . . ."

"You wouldn't be ashamed to let her drive you around?"

"No. Not at all. I mean . . ."

Kole's grin emerged slowly. "Course your last partner was a dog, so what do you know?"

Heather rolled her eyes.

The policeman's laugh was tentative. "I know you've got yourself a great looking driver and a nice dog."

"That's very reassuring, Officer," Kole said innocently. "I've always depended on the vision of strangers."

"As long as you've got the dog, I don't think anyone else will bother you."

"I depend on him, too." Kole reached back. Woof sniffed his hand, and Kole ruffled his fur.

"Sorry for the disturbance."

"It's more like a reassurance," Heather said. "Thank you for keeping the peace, Officer."

The only laugh that didn't sound nervous was Kole's.

"God, you're good," Heather whispered as she locked the camper door from the inside. "Have you ever done that before?"

Kole puffed out his bare chest as he peeled off the sunglasses. "Which of my many skills are we talking about?"

"The blind act. That was a stroke of genius."

"Then Officer Dan is smarter than he looks. It was all his idea."

"But the sunglasses."

"It was either that or a paper bag, which I thought might look suspicious."

"I was handling it just fine. You didn't have to inter—"

"Yeah, I did." He drew her into his arms, his hands slightly unsteady. "Woof knows damn well the policeman is no friend of ours, and he didn't much like the way he was flirting with you."

"Woof?"

"You take a bite out of a cop's leg and you go to the head of the line on death row. Interference was necessary." He leaned back to make eye contact. "I was good, wasn't I?"

"I don't know anymore. Were you doing a blind man, or was he?"

"Ah, you can't be sure, can you? You're so beautiful when you're bewildered." He grinned. "Did I say I was blind?"

"You said . . ." She looked down at Woof, trying to remember exactly what Kole had told the cop.

"I told him no lies," he said, reading her mind. "Kola, the blind flute maker. I like that. It's going right into my repertoire."

"You have a repertoire?"

In the dark his smile was soft and inviting. "How else can I hope to keep you entertained?"

◆ ◆ ◆

Despite her protests earlier, Heather felt that Kole had planted a worry seed. She was sitting on an irritating grain of sand, and it had her squirming in the driver's seat. Could she write this story objectively? How much of herself had she compromised by sharing his bed?

In the past she'd taken many less-traveled roads—some high,

some low, some just plain bizarre—and she'd been labeled crazy almost as often as she'd been hailed as a master at finding out where real players got their scripts.

The truth was, she was both. She knew it, and she reveled in it, because in the end it was never about her. She could take risks and produce something masterful and revealing, while she also remained separate from everything but the success of the piece.

But this story was different. The dream of this story had always been different. If she was honest with herself, she'd have to admit that she'd never been objective about this story—no more objective than she could be about the memory of two young women with big dreams. A struggling model and a hustling journalist. Whenever one had faltered, the other had shored her up, made her believe.

They'd made up for each other in other ways, too. Heather liked the way it worked, the way they'd divided the territory. Savannah was the pretty one, Heather the smart one. They'd even shared their interest in Kole, dividing him up the way adolescent girls divided up the members of a band or the cast of a TV show. Savannah had Kole's friendship, his trust, eventually his child, but she left his mind—or more precisely his politics—to Heather. And that was all she wanted, for therein lay his story.

Which was getting better all the time. It might have ended in the north woods, the way Savannah's might have ended in the bedroom of her last apartment in New York. Not with a bang, but a whimper. Heather remembered the last time she'd seen Savannah, before her friend had finally tucked her tail between her legs and gone home to Wyoming. Savannah had stopped answering her phone, and Heather had run out of pep talks. No, she didn't know how it felt to lose her breast, but it had to be better than dying. And Savannah had a fabulous face.

Heather didn't know what *that* was like, either. Few women did—not that kind of a face. Why waste it? Pick yourself up, put on a few more clothes, and get back out there, Heather had said. Do what you were meant to do.

Heather had to admit, she'd lost patience with Savannah's self-pity. She'd gotten a little disgusted. True, Heather had never been sick. True, she had never been really good around sick people. But Savannah had been at the top of the modeling game, and Heather believed she could have climbed right back up there if she'd had a mind to.

The mind was Heather's territory. And maybe this time she'd lost it. If she had, the answer was no, she could not write Kole's story. It would turn into a trivial piece of romantic trash.

10

Heather's reporter's instincts had gone dormant.

They ought to get back on the interstate and head into the wind, she muttered as the motley caravan of "Indian cars" made its way down the neatly manicured Midwestern Main Street, drawing curious stares like a parade of motorcycles in pickup country. Story or no story, Canton, South Dakota, simply felt like a risky place for Kole to show his face.

The little town, perched on the bluffs of the Big Sioux River not far from the three-way demarcation of Minnesota, Iowa, and South Dakota, enjoyed a clear view of forever across the prairie sod, where the West began. The sky billowed on a blue day, pressed and pushed when it turned gray, and promised next-day miracles with the glorious pinks and purples of a setting sun. To the west lay the memories of the Great Sioux Nation.

While most Americans were unlikely to have any connections or associations or even any knowledge of Canton, South Dakota, many Native Americans, especially the elders, shuddered when they heard the name. Canton had once been the site of the Hiawatha Insane Asylum for American Indians. Only the cemetery was left now, and the presence of its ghosts, the lure of their secrets, was almost palpable.

Heather had never heard of the asylum, and she considered herself well versed in American Indian history. Established by an act of Congress, it was run by the Bureau of Indian Affairs from 1902 until 1934, when the Roosevelt administration overhauled Indian policies. Little had been written or published about the institution, but Kole explained as they drove into town that the institution was remembered by the older generation as one of many places to which people were "sent away," never to be seen again. They were as likely to be committed to the asylum by the Indian agent, later known as the agency superintendent, or by the principal of an Indian boarding school as by a medical doctor.

After the asylum was closed, the facility had been used for, among other things, a minimum-security prison. Eventually it had been demolished, and the grounds were given to the community of Canton. Now the burial place for 128 former patients of the asylum, surrounded by a rail fence, was the centerpiece of a nine-hole golf course.

A small group of people who were determined to have the grounds designated a historical site regularly held memorials to honor the dead and call attention to a forgotten chapter in America's history. At the moment, no one seemed to be listening, but it was the kind of political issue that might attract Kole's friends to gather. It could also attract his enemies. The real trouble was—and this Heather noted without remark—he didn't always know the difference. But Jack had intended to cover the memorial ceremony for *Native Drums* anyway, so the event was on the caravan's itinerary.

After the mourners and the grounds had been purified with burning sage, after the drums had been played and the prayers had been said and sung and sent to the heavens on drifts of white smoke, most of the people adjourned to a public picnic area, where they would be fed and fueled with food and fine words for the cause. Jack would be their host.

But Kole seemed reluctant to leave with the others. He and Heather took a closer look at the large chunk of stone that served as a common grave marker, listing the names of the dead. They remarked on the names, the dates, the curious fact that unnamed infants had been interred there.

Crazy Indian babies? The absence of any mention of the asylum's existence in anything she'd read was more remarkable to Heather than the fact of its existence—she'd researched so many abominable federal policies and deeds that she was no longer shocked by the facts. Her aggravation over the lack of public knowledge about Indian affairs—to which the American government devoted a whole bureau—was the seed of her mission to inform. But how had this institution been kept secret?

"Lack of interest, most likely," Kole said as they picked their way among the depressions in the ground that were the only evidence of individual graves. "That and fear. This was a place Indian people whispered about. It was a bogeyman kind of place that they used to warn their kids away from misbehaving or even speaking up for themselves when they went to boarding school. I've heard of kids being sent here because they had trouble learning English—or maybe they just resisted—which made them mentally incompetent.

"There are plenty of records of the place in government archives, but who looks at those? Back then, people didn't talk about it. It never makes it into the history books or the popular media, so not many white people have heard of it," Kole said as he swung his leg over the rail fence. "And if they have, it's one of those so-sad, too-bad, get-over-it-lad kind of things. What difference does it make now, you say?"

"Did I say that?" Heather braced her arm on the rail and kicked her left leg up and over.

"That was a general 'you.' "

"I don't think you'll get a rise out of me this time. I just don't feel like saluting General You today." She turned to survey the cemetery in shadowy twilight. Scraps of black, white, red, and yellow cloth, tied to the fence to honor the four directions, fluttered in the chilly autumn breeze. Heather hugged herself. "I don't know anything about what happened here, and I want to know. So give me a break, just for today."

"One day at a time." Kole slipped his arm around her, shielding her from the wind. "Sorry, Little Cherokee."

"Whoa, an apology. Where's my notebook?"

"You wanna know the truth?" He shivered. "Places like this give me the willies."

"Really?" She could have sworn he was fearless. If this kind of place was his weakness, she could protect him. The only ghosts she believed in were the memories of the living and records of the dead. If the names on the stone haunted this place, it was only to declare that they had once lived, and that the story of their lives was due the respect of remembrance. The place itself was peaceful now, except for the rustling pines that had been planted long ago as a screen. "It just makes me angry that they built a golf course around it," she said.

"No willies?" he asked in disbelief, giving her a quick squeeze.

She shook her head.

"Ghosts don't bother you?"

She shook her head again.

He chuckled. "You've gotta be *very* little Cherokee. I used to try to scare Clay with some of the ghost stories I grew up with, but they never worked on him the way they got to me. Graveyard stories, stories about the spirits stealing into the house in the dead of night, demanding their due." He made a sweeping gesture. "Imagine what these spirits are due, how restless they must be. Look at these depressions in the earth. They've been coming out at night a lot over the years."

"There are no vaults."

"They're not in a good place. They're trapped in this pitiful excuse for a resting place, surrounded by the echoes of their anguish." He glanced down at her, peering through the deepening shadows. "You don't believe me?"

"About their suffering in life? I can certainly believe that, but I would want to see the records. I would be interested in investigating the—"

"You don't believe me about the ghosts," he said, sounding disappointed. "Fine. We'll come back here later tonight, when it's *really* dark and the *gigis* are out in full force."

"No, I'll take your word for it."

"But you said you wanted to investigate."

"The *records*. I'd like to read up on the history."

"These people didn't write the history. They lived it, but somebody else did all the writing. You want their version? I dare you to come back here with me tonight."

"Well, fine. I'm not the one with the willies."

He grinned. "Then you can take care of mine."

They turned to leave and were both startled by a young woman emerging from the stand of tall pines. Exchanging where-did-she-come-from looks, they paused to find out. From her purposeful stride it appeared that she had sought them out, but she greeted them curiously.

"Isn't the golf course closed?"

"We're not on the golf course," Kole said. "You work here?"

"No. I was just . . . I came for the ceremony today, and I think I dropped something somewhere between here and the parking lot. I'm Abby Wendel." She offered her hand as though to either or both of them, whoever was willing to accept it.

Heather made the move.

"I'm from the Twin Cities," the woman said. She wore a long, shapeless skirt with a bulky sweater that hung almost to her knees. She wasn't old enough to be an original hippie, but she was dressed like second generation. "I saw a flier about this ceremony on the library bulletin board, and I came down to find out what it was all about. I'm getting my doctorate in history."

Heather introduced herself. Kole did not.

"I understand there's a group of you marching in protest on . . . Hollywood, is it?" Unflustered by Kole's reserve, she turned to him. "Why Hollywood?"

He lifted one shoulder. "They've got a lot of cameras there."

"What will you do when you get there?"

"You'll have to wait and see." He glanced at Heather. "Just like the rest of us. We've gotta get there first."

"I was very moved by the ceremony," Abby said, a little too eagerly. "Is any of your family buried here?"

"Family?" Kole glanced over his shoulder toward the monument, a shadow among shadows in the waning light. "Sure."

"Someone who was a patient at the asylum?"

He turned to give her an icy look.

"I'm sorry," Abby said quickly, her eagerness undiminished. "I don't mean to pry. I'm working on my dissertation in—"

"See what I mean?" Kole said to Heather. "Somebody else writes the history."

Heather's quick frown warned him to behave himself as she encouraged Abby. "Your dissertation in what?"

"The role of intertribal rivalry in the defeat of the Plains Indians," she said quietly, turning to Kole. "The truth is, you've always been your own worst enemies."

"Is that the latest version?" He chortled. "They'll call you 'Doctor' for comin' up with that one?"

"I don't say we didn't take advantage of that truth in the worst possible ways. This place might very well have been one of them." Abby Wendel folded her arms and took a step toward the fence, scanning what little could be seen of the cemetery. "But I'm afraid it's the way of the world. Close neighbors, ancient rivalries. You find it in Africa, the Middle East, the Balkans . . ."

"Western Europe doesn't jump to mind?" Kole challenged.

"Of course. There's—"

"Shhh." The sound of what might have been a footstep within or beyond the stand of pines brought Kole's finger to his lips. The women froze their bodies and tuned in. "The *gigis* are restless," he whispered. "They're bored with this whole discussion."

"I don't hear anything," Abby whispered back.

"That's because you're talking."

"I'm sorry."

Flapping wings lifted a large, hooting spy above the pines, above their heads, and into the night.

"That's only an owl," Abby said dismissively.

"*Only* an owl? Jesus, lady." Turning to Heather, Kole wagged his head. "Only an owl."

"It does sound like an owl, Kola."

"And an owl is an owl is an owl," Abby quipped.

"To you, maybe," Kole said. "Which is why that dissertation of yours will be nothing but words, words, words."

"I didn't say it was *just* an owl."

"Heather's a writer, too, but she's part Cherokee." He nudged Heather with his elbow. "What, about nine parts writer and one part Cherokee?"

"You're impossible."

"But aren't you also a writer?" Abby asked. "I recognize the name Kola from one of the periodicals I subscribe to."

"*Subscribe* to? Jeez, you're really into this project, aren't you?"

"That's the way it is with a dissertation. You pretty much eat it, sleep it, and wear it until you've successfully added those three lovely letters to the back of your name. Your latest article on Indian entitlements was interesting."

"Entitlements?"

"I don't think you used that word. Treaty rights, I guess. Health care was the main focus. You were complaining about—"

"My arthritis was probably acting up, so I felt like going after the Indian Health Service. Just like any other crank who writes in to the paper when he feels like sounding off." He shook his head. "I don't call myself a writer. I'm a flute maker by trade. I might scribble something and send it in when I've got nothin' better to do. Jack might put it in the paper when he needs some filler."

"And I might follow you guys to Hollywood just to see if you can actually pull this off. That's how important this project is to me."

"You're betting we'll come unraveled," he charged flatly.

"I'm not betting anything. I'm observing."

"That makes two of you. Watching us through the glass." He shrugged, slid his arm around Heather's shoulders with a casualness that belied the strange tension she sensed in him. "As long as they send us the good-lookin' females, I won't complain."

"Who's *they*?" Abby wanted to know.

"I haven't figured that out yet." He nodded toward the gravel road that would lead them to the area where the caravan was parked. "I think the group plans on headin' out after everybody's had time to meet, eat, and gas up. We can't camp here. They're closed for the season."

"I thought you wanted to—"

Kole cut Heather off as he glanced at Abby. "So we'll take the show back on the road and see what we can pick up along the way."

"Your flutes should come in handy. Are you taking the children with the rats?" Abby chided.

"Not rats." In the dark he gave the first show of teeth, which Heather was pretty sure constituted a smile. She couldn't tell whether it was a friendly one. "Pretty white mice," he said.

Abby laughed. Heather didn't.

◆　◆　◆

In the dark the caravan made its way west along South Dakota's mostly straight and narrow county roads, headed for the Pine Ridge Oglala Sioux Reservation. When they reached the Missouri River, they stopped for their first sleep since Minneapolis.

Heather spoke of needing rest, wanting rest, welcoming the chance to rest awhile, but rest wasn't the same as sleep. Rest meant freeing their bodies from jeans and shirts and shoes and easing into each other. Rest meant giving and taking with whispered words and intimate touches and holding each other, taking comfort in closeness, resting in pure satisfaction.

"I've never felt this way before," Kole said. "Never fit this good with anyone."

"Not even with . . ." Heather caught herself. *Stupid, stupid, stupid.* What, was she back to being sixteen again?

"Women." He squeezed her as she lay in the crook of his arm. "Why do you wanna go and get specific on me? Can't you just accept the spirit of what I said?"

"I guess I'm trying to figure out exactly what it meant. The physical fit is pretty much—"

"Put it this way," he began, then paused, measuring his words. "It's like we're moving together, the way we did in the canoe. I feel like you're all of a sudden part of me." He pressed a warm kiss against her temple and whispered, "A nice new part."

"You didn't want a new part."

"I do now," he said solemnly. "For now, I do."

"For tonight?"

"And tomorrow."

She tucked her head under his chin, her face against his warm neck, and inhaled his scent. Sage and smoke and sex. "You've been part of me for a long time."

"Until now it was all in your head."

"A safe place to start."

"Yeah, you're right. I hope you haven't gone from safe to sorry." He leaned back to look her in the eye. "I might not be a nice part, and God knows I ain't gettin' any newer, but I really like being part of something besides your head."

"I'm not sorry."

"And you're not safe."

"Are we back to your ghosts?"

"My ghosts won't hurt you, but my enemies are very much alive. And I don't think they care who they hurt."

" 'Enemies' sounds so . . ."

"Bigheaded, I know." He chuckled humorlessly. "Like I'm important enough to have enemies."

"Maybe you don't anymore. Maybe they've found someone else to hound." She lifted her chin, her turn to search for answers in the eyes of her lover. "What do you think of our new friend?"

"Interesting segue," he said. "I was thinking about her, too."

"Really."

"She doesn't look like any college professor I ever had. Granted, my experience is limited. I only had two."

"Really."

"And they weren't that good-looking. They definitely weren't in that good of shape. Or shaped that good."

Heather wasn't humored, either. "How could you tell? It was dark."

"The way she walks."

"Maybe she plays racquetball." And then, out of nowhere, came, "I belong to a fitness club. I'm a pretty good racquetball player."

"I don't think Abby Wendel's sport is racquetball."

"I stomp when I walk, don't I? Savannah used to try to get me to take it easy, but I told her we were never going to get anywhere unless we really *pounded* the pavement." She laughed, but only a little. The nice part of him that she was supposed to be was all female, all soft and pretty. There were many ways to move together, and she wanted to be the feminine part of the motion. The graceful part, a part she'd thought was fine for someone else, unimportant for a woman like her. "I walk like a man, don't I?"

"Anyone walking next to Savannah would look . . ." He chuckled. "I can just see you two heading down the street together, Savannah in a world all her own and you with places to go and things to do."

Heather felt a little sting. She knew which of his visionary women was the prettier.

"My mother used to tell me to walk like a lady. I never knew what that meant until I met Savannah." And even then she hadn't cared. But now she wondered how she'd look if she tried it. "Does Abby Wendel walk like Savannah?"

"No."

"*Nobody* walks like Savannah."

"Nobody walks and talks and thinks like you, either," he told her softly. "You asked me what I thought of Abby Wendel, and I thought you were thinkin' what I was thinkin', and it had nothing to do with Savannah."

"You were thinking she's attractive."

"Savannah?"

"Abby Wendel."

"I was thinking . . ." He sighed. "I was thinking what I always think when somebody pops up out of nowhere. *Who the hell are you, lady, and how much do you know about me?* It's part of my drill, part of the spin. Round and round in circles. Do you know me? Do you *really* know me? What do you know? What do you want? Who do you work for? Are you the one?" And then, his voice slightly hoarse, "Is it over yet?"

"No."

"It's up to you, Heather."

"No."

"You're writing the story. It's your call."

"I'll make you safe, then. I'll make you happy."

"You're the only one who can. Don't ever walk beside anyone else, honey." He kissed her temple again, then smoothed her hair with his lips. "Next to me, you'll always look like a fine lady."

"You're impossible."

"*We're* impossible."

"But we're making it anyway."

11

Kole had not set foot on home ground in many years.

Pine Ridge was his mother's reservation and the scene of his own public activity back in what he fondly called his "wild Indian" days. As a wanted man, he had had the good sense to stay away from South Dakota—until now. He had, in fact, spent much of his recent time—literally his free time—developing his newfound good sense. Then he'd met Heather Reardon, and all bets on being sensible were off.

Still, he'd followed the news from home. He read *Native Drums*, and so he knew the issues of the rally that they were about to attend at the high school gym.

As Kola, he had written several pieces on the current controversy at Pine Ridge, which was a dry reservation. Oglala activists had been protesting the lucrative beer and liquor trade in nearby White Clay, Nebraska, a tiny off-reservation town that thrived economically on the misery of those residents of the Indian communities just across the state line who suffered from alcoholism. A "beer run" meant getting a ride to White Clay. The ride home might be harder to find. The people of Pine Ridge had few friends in White Clay.

A town of few people and many liquor stores, White Clay appeared to exist for the sole purpose of turning a profit on the sale of alcohol to a group of people for whom drink had historically meant physical, emotional, social, cultural, political, spiritual, and every other kind of human calamity.

The town's notion of earning an honest living was a throwback to the frontier liquor trade, recalled by most Americans a century later as a national shame. But it was immensely profitable, and it endured, despite tribal protest. After all, it was perfectly legal.

"Most towns have a bar or a liquor store," Kole acknowledged, as though Heather had said something to justify such businesses's right to exist rather than nod in agreement as he explained the situation. "But that's *all* White Clay is."

"I've checked it out myself, and that's all I saw," Heather said quietly.

"You *went* to White Clay?" He challenged her with a glance.

"I saw a television report about it, so when I was here interviewing people during President Clinton's visit to Pine Ridge a couple of years ago, I went down there to see for myself. It's not a pretty place."

"Not your picturesque little town on the prairie?" He parked the camper behind the school he'd assumed he would attend—until the day his mother had packed him off to his father's ranch.

A steady drumbeat penetrated the walls of the building, proclaiming that they'd come to the right place. Kole's pulse was reinforced by the rhythm, and when he turned to the woman sitting next to him, he saw no judgment in her eyes. But he was embarrassed anyway, even as he told himself not to be. She had gone looking for White Clay, and now she was the proud owner of the memory of a place that should not be.

"The business of White Clay is to sell firewater," he said matter-of-factly. "It's like selling cigarettes to kids. Worse, maybe, because you know the stuff is *already* killing your customers. But it's legitimate retail and you're a legitimate businessman."

He didn't mean *you* the way it sounded. He didn't know why he kept saying it. He didn't want Heather's tent pitched in any other camp but his own.

"Moral is a step beyond legal," she said.

He nodded, surprised she hadn't jumped on the chance to take that damn *you* wrong. In fact, her eyes fairly glowed with enthusiasm for the topic. Not sympathy, not pity, but a kind of enthusiasm for knowing and understanding, like she was on some sort of fascinating anthropological field trip. And where did that put him?

"Do they have any churches in White Clay?" she asked. "Business is probably pretty good there, too." He questioned her logic with a look, and she clarified as she shut the camper door. "Saturday night confession."

"I wouldn't know. I don't know how those people live with themselves. We've been fighting it for years."

And now he was fighting something else. Embarrassment, for God's sake. He didn't like it, but there it was. Naked in the dark, she could be part of him, but not in White Clay. The people lying in the street were more part of him than she was. The people behind the cash registers were more part of her than he was.

Kole hissed at a scrawny rez hound threatening to lift its leg on the camper's rear tire. Woof's face appeared in the window. The skinny dog took off at the first warning growl, leaving no trace of his visit to Woof's territory.

Her people were behind the cash registers in territory once his people's home.

He shook off that poisonous thought and reached for the standard antidote. Humor. They were in Pine Ridge, not White Clay. He was home.

"How 'bout this?" He tapped her arm with the back of his hand as they walked toward the door. "When we get to Hollywood, how 'bout we ask Clint what he'd think about taking a ride into White Clay with a few buckets of red paint."

"The old High Plains Drifter himself?" The shift from White Clay to Hollywood made Heather laugh. Tension drained from her neck and shoulders. She could just imagine what kind of news coverage a reenactment of Eastwood's classic western morality tale would prompt. "I'm surprised Barry Wilson hasn't thought of it."

"Clint would get top billing." Kole ushered her through the side door to the high school gym in the reservation town of Manderson, where the powwow was already in progress. According to Jack, who knew what was shaking in any given week on any reservation from Leech Lake to White Mountain, the customary call to rally round a boycott of White Clay would be part of the powwow activity and the perfect springboard for their own pitch. "Besides," Kole said, "Wilson's gotta be careful about his image nowadays. I read where he doesn't wanna always be playing the Indian."

"Lately he has been *the* Indian. They must call him every time the script calls for one."

"One little, two little, three little Indians," Kole quipped. "Wonder what they do when it calls for more than one." He picked up an invisible phone. "H. R., get me a couple of actors who look Native American. Like, you know, American Indian," he said into his fist. "But not *too* Indian. More American. Brown but not crisp, if you catch my drift." He did a mock double take. "Wait a minute, H. R. Did I hear you say you're a little Cherokee? Have you done any acting, H. R.?"

"Please stop it," Heather pleaded with a sigh. "I don't claim—"

He bumped her shoulder with his. "Just kidding. You're right, Wilson wouldn't mind playing two or three parts. My uncle Fuzz was an extra in a movie they shot not far from here. He got shot off his horse and killed seven times in one movie."

"Lucky guy."

"He was. He got paid by the kill."

"Brings new meaning to the term 'kill fee.' "

"Yep, ol' Fuzzy Wuzzy got a fee to do a fie on a foe and then die. Plus, he got paid an extra *fum*." He laughed, feeling full of himself as she gave him a slow groan and a quick shove. "No lie, for playing a Pawnee," he protested.

"Because they're your traditional enemies?"

"Because he had to shave his head. No shame, that guy. He went around wearing a stocking cap for a month to cover it up, but they still called him Fuzz."

"True story?"

He shrugged. "You decide."

Once inside the school gym, they were surrounded first by their fellow pilgrims, including Jack, who had done the advance work to make sure there would be no unwelcome surprises waiting for Kole. Unlike with the stop they'd made in the city, Jack had put out no word of Kole's impending visit to Pine Ridge.

The reservation had a history of protest and activism. Not only was it the home of Kole's closest friends and relatives, but it was also the site of myriad unsolved murders, including that of Lana Kills Crow. Kole recalled several nights when he and his mother had been terrorized by gunfire from shadowy vehicles racing past the three-room house they'd shared with his grandmother, his aunt, and several cousins.

Thanks to the FBI, the American Indian Movement, and the shifty tribal chairman's notorious gang of thugs known as the Goon

Squad, the 1970s had been a violent time in Pine Ridge. But it had also been a time of Lakota revival.

"Hey, Kole, how's it goin'?"

"Hey, Red Butt. *Waste yelo.*" *Good.*

With a handshake, Kole greeted Robert Red Bull by the nickname with which the big man had long since made his peace. There was never any choice once a nickname stuck. And since the day Robert had shown up late for basketball practice after losing his cherry with Reva McLane in a patch of poison ivy along the river bottom, he'd been Red Butt.

Kole had been in the seventh grade at the time—not long before his mother had taken him to live in Wyoming with his father—but he'd already made the junior varsity team, so he'd been a witness to poor Red Butt's humiliation. Cheeks flaming at both ends.

"Let me take your pulse, man." Red Butt squeezed Kole's forearm and craned his neck to take a sniff. He'd put on at least fifty pounds since Kole had last seen him, and his grip was powerful. "Hell, you don't *smell* dead."

"Is that the latest?"

"Nah, your death is old news. The latest is what I'm gonna be tellin' around next. Would you rather be back from the grave or a dead ringer for yourself?"

"I'd rather be Kola, the flute maker. And since not too many people know what he looks like, you might have to introduce me around."

"I can do that." Kole's old friend jerked his chin to point to Heather, who'd been sticking close to Kole's side since they'd left the camper. "Is she with you?"

"Heather Reardon," she said, offering a handshake. "I'm with the caravan."

"She's with me." Kole laid a hand on Heather's shoulder and nodded toward the kettle-laden tables at the far end of the gym. He leaned close to her ear. "How about getting us some coffee, there, Cherokee?"

She whipped her head around so fast she nearly clipped his nose. *Are you serious?* her wide eyes challenged. He smiled, nodded once, and to his amazement she asked, "With sugar?"

"You know what I like."

She flashed Red Butt a fixed smile. "He's just so sweet already."

The two men watched Heather saunter across half-court. There was no hip-swaying from her, but neither was there any of the stomping she'd worried about. There was poise and purpose. Heather always moved with purpose. Kole glanced up at the faces in the bleachers, noting that his and Red Butt's wasn't the only notice she was getting. She was a standout in any crowd, he thought, but here—hell, she was white.

"You're takin' a big chance, cuz," Red observed quietly.

"It's something I haven't done in a while. Gets the blood pumping."

"Is that what she does? Get your blood pumpin'?"

"Oh, yeah."

"You sure you can trust her?"

A few feet short of the food tables, Heather was just hooking up with Abby Wendel at the end of the line, striking up a conversation right away like two chirpy chickadees finding each other among a flock of sparrows. Abby *really* stood out. She was the only blonde in the gym, for one thing, but there was something else about her that stood out, something that made him feel uneasy around her.

"About all I know for sure is that nothing's for sure. But what the hell, you either take a shot once in a while, or you might as well pack it in."

Red Butt grinned. "Use it or lose it."

"I'm trusting her. As to whether I can or not . . ." Kole watched the two women share a piece of frybread after Heather tore it in half. They sure seemed to have a lot to talk about for two people who'd just met. "Guess that'll be up to her."

"Yeah, I can see why you'd chance it." Red Butt hiked one foot up to the second step at the end of the bleachers as he, too, watched the two white women. "What about the other one?"

"I don't know. Heather seems to think she's cool. You know how women are. They like to run in pairs."

"Or little bunches. Nice little handfuls of round, ripe . . ." Beefy, upturned hands scratched some imaginary flesh. "So the other one's unattached?"

"For all I know, she's got more strings tied to her than Howdy Doody."

"Who'd be pulling 'em? I heard Buffalo Bob went to the Happy Hunting Ground." Red Butt's facial expression went from utterly straight—"The Old Ones ate good that night, they said. Tanned his hide and painted a big grin on it. All teeth."—to a wooden smile.

"Damn, Red Butt. You'd make *papa* out of Bambi," Kole teased, referring in Lakota to jerked meat.

"A rash on the ass'll do that to a guy." Red Butt eyed the women, who had finally reached the coffee urn. "I don't know, man, she looks pretty harmless."

"Maybe she is. Maybe they all are."

"You talking about women or *wasicu*?"

"I'm talking about hunters." Kole shrugged. "Figured it was time to step out in the open and see if they're still looking for a trophy buck."

"You're a trophy buck, all right. Brave, too."

"Half-breed to boot. How many ways can you spell *target*?"

"You gotta practice up for Hollywood, man. Get the vocabulary down."

"I've got it all memorized. Why don't you come along? You working?"

"I had a job at the school, but the funding for the program got cut. I guess I could go."

Kole grinned. "I need some rabble to rouse."

"Red Butt the Rabble, that's me."

"Nobody looks meaner when he's roused."

"How the hell do you know what I look like roused? You been hiding in my closet?"

"That would be *aroused*, and I don't even wanna go there."

"Damn right you don't." Big Red gave Kole a friendly slap on the back. "A red-ass stud like me puts a little brown buck to shame."

◆   ◆   ◆

By the end of the evening, they'd all become a little too chummy for Kole's taste. Red Butt had hit it off with Abby Wendel right away. He was "just too funny," she kept saying. So they'd all had supper together, and they'd joined in on a traditional circle dance, *kahomni*, together. Before Kole knew it, Heather had suggested that Abby and Red Butt ought to ride in the camper the next day, "just so we can chat some more."

Kole didn't feel like chatting. Neither did he feel like playing cards, which probably showed in the mechanical way he handled them, sitting across the table from Red Butt as Heather piloted the camper westward. In the interest of "chatting," Abby had claimed the navigator's seat. Kole longed for the seat next to the fireplace in the quiet north-woods cabin he'd abandoned.

Over the years, he'd gotten used to getting up in front of a crowd to give a talk, and he'd taken part in the round-robin speech-athon at the powwow. That was his role. But he considered himself a private man, and social chatting put him to sleep. He'd rather be talking with just one person. Heather would have been his first and only choice. In about two minutes he was going to stretch out on the back cot, close his eyes and his ears, and shut them all out. He was going to take a hint from Cat, who was stretched along the top of the back cushion between Kole's shoulders and the window. She had it made.

Woof lay on the floor behind the driver's seat. He'd taken a real shine to Heather. When they went their separate ways, Kole wondered whom the wolf-dog would follow.

To torture himself further, he half listened to the college-days stories Heather and Abby were trading. They'd both been to school back East, of course, which was like another country altogether as far as Kole was concerned. Damn Heather, she knew he hadn't planned on letting anyone ride with them. The extra passengers and the happy chitchat felt like a wedge between them—a cold steel wedge, and her world was the fat end. He could almost manage to forget that reality when it was just the two of them.

But that thought galled him, too. Forgetting their differences was the stupidest thing he could do right now.

He tossed a card on the table, trumping Red's jack. When had he started feeling so flush that he'd taken to wasting his trump cards? He didn't know *jack* about this Wendel woman, and he wasn't too sure about Red Butt, whom he hadn't seen in years. If push came to shove, he wasn't too sure about anybody.

He didn't know much about Heather, either, but he knew her. Intimately. He knew the way her eyes brightened when something piqued her interest, the way they softened when he sweet-talked her, the way they closed slowly when he kissed her. He knew that she liked to sleep on her side with one knee cocked. Early in the morning he'd taken to hooking his leg over her, tucking his knee in the hollow of hers and nesting his stiff cock in the swell beneath her buttocks, letting her sit on his eggs. He loved the scent of dewy night on her skin.

Damn her. He glanced at the hiked-up bunch of auburn hair bobbing above the back of the driver's seat with each bump in the road. Abby Wendel and Robert "Red Butt" Red Bull were going to have to find themselves someplace else to sleep.

"I got a cousin in Casper I think I could borrow a car from," Red

Butt said quietly without taking his eyes off his hand of cards. "I could give Abby a ride."

"You readin' my mind?"

"Don't have to. You got it written all over your face." Red Butt glanced over his cards with mischief in his eyes. "Just don't tell my ol' lady."

"What's not to tell?" Kole didn't even know who Red Butt's old lady was.

"But be careful, man."

"I'm always careful."

"It's been a long time, Kola. All the warriors we used to know have either gotten old and paunchy, or else they've gone mainstream."

"There's a few still locked away."

"I hate to see you—"

"You won't. I ain't goin' back to jail, man. No way." He gave Red Butt a meaningful look. "But I'm tired of sittin' quiet. The rumors of my death could just as well be true. I've gotta say my piece somehow, you know?"

"You've been sayin' it. I've been readin' it." Red Butt shrugged when Kole's face expressed some doubt. "Sometimes. I saw that one about the people who got moved off their reservation into a place that turned out to be contaminated with radiation. Were they Hopi?"

"See, you don't even remember."

"I get 'em mixed up with some of the Pueblo people. I've never been down there, myself. I was hoping we'd be passing through that country on this trip." Red took a card and discarded a seven of spades. "Are they getting any compensation, those people?"

"Somebody in Washington said 'Whoops.' "

"So they'll get something."

"How do you get a life?" Kole wagged his head. "You know that expression 'Get a life'? People say it all the time. 'You need to get a life.' When they've been moving people around like pawns for a hundred years, what does it mean to get a life? How do you get a life in a poisoned body?"

He suddenly realized the women had stopped talking. Time to answer his own question.

"You stop feeling sorry for yourself is what you gotta do, Red."

"I ain't feelin'—"

"You take the bull by the horns and march on the bull-throwing capital of the world. You turn all their best lines on them. 'I'm mad as hell, and I'm not gonna take it anymore.' "

"Jack would love to hear this," Heather tossed back from the driver's seat.

"Well, we oughta be practicing up. There's no progress without protest, right? We're the only counterculture left."

"I wouldn't say that."

"It doesn't matter what you'd say, honey. It's my quotes you're supposed to be collecting."

Heather glanced at Abby. "He's pretty insufferable for a flute maker."

"Flute making is an art," Kole reminded Heather. Then he took a verbal stab at Abby. "The temperament of an artist is one of my *entitlements.*"

"Ah, but is it a treaty right?"

"No. Entitlements are for everybody. A treaty right is something special. At least, that's what they claim."

"Who's 'they'?" Abby wanted to know.

"The insufferables." Kole grinned across the table at Red. "Hey. That sounds like a good movie title. *The Insufferables.* Based on the dissertation of Dr. Abby Wendel, Indian expert."

"Ko—Kol*a*," Heather scolded, catching herself in a near slip. "Some of the most effective voices being raised in your behalf these days are academics."

"*My* behalf?"

"In behalf of the American Indian," Heather said. "Abby was just telling me about—"

Abby turned in her seat, looking for Kole. "I think we got off on the wrong foot, and I'd love to find a way to backtrack and start over. Switch feet, as it were. Which words would you like me to take back?"

"None. I was just kidding."

"You were?" She turned to Heather. "He sure didn't look like a man who was kidding."

"What," Kole barked, "you expect me to smile when I'm kidding? That would take all the fun out of it."

♦   ♦   ♦

They had their privacy back by day's end after the caravan had swung through Casper, Wyoming. Red Butt had borrowed an orange and white VW bus from his cousin, who had thrown in an extra spare tire when he found out there were to be passengers. Red had said he'd be picking up another relative on the way out of town. Kole figured the suggestion of a chaperone was for the benefit of the moccasin telegraph, to which Red Butt's old lady—whoever she was—was bound to be connected. From Casper they'd driven to the Wind River Shoshone Reservation, where the eighteen vehicles' campsites dotted the otherwise deserted powwow grounds.

"Back to you and me, babe," Kole quipped, surprised by the contentment he felt in saying it as he parted the camper curtain and peered out at the moonlit plain. Red Butt had been kind enough to park a good twenty yards away with his little party. He'd built a campfire, and already several people had pulled up a chunk of firewood and sat down. "I was feeling pretty cramped," Kole muttered.

Heather slid her arms around his waist. "He's *your* friend."

"Is she yours?"

"I think she's pretty interesting. Pleasant enough." She kissed the back of his neck and whispered, "Harmless."

"You sure?"

"I have pretty good instincts about these things. She strikes me as good people."

"She probably is," he said, turning to her. "One of the good guys. The trouble is, I'm one of the bad guys." He undid the top button on her blouse. "So from my perspective, she's anything but harmless."

"You are *not* one of the bad guys."

"I didn't think so, either, until I saw my own face on a Wanted poster." He lifted his hand, examined his empty palm. "Damn, that's me. 'Escaped from federal prison, suspicion of murder, possibly armed, considered dangerous.' Sounds like one bad hombre."

"I know better."

"Whatever." He slid his arms around her. "It's the good guys who want me behind bars, honey. Now, I don't know whose side you're on, but—"

"*Yours.*"

"But I'm real fussy about who I hang out with. Good guys make me nervous, and this new friend of yours definitely makes me nervous."

"What about me?"

"I feel pretty comfortable around you." He returned her favor, nuzzling her neck. "You must not be too good."

"Not *too* good."

"Maybe even a little bit bad?"

"Sometimes."

"As long as you're with me, you won't be making too many new friends." He leaned back, gave her an apologetic look even though he was hardly sorry. "That's the way it's gotta be."

"How about seeing old friends? Family?" He started to pull away at the suggestion, but she held on. "We're so close, Kole. You said you wanted to see them."

"It might be too dangerous."

"We can call them and have them come to the reservation where—"

"Not for me. Dangerous for them. For my daughter. It's bad enough she's living with my brother."

"He's a wonderful—"

"I'm sure he is," he snapped. "Top of the good-guy list. Father of the year. I just meant, it's bad enough that somebody might . . ." He sighed. He never allowed himself to take too close a look at his feelings for his only brother. It wasn't Clay's fault that he reminded Kole of things he didn't want to think about—like their white father. "Somebody might link her to me through Clay. My daughter's mother was murdered, Heather. And I don't know whether the good guys did it or the bad guys. Good and bad don't mean much to me."

"How about friends and family?"

He nodded. "They mean a lot. I need to be careful for them."

"Kola," she whispered. "True friend. You need them, too, you know. You need your family. You're just like anybody else, Kole; you also need friends."

"Like I said, I'm real particular about who I hang out with. Mostly nobody I really like, except maybe Jack. But I couldn't chase him away with skunk spray and a sharp stick."

"Me neither. I mean, you couldn't chase me away."

"I wasn't expecting you." He tightened his embrace, wishing he could just crawl inside her and let her absorb him completely. "You took me by surprise. I'm gonna have a hell of a time letting you go, lady."

"I going with you," she whispered. "California or bust."

"I'll take some of that bust."

He began by undoing the rest of her buttons.

12

Heather had eaten more than a few of the words she'd peppered Savannah's plans with a year ago, mostly over the phone. Savannah had been one of the best-known faces in the fashion industry. At the time, Heather couldn't believe her chic, sophisticated friend could go home again. Not happily, and surely not ever after.

But every time Heather had seen that dearly familiar, not-so-secretly coveted face in the last year, she couldn't deny the contentment she saw there. Savannah and Clay had saved his ranch's financial bacon with her crazy idea of a retirement home for horses. The wealthy paid handsomely to put their geriatric horses out to pasture, and horse lovers' charity took care of the needs of the neglected horses Clay continued to take into his care.

Savannah had become a spokesperson for horse causes and women's causes—breast cancer awareness in particular—and she had found innovative ways to integrate the two through what she called "horse therapy." She maintained that a woman didn't have to be a rider to enjoy the consoling company of horses.

Seeing Savannah now, Heather was pleased to eat every doubt she'd had. Savannah was her sister in every sense of the word but blood. And when she confided to Savannah that she and Kole were together, it was Savannah's turn to be dumbstruck. When she found her voice, there was no shortage of words—questions and cautions, admissions and advice, punctuated by the occasional "Omigawd!" and "Are you serious?"

Oh, yes, Heather was serious. She'd always been serious about the lives around her, lives that interested her or meant something to her, but she'd never been this serious about anything in her own life, other than her work. And no one knew that better than her friend Savannah.

♦ ♦ ♦

Kole met Heather at the door of the camper, where he'd been waiting. "What did they say?" he demanded before she even got inside.

"They want to see you, Kole. They're dying to see you."

"Who is?"

She slid into the booth, hoping that he would do the same. "I spoke with both Savannah and Clay. They were surprised, of course, and relieved and actually delighted that I'd . . ." She looked up, hoping he'd settle down beside her. But he was waiting to hear what she'd done to please Savannah and Clay. "They really, truly did not know that I was trying to track you down."

"What about the baby?"

"She's not—"

"I know, not a baby." He turned away. This was the first time she'd seen such agitation take hold of him. "Will they let me see her?"

"They want to see you first."

"Why?" He whirled on her, a new hardness in his eyes. "So they can tell me what to say to her? How to act?"

"Do you realize how long it's been since they've seen you? You were in prison the last time Clay saw you. And Savannah hasn't seen you since—"

"I gave her my baby."

"Who's seven years old now, Kole. You don't have to explain anything to a baby, but now she's old enough to—"

"I trusted Savannah completely then. She can damn well trust me now." He sighed, finally gave over to taking a seat, as though his own body were his heaviest burden. "If we're gonna do this at all, we're only doing it once, Heather. This kind of rendezvous is risky. I don't want anyone knowing about it."

"Not even Jack?"

"I don't talk about my child with anybody. *Ever*." She denied his claim with a simple look, and he sighed again. "That's right, I broke that rule with you. You're the crack in my defenses. So." He shrugged, glanced away from her, toward the door. "If anything leaks, I'll know why."

She refused to take his bait. "I think a lot of people in Sunbonnet have already made the connection to you."

"I don't worry about them." He nodded toward the campground beyond the camper door. "I'm more worried about this bunch we're traveling with. The rednecks of Sunbonnet have about as much interest in Indians and Indian issues as they have in lobster fishing."

"You don't trust your own . . ."

"I've read a little history, rubbed shoulders with a few killers. If you're gonna get stabbed in the back, chances are the doer is somebody close, somebody you thought would cover you in a crisis."

"What did Abby Wendel say about Indian people being their own worst enemies?"

"Isn't she a clever girl? Like we're any different from anybody else." He snorted contemptuously. "Who killed Gandhi? Sitting Bull? Caesar? Jesus and Jesse James? And, *no*, I'm not comparing myself," he assured her. "I'm just sayin', I don't even have to look over my shoulder anymore. Trouble has a certain feel about it, a certain smell."

"Do you smell it now?"

"You're sweet trouble." He leaned close to her and inhaled deeply. "No, it's not the same."

"I mean here. Wyoming. Wind River. This particular campsite."

"Yeah. I do. And I'm not about to lead it to my child." He closed his eyes, shook his head, finally slammed his palms on the table and pushed to his feet. "Goddamn it, yes, I am. That's exactly what I'm about to do."

Nearly tripping over Woof, he fled to the back of the camper. He returned cradling a long, slender flute decorated with carved turtles. He extended it to her across his palms. "Take her this. I made it for her. Just tell her you got it from a gift shop."

"No." She pushed his hands and the pretty instrument away. "No, Kole, you give it to her. It should come from you."

"Like my story should come from me, and this crazy caravan, and the truth, the whole truth. It's going to set me free, right? I *was* free. Then along comes my sweet trouble."

"No, you weren't. You were—"

"I like that," he said, ignoring her protest. "My sweet trouble. Good title for my book."

"What book?"

"The one I'm workin' on about you."

He almost had her, but she quickly shook off the credulousness only he could produce in her. "You weren't free, Kole."

"Free to keep to myself. But now you've got me all riled up inside. I want things I can't have, and my feet itch to go places, and I dream about—" A knock on the camper door nearly blew his fuse. "Who the hell is it?" he bellowed.

"A friend."

They looked at each other. It was the one voice common to their lives and memories.

"Shit. Didn't you tell her not to show that face of hers here?"

Heather moved past him. "Maybe we should let her in before anyone sees it. How about that?" She opened the door and waved their friend inside.

Kole stepped back, shaking his head even as his eyes welcomed the woman who was more sister to him than friend. "Damn you, Savannah, you shouldn't . . ." Whatever she shouldn't be doing couldn't stop him from grabbing her in his arms. "Damn, you look good. Damn, damn, damn."

"Nice talk," the lovely, lithe blonde said with a giggle. "It's so good to see you. Alive and well, walking, talking—even if it's just to cuss me out."

Heather stepped aside, smiling through the twinge of jealousy she'd always felt when she watched Savannah float into a man's arms. You could almost hear the guy's libido gasping for breath.

Kole took hold of Savannah's shoulders and peeled her off his body. "You shouldn't be here, honey. We shouldn't connect. We don't want anyone connecting . . ." He glanced at the door behind her. "Where's Clay?"

"He's at home. Waiting. Hoping you'll come back with me."

"Are you crazy?"

"After it gets dark." Savannah reached for Kole's shoulders, nearly even with hers. She tried to shake him, didn't seem to notice that he wasn't budging. Not even for her world-famous smile. "C'mon. Nobody'll see."

"It's a stupid idea." He pulled away. "I let myself think about seeing you guys, and it's like opening a window and saying bye-bye caution. I can't go soft now." He turned his back on both women. "You don't want her seeing me now, Savannah. You know you don't." At war with himself, he turned again. "Just tell me about her. Like today— what's she up to today?"

"She's in school."

"School," he marveled. "Damn. Is she smart?"

"She's very smart. Which you would know if you called once in a while."

"You adopted her. Your terms were 'no strings.' I gave you my . . ." He raked his hair back with an unsteady hand and nearly lost his voice on the pathetic assessment. "Her father is a convict and a god- damn coward."

"Clay's her father in all the important ways," Savannah gently pointed out. "For him it was love at first sight—partly, I think, because he saw you in her face. She looks just like you, Kole."

He smiled, but he couldn't look at Savannah. His eyes glittered. "You never saw her mother."

"I'm her mother."

Clearing his throat, he took a seat at the table. "Did you bring any pictures of her?"

"No." Savannah sat across from him. "I think you should see her in person, Kole."

"Now that you've checked me out?" He nodded as he reached

across the table for Savannah's perfect hands. "You were right. It's a bad idea. It could still be dangerous, for one thing." He studied those hands for a moment before adding, "And the other thing . . . I know she's got a good life. Mother and father, safe home, school."

Heather was beginning to feel like the fly on the wall. She slid quietly into the front passenger's chair. What could she do but listen?

"She's going to need you, too, Kole," Savannah insisted. "Not long after she started school she told me she didn't want to be an Indian." She gave a tight smile in response to his inscrutable glance. "Of course, I got all shook up about it, trying to come up with the right thing to say. But it has to come from you. I can teach her about being an American, a woman, a bicycle rider, a cookie baker, a hundred other things. I can take her to museums and read her books. But I can't . . ." Savannah looked him straight in the eye. "Kole, I don't live in Lakota skin."

"Yeah, well, I do, and maybe that's part of the reason I had to give her up. It was the only way I could protect her, give her a life," he said, looking for validation. Savannah nodded, happy to oblige. "You need to keep her away from me now, Savannah. I'm bound to get caught soon."

"On purpose?"

"I've got a purpose for making this trip."

"Not to get caught. You've been so careful for so long." She reached across the table to touch his hair.

A motherly gesture, Heather told herself.

"I doubt they're even looking for you anymore," Savannah assured him.

How would she know? Heather asked herself.

"If you say so," he muttered.

My, how the mighty have melted.

Savannah smiled at him. "Would it be disappointing to find out that you're really not material for *America's Most Wanted*?"

When had the world-famous smile gone from Mona Lisa–like to Madonna-esque?

"Not at all," Kole said. "But stuff like that doesn't go away, not even with time. Some things don't change."

"Maybe not, but apparently your life has suddenly changed quite a bit."

"Do I have you to thank for that?" he asked Savannah as he slid Heather a quick glance.

Did I buzz? Heather returned a perfectly innocent look. *Don't mind me.*

"I would gladly take credit if I had it coming." Savannah squeezed his hand. "Your family hasn't gone away, Kole."

Heather stifled a sigh. *Buzz, buzz, you two, while we flies mind our own business.* But it was hard to ignore all the motherly petting and squeezing reflected in every facet of her big eyes. It was enough to make even a fly puke.

"*You* have a family now," Kole was saying. "I have the memory of one."

"Oh no you don't. You will not deny her."

"What do you want me to do? You want me to take her back?"

Savannah answered him with a daring look that bore no resemblance to anything on paper or canvas.

"You don't think I've thought about it?" Kole demanded.

"I'm sure you have. I'm just as sure you won't."

He drew a deep breath. "Does she ask about me? What do you tell her?"

"We've answered her questions as they came, told her as much as she was ready for. Clay insists on being absolutely truthful with her."

"He wouldn't know how to do anything else."

"He misses you."

"Why didn't he come with you?"

"Being straight with Claudia about who you are is one thing. Letting her meet you now and make up her own mind is a little scarier for him."

"Not for you?"

She was not so quick to answer that one. Finally she admitted, "It would be if your wife were alive."

"If she were alive, we wouldn't be having this conversation. I wouldn't be going on this damned crusade, and you wouldn't be—" His eyes met Heather's. Oddly, the look in them softened, almost like an apology. He pressed his lips together, drummed his fingers on the table. Finally, almost inaudibly, he said, "This could be the only chance I'll ever have." He had to clear his throat. "To see my . . . to see Claudia."

"Then we have to take the chance," Savannah said. "For her sake more than yours."

13

The acoustics in the rocky den high in the foothills northwest of the Lazy K Ranch reminded Heather of Colorado's Red Rock Amphitheater, where she'd once attended a symphony concert. But instead of exploding against the rocks, Kole's plaintive flute music ascended in sinuous spires, like the smoke from the fire they'd built, reaching for the star-studded night sky.

They had come to this magical place earlier than the appointed time because he wanted to show her its secrets. Myriad petroglyphs, carved on the surrounding moon-washed rockface by the ancestors of his ancestors, were signs of the sacred. It was impossible to feel anything but inspired by the ageless message of the marks and the echoes of the music. Here the light from the fire and the night sky made little of color and less of time. Here the only race was human; the only religion was a private discovery of the creator of this place in the surrounding rock, the night sky, and the face on the opposite side of the fire.

When the music stopped, only the crackling fire disturbed the quiet. The distant call of a coyote briefly brought Woof's ears to attention, but then he stretched and declared the lack of a threat with a yawn.

Kole tapped the flute against his palm. "This was our secret place."

"You and Savannah?"

"The three of us. It was theirs, really." He draped his forearms over his upraised knees. The flute linked his hands. "I was too old for a 'secret place,' but I played along when there was nothing better to do. I liked it up here. It's the only part of the ranch that feels like home to me."

"You knew she had a crush on you."

"A crush? That sounds pretty trivial considering the way I used to have to beat that girl off me with a stick." He enjoyed the look she was giving him, kept a straight face as long as he could. "Truth is, she was about as independent as any woman I've ever known, with the exception of my mother. But if she ever belonged with anyone, it was Clay."

"I'm devoting a whole chapter to this beating people off with a stick fantasy of yours," Heather warned.

He smiled and waggled his flute at her.

"I take it your mother was her own person."

"Totally."

"Funny you should compare her with Savannah, then." Her tone was all innocence. He liked that about her, the way she forgot herself and went utterly female with him. She didn't seem to know how obvious she was, so it didn't feel like she was putting him on.

He tipped his head to the side, peered past the fire to offer an invitation with a bemused look. *Let's have some fun. Tell me why you don't want me comparing Savannah with my mother.*

She poked at a burning chunk of mesquite with a stick. "I love Savannah. She's my dearest friend. But I'd hardly call her the epitome of independence."

"What would you call her? Besides your dearest friend."

"Good friend, good mother, good wife, great spokesperson for the horses she and Clay protect and defend. Terrible model."

He said nothing, but she caught the raised brow.

"It's true, when you think about it," she insisted. "Nobody looks like that. Not even Savannah. You look at her picture, and you think *perfection*, right? How can anybody really look like that?"

"Is it true when you don't think about it?" He chuckled at the scowl she flashed him. "I just saw her. She looked like Savannah to me."

"Which is not good for the rest of us. And she did it all for Lady Elizabeth—whoever *that* is. For God's sake, Kole, you know she wasn't doing it for herself. She did it for her mother. And for her friends, her rivals, for every masochistic female who ever ordered from Lady Elizabeth's hoping that something skimpy from the latest line of so-called *dreamwear* would make her more attractive to some slavering male like you."

He wiped the corner of his mouth on the back of his hand, which he examined, then glanced at her. She gave him a puckish smile. He scooted around the firepit, touched the pad of his thumb to the corner of her mouth, showed her the moisture he'd gathered. He shook his head, chuckling.

She gave a theatrical sigh. "Men don't get it."

"You can say that again." He looked up at the stars—speaking of heavenly bodies—and noticed that they'd already shifted some over-head, which made him feel restless. Rejected, maybe. "I don't think they're coming. We ought to just go."

"It'll be fine, Kole." Heather put her hand on his arm. "You'll be fine."

"Sure I will." He sighed, shivered at the thought of being anything but fine. "I haven't been around kids much. I don't know what to say to her."

"It'll come to you." She slid her hand over his. "Are you cold?"

"No. Yeah. I don't know. Am I?"

"Your hands are always warm, but not now."

"That's what I hate about this place. At night especially, it gets so damn cold."

"Says the man who's been living in a cabin in northern Minnesota for how long?"

"That's different. Different kind of cold." He smiled for her. "My bed's been a lot warmer lately."

"I'm glad I'm good for—" Woof barked. Heather lowered her voice to a whisper. "—something." They both turned in the direction that claimed the dog's full attention. At the sound of approaching horses, she smiled. "After all goes well, I'll take credit for this, too."

"And if it doesn't?" Damn, he had goose bumps.

"How can it not go well?" Anticipation jacked her voice up an octave. She hugged his neck, bussed his cheek to reassure him. She obviously thought she was the fairy godmother here, granting him some big wish.

He caught her arm before it slipped away. He needed something more from her, or thought he did.

"How can it not?" she repeated as she leaned back, grinning. "Unless you lose your cool-a."

He nodded, her joke slipping past him. They could hear voices of the three on horseback. The words were inaudible, but the three separate tones were distinct, and the conversation sounded lively. Unmistakably family-talk. Papa Keogh, Mama Keogh, and Baby Keogh.

How could it not go well?

Kole had been counting the ways. For starters he could crack and break apart right there in front of everybody. He resisted the urge to physically try to hold himself together while they watched and waited. Woof growled, and Kole tried to remember whether the dog had ever been around horses before this trip. One more way things might not go well. How about kids? What if his dog bit his kid right off the bat? He ordered Woof to be quiet and get behind him. He understood exactly how hard it was for the dog to control his growling. He wanted to make some kind of sound himself, but he swallowed it back down into his churning gut. Any sound he made now was bound to scare everybody away from him.

Christ, what was he doing?

Sitting there, trying to breathe steadily. He was waiting for vague silhouettes to become heartbreakers. Waiting to sacrifice himself and his friend—two wolves who belonged in the woods. Then he saw them.

Savannah and Claudia rode double, while Clay led the way on a big gaited horse, prancing across the natural plaza like he owned the place. Which, according to the laws of the Keogh forebears, he did.

Kole stood slowly as his younger brother strode purposefully, as though he might pick a fight first thing. His "little" brother, the one who outweighed him by thirty pounds and stood nearly a head taller, the one whose farrier's hands would never outshoot him in hoops but never failed to take him down in any form of wrestling. His loyal brother, who refused to be turned away by Kole's refusal to accept company on visitors' day. His only brother extended him the hearty, pump-handle greeting of a white man.

"What the hell are you doing here?" Clay demanded as he threw an arm around Kole's shoulders. "You could get picked up anytime."

"I already have, by your wife's friend. I couldn't beat her, so I joined her."

"We didn't know where you were, I swear. You okay? You're supposed to be eating well. I hear Heather's a good cook."

"She talks like she is, but I can't make a meal off words."

Heather groaned.

Clay laughed. "What's this about you guys marching on Hollywood? Have you lost your mind?"

"A little stir-crazy, but at least I've got an excuse," Kole said as he eyed the moving shadows behind his brother. Savannah was messing with something tied to their saddle. "I hear you're runnin' a retirement home for horses. I knew you had a soft heart, but soft in the head is something new."

"It was Savannah's idea, and it's working out better than I ever dreamed. The more you charge, the more people think you're worth."

Claudia took the first step, cutting the distance between her parents in half as she emerged quietly from the shadows. Wide-eyed and plainly curious, she stared at Kole. He knew he was staring, too, but he couldn't seem to do anything about his own rudeness. His consciousness had somehow stepped out of his immobile self. All he could do was watch and witness.

His baby had a new face.

He remembered Linda. He remembered his younger self. The day their child was born replayed in his mind. She'd slithered into his hands like a little mermaid, all slick and gooey, bloody and bawling. *It's a girl, isn't it?* Linda had said, her voice reedy from her enormous effort. *I knew I was carrying a girl. I wanted one so bad. Is she okay?*

Yes, she was. She was fantastic. Once again his daughter had totally blown his mind.

"Go ahead and say hello," Clay whispered to him. "She knows who you are."

But Claudia's attention shifted abruptly. "Daddy, can you help us? You tied the ties too tight, and it's going to make Mommy break her fingernails."

"I don't have any nails worth worrying about," Savannah called out from the shadows. "I just can't get this knot out, Clay. Heather, what do you think of our secret place?"

"What a wonderful place for a picnic," Heather said, but her mind wasn't on food. Kole could feel the way she was all tuned in to him. He couldn't look over at her just now, but he had no trouble sucking up all the good vibes he could get.

Claudia took another step closer. "You're my . . ." She gave Kole an overt once-over. "You're Daddy's brother, aren't you?"

"Yeah." When she reached him, he sank to one knee. The sudden change in altitude made him dizzy. "I am."

"You gave me to my mother when I was a baby."

"I did."

"Because she was your friend, and you knew she'd take good care of me."

"That's right." He extended his hand to touch her, but he quickly fisted it and pulled it back to his chest. He needed permission from her. Not necessarily in so many words, but he would know it when he saw it in her eyes. He cleared his prickly throat. "You've gotten so big."

"I'm seven. I skipped the first grade, so I'm small for my grade. But I'm still the smartest one in my class. Well, sometimes the second smartest. Sometimes Jessica Stone beats me in math. But I read better than her."

"Can you show me?"

"I didn't bring a book. Did you?"

"No, but I mean . . . I'd like to listen to you read sometime."

"Were you sad?" She glanced over her shoulder toward the sound of footsteps. Savannah had apparently undone the knot herself. She handed Clay a saddlebag, but she was clearly all eyes and ears for her daughter, as were they all. Claudia turned quickly back to Kole and said, "When you gave me to my mom, were you sad?"

"I was. Very sad. Your real mom . . ." He, too, glanced at Savannah. "Your first mom was . . ."

"She died," Claudia recalled, clearly willing to help him out. "I know you were sad about that."

"I was sad about losing both of you." He looked into her dark eyes. Permission granted. She stood very still while his fingertips grazed her soft cheek. "I still get sad over it sometimes."

"I don't want you to be sad, but you can't take me back."

"I know."

"I'm adopted. That means I belong to my mom and dad as much as other kids belong to their moms and dads. So even if you wanted to, you couldn't take me back. It's the rules."

He nodded, lightly running his forefinger down the center line of the long braid that dangled in front of her shoulder, past her collarbone. "You must be happy here on the ranch. I see you're already riding horses."

"I help my mother take care of them. Mostly we take care of them, except Daddy takes care of their hooves." She scrutinized his craggy face. "You're an Indian, aren't you? That's why I'm an Indian."

"Your mother was, too. I mean, your first mother." He smiled wistfully. Her hair warmed his finger the way the fire warmed his back and his memories warmed his heart. "You look so much like her. I saw some pictures of her when she was a little girl, and they could have been pictures of you now."

"Where are they? Can I see them?"

"They were in the house when . . ." The fire seemed to mushroom, like a genie escaping its bottle. Kole swallowed hard, glancing away quickly, sending remembered heat and light into the darkness. When it was gone, he recovered himself in the child's small face, gently brightened by fire. "Maybe I can get some more. I'll try."

"You don't have to." Claudia turned her own smile on Savannah, who was laying packages of food out on a blanket. "My mother used to be a model. Her pictures were all over the place. Magazines and everything. Mommy says you really like my aunt Heather. Is she your girlfriend?"

"Sort of." Kole turned to Heather, who was watching him with a smile he'd never seen on her before—one of those motherly smiles all women seemed to have tucked away for times when a guy's legs went out from under him and he looked like he needed mothering. He had to laugh at himself. "I don't know. You should ask her if I'm her boyfriend."

"You have to be if she's your girlfriend. She's almost as pretty as my mom. And see, we brought a picnic. Is that your dog?"

Woof had been consigned to the shadows.

"Sort of," Kole said.

Claudia gave him a curious look. He figured he sounded about as know-nothing as he looked right about then. She noticed the flute in his left hand and generously offered him another chance. "What's that?"

"This is what I brought for you."

She squatted on her haunches. "What is it?"

"It's a flute." He laid it across her knees.

She sat cross-legged on the ground, examining her gift. "It doesn't look like a flute. They're silver colored." She looked up at Kole as he sat, too, mirroring her position. "I'm learning violin. I want to learn to play the piano, too, but we haven't found me the right teacher yet. I started in Suzuki when I was only three, and I know all my Twinkles."

"That's great." He glanced at Savannah.

" 'Twinkle, Twinkle, Little Star,' " she supplied.

"Well, this really is a flute," Kole said. "I know because I make them. I made this one especially for you. These turtles will bring you long life. And see this little bird?" He touched the carving he'd attached with a strip of deerhide. "It's a mourning dove."

"We have those in our yard sometimes."

"Whenever I hear a mourning dove, I think of you." *Don't go there,* he told himself, but the delight in her eyes said, *What about me?* And he wanted her to know that part of her life still belonged only to him. "I used to fall asleep sometimes rocking you," he remembered for her. "And when I'd wake up, it would be early morning, soft gray and quiet out. Except for the mourning doves calling back and forth under the window. You'd be asleep in my arms."

"Did you sing to me? My daddy sings to me."

Kole closed his eyes briefly and shook his head, then managed to smile. "Clay sings real pretty, doesn't he? I didn't get his singing voice. Must be from his mom's side."

"I don't think so. I've never heard Grandma sing. Maybe if you practiced every day for about a month your voice would be nice for singing. You should try, just in case you get another baby someday." She offered the flute up to him. "Can you play this for me?"

"Sure." He busied himself with the instrument, taking it in his hands like a newborn, positioning his blunt-tipped fingers just so as he moistened his lips and tried to imagine where another baby might come from. Maybe the turtle would drop one off on his doorstep, or he'd find one in the mourning dove's nest. "This is a night bird song, for going to sleep."

He felt as though he were trying out for some small part in her play, blowing long, solitary notes as deep into the night as he could make them go. *See what your father can do?* he thought, but he knew there was nothing, had been nothing of him for her to see. He was not surprised by the silence when the last echo of his song drifted beyond their ears.

He stared at his own rough hands on the smooth wood until someone spoke, as though waking him from a dream.

"Can you play the dove's song?"

He lifted his head and met the child's eyes, alight with unqualified approval. A dream fulfilled. He raised the flute to his mouth and played for her again.

Food eased the mood. Their picnic was a family meal, replete with all the joy of a homecoming. They had chosen a good place to come together, and it felt like a natural part of a surreal journey, another stop for fuel. Kole was beginning to understand why he hadn't been anywhere lately. It wasn't fear so much as the lack of fuel. This was a journey that required high octane, and with Heather he seemed to have hit on a new source.

Damn, if he didn't feel thoroughly juiced.

Claudia kept tapping him on the arm or knee to get his attention. She didn't know what to call him, and he couldn't bring himself to tell her to call him by his name. Let it ride, he told himself. She'd come up with something. She was bright and beautiful and happy, even if she was no longer his. He'd done right by his baby, and no one knew that better than Claudia did.

"Do you have any horses or anything?" she wanted to know.

"No horses. There's a cat who lives with me." He reached back into the shadows for Woof, who hardly stirred after proving what a good catcher he was on chunks of chicken and oatmeal raisin cookies. "And this ol' wolf."

"He can't be a real wolf. Real wolves don't live with people. Do they, Daddy?"

Kole drew back his empty hand and stared at it, anticipating his brother's answer. When it didn't come, he looked up, impassively meeting Clay's glittering eyes. *Damn.* His brother hadn't changed. Never could hide his feelings, didn't even bother to try. Kole remembered how mean that damned look used to make him feel. *Big baby.* He didn't know whether he'd said it, but he'd sure thought it enough times. *You let people see inside you like that, you're just asking for more pain.*

The pain was his to bear, not Clay's. His loss was Clay's gain. But there was sorrow in his brother's eyes. Or pity, which Kole didn't need. He'd done right by his daughter, and it was hard, but he was no sad case, no damn bellyacher.

He wanted to punch his brother in the face for being the daddy here.

He wanted to kiss his feet for being a good one.

His face betrayed neither impulse. He simply gave a nod. *She means you.*

"Only special wolves," Clay said quietly. "Does he have a name?"

"We call him Woof." He glanced at Heather. "Don't we?"

"We should have brought the cat with us, too," she said. "Claudia loves cats."

"But a real wolf? This is the first one I've ever seen, except at the zoo. I've seen coyotes outside the zoo, but you can't get this close to them."

"Dogs are just tame wolves and coyotes," Kole said.

"Well, there's a little more differ—" Clay cleared his throat, backing off. "You've sure done a nice job taming this one."

"We decided to hang out together is all."

"What's your cat's name?" Claudia asked.

"Cat."

The child laughed. It was such a sweet, musical sound, it made Kole laugh, too. "That's silly," she said. "You can't just name it Cat. It *is* a cat."

"That's why I call her that. She came in without introducing herself and made herself at home. Just like a woman." He smiled at Heather. "If she has another name, she hasn't told me."

"You call her Cat because she *is* a cat?"

"So you can call me Man if you want." He laughed when she screwed up her face to let him know what a silly idea that was. It would only make sense to her if she'd been with him the last seven years and thought the way he did. He shrugged. "Or Kola, which means 'friend' in the Lakota language. That's the name my mother gave me. Kola."

"I didn't know that," Clay said.

"Secret name. Power name." Kole was still smiling at Claudia, piling on words that might impress a child. He gave a quick jerk of his chin. "You call him Dad because that's what he is. I'm Kola. Don't forget that. If you ever need anything, anything at all, I'm your friend."

"If you ever need someone to take care of your wolf for you, I could—"

"Whoa," Clay said to his daughter. "No way. No wolves. We're ranchers, remember? Wolves and cows don't mix, so I'm afraid I'm gonna have to put my boot down on that idea, Kitten." He dug his boot into the dirt. "Squashing it right under my heel."

"I can feed him, can't I? Can I just give your wolf a piece of chicken, like you did?"

"He's never been around kids much, which is why I'm keeping a close eye on him," Kole said. "He might bite."

"You're just trying to scare me. I'm not so easy to scare."

"Kole's not nearly as scary as he thinks he is," Heather put in.

"Yeah, well, Woof's mouth is even bigger than yours, woman. And his teeth are sharper than mine."

Claudia laughed again. "You *do* go by what things are. Don't you know her name?"

"I have several names for her."

"Secret names?" Claudia giggled. "C'mon, Aunt Heather's really your girlfriend, isn't she?"

"*Woman* friend," he said. "And you're a girl. I don't know why my brother thinks you're a kitten. I would think he'd know different by now."

"If my dad's your brother, that makes you my uncle."

"Whatever you say, Claudia. But when you were a little baby, you were . . ." He glanced from Clay to Savannah, then smiled at Claudia. "You were beautiful."

"I'll bet you called me Baby."

"You were named for one of your grandmothers." Again he touched her braid, recalling the single braid his mother had worn over one shoulder. "Girls should wear their braids in back, until they become women. I can make you some special hair ties to hold them in place if you want. Beaded hair ties. What's your favorite color?"

"Blue," she said. "But I don't have a grandmother named Claudia."

"You have many grandmothers. Grandmothers are very important. You're a lucky girl to have so many."

"I only know one."

"Heather's writing it all down, all about the ones who came before you. So when you're ready, your mother will have this story for you."

"Is it about Indians?"

"Yes. It's partly about your Lakota grandmothers and your Ojibwe grandmothers. Partly about me and why I've done some things that brought trouble into my life. I don't want that trouble to touch you."

"I'm not afraid," Claudia insisted. "I know how to act around all kinds of animals. Daddy taught me." She peered into the shadows. "If he doesn't bite Aunt Heather, I know he won't bite me."

"Maybe not, but it's better to be safe. You never can tell about things that are mainly wild."

"Can I tell you a secret?" Claudia scooted close to Kole. He shivered when she cupped her hands around his ear and whispered, "If you need me to help you, I can usually get Daddy to change his mind."

14

Kole claimed the captain's chair and revved the camper's engine. "We're getting out of here."

"Where are we going?" Fine question for a copilot, but Heather's weary body was expecting bed after the nocturnal mountain climbing.

"Someplace that's not Wyoming." He already had the camper crawling through the grass without benefit of headlights. "We're getting out of Keogh country."

They had used Kole's pickup truck for the off-road rendezvous, leaving the camper with Jack, who had asked no explanation for all the odd comings and goings. He hadn't even questioned being sent back to his own sleeping bag in the middle of the night when they reclaimed the camper. Blanket wrapped around his shoulders, he had stumbled off like a kid who was sleepwalking.

Kole had written off Heather's sympathetic noises. "Jack's a good man."

"But it seems so unreasonable, sending him out in the middle of the night."

"Only to a woman. Times like this, guys don't ask for reasons."

In the side mirror, Heather now watched the camp quickly become indistinguishable from the rest of the shadows hulking against the horizon. She felt as though she were leaving all but her last friend behind. "I think we should stay with the group, Kole. There's safety in numbers."

"For you, maybe, but there's no safety for anybody else in this group as long as I'm around. No safety for my kid. I had good reasons for keeping to myself all this time."

"The real risk here is that somebody with a badge is going to walk in and handcuff you. The rest of us are only . . ." Her delayed hearing registered another sting as the camper bobbed over wheel ruts in the Wyoming clay. "Why me, Kole? Why am I different?"

"You tell me." Bouncing in his chair, he didn't give her much chance. He was rolling. "You are who you are. And who you are is different from us."

"Is that why you trust me?"

He did a double take to see whether he'd heard right.

"You *do* trust me," she said. "You let me be with you today."

"I trust you as long as you're right in front of me and I can watch every move you make." He laughed, shrugged, acknowledging the joke on himself. "No, you're right. I seem to be trusting you."

"Any particular reason why?"

"You're a good lay."

"True, but what does that have to do with trust?"

"Gotta offer you something. You don't seem the type who'd go down for money." They'd reached blacktop. He spared her a glance as he gunned the engine, back tires churning up a spray of roadside gravel. "Trust is nice, isn't it? Kind of a woman thing. You like it that I took you up there today and let you watch me break my heart over the kid who calls my brother Daddy."

"You don't exactly wear your heart on your sleeve, and I didn't hear anything crack. I could've sworn you weren't the type who'd *go down* for pity." She knew she was pushing. He needed pushing. He needed a smug smile and a kick in the ass. "But maybe I'm wrong. Are you looking for a sympathy fuck?"

"Nice talk."

"I give as nice as I get."

He gave her a quick, hard look, then set his jaw and suddenly arced the wheel, hard right. Heather grabbed the arms of her chair, looking for the eyes in the headlights, bracing herself for a road kill. The camper rocked as Kole pumped the brake. Gnashing gears brought the vehicle to a lurching stop. Kole bailed out, slamming the door behind him.

Stunned, Heather released her seatbelt. Warring impulses paralyzed her when he ripped her door open and pulled her out of her chair. She fairly tumbled into his arms. "Get this," he growled and took what was left of her breath away with a hungry, desperate kiss. "Now give it back."

Not sympathy, she realized. Acceptance. He needed what he felt he didn't deserve. She took his face in her hands and gave the kiss he needed, the one that fed the hunger of an empty heart. She gave a woman's kiss, then drew back, anticipating some change in him, some new awareness or awakening, some kind of love light in his eyes. She wasn't sure what that was, but she'd know it if she saw it.

She didn't. Maybe it was because he had such dark eyes, and the night was so close around them that the darkness had seeped into him.

He took her hand from his face, touched his lips to her fingertips, and asked quietly, "Did I scare you?"

"A little."

"I'm sorry."

She knew he wasn't.

"I'll take you back if you want."

"Back where? Where would I go back to?"

"Anywhere you want. You can go anywhere, Heather." But he was still holding her, and she wondered what he would do if she tried.

"But not back. I might be able to stay where I am for a while, or I can go on. But not back."

He groaned. "Don't try to go worldly-wise female on me, Little Cherokee. I might take you up on that sympathy fuck."

"I don't recall offering you one. And don't you try to go ruthless male on me, Kole Kills Crow. We both know you can't pull that one off."

"I used to be able to. You better hope you haven't ruined me for other women."

"Charity workers tend to be pretty gullible."

"Naw, we're just plain hard up."

She whacked his arm. "Would you ever have said a thing like that to Savannah?"

"Ugly ol' Savannah?" She whacked him again, and he laughed. "Ol' nobody-looks-like-that Savannah? Jesus, honey, that girl used to follow me around like a puppy. They all did. Back in those days, I didn't even know what 'hard up' meant." He pulled on the passenger door, standing open behind her. "Jump in."

"And let *you* drive?"

"Come on. You know I was in control the whole time."

"Right." She mounted the camper step. "Where are we going?"

"Hell, if it's open this late. If not, we'll try Nevada."

Soon after they got back on the road, he surprised her again.

"You got your tape recorder handy? I feel like talkin'. I feel like get-tin' down and dirty in the confessional."

"I'll use the one in my head," she said, turning in her seat. "Shall I pull the curtain?"

"Is that how it works? Shouldn't one of us be kneeling?"

She groaned. "And I was all set to let you suck me in."

"Stay set and let me try. To start with . . ." His tone suddenly went flat, seemingly unfeeling. "I didn't want the baby."

The engine whined in Heather's ears as she shifted her own gears. She was of two minds—a brain and a heart—and at least one of those parts was tempted to wave this tale off, turn it back through the door he'd reluctantly opened. She wasn't ready to let go of that tender image of him rocking his baby to sleep. But some other part of her took hold. She turned to him with an experienced ear, an encouraging expression in her eyes.

"When Linda told me she was pregnant, I said, 'Now's the time for the old termination policy to kick in. There is no way we can handle a kid.' But she wouldn't listen. Sound reasoning was out of the question for her."

Heather smiled at his reference to a failed mid-twentieth-century attempt to eradicate the reservation system. A joke about a mistake. She shrugged as she replied in kind. "What do you expect from a woman who runs around with an escaped convict?" *Go easy; keep the story coming.*

"She was married to him. What's your excuse?"

"I'm writing a bestseller."

"Yeah, right." He took a two-handed grip on the wheel. "So she had the baby. Nearly killed her. She was sick all the time. She had these bad headaches. And when the baby came . . ." He shook his head. "I don't know how she stood it. It took hours and hours. All that monster pain, and she was so small. Linda, not the baby. But she came through—they both did—so I thought the least I could do was help out when Linda was having those headaches.

"We had a canvas carrier that you strap on with the baby in it." Hand to his chest, he showed Heather where he'd carried his new burden. "I got so I could do anything with the baby strapped to me. I could work, read, sleep. I could do anything but nurse her. She was a good baby, except when she'd get this gut ache right around the same time every night. Man, could she wail. The only way I could settle her down was to drive her around. That's why we were out of the house when it blew up." The last came reverently; clearly still a wonder to him.

"What makes you think that was anything but a tragic accident?"

"The furnace had just been fixed. It was working fine."

"You'd had it professionally repaired."

"There's only one guy in Blue Fish who works on stuff like that. He's lived there all his life, name's Al Chaud. Al knows what he's doing. And, hell, I watched him the whole time. He showed me what was busted, and I watched him replace it. When I questioned him after the fire, he said there was no way it was caused by the furnace or the gas line. But the federal investigators told Linda's father there was probably, *probably* a gas leak."

"There was an investigation," Heather reflected carefully. "But you were not . . ."

"I talked to the tribal cop, but, no, I was not available to the feds."

"But they questioned Linda's father."

"He told any outsiders that the men's clothes from the house were all his. Said he had the baby with him, said he didn't know who the father was. He also told them the furnace had been working fine. They told him it worked fine for a bomb."

"But there *could've* been a gas leak."

"Something sure as hell leaked, didn't it?" He flashed her an odd look, as though she had the inside track on all leaks. Then, just as quickly, he shrugged off all suspicion. "But in another way, that explosion plugged up a huge hole. I finally stopped hating my mom for dumping me off in Wyoming."

He paused to allow for some reaction from her. If her simple nod was less than what he expected, he didn't show it. She hoped he understood that she knew what she was doing when it came to confessionals.

"Because I finally, truly realized she had no choice," he said, as though she'd asked. "Even if she'd gotten out of the Indian movement, traded in her bullhorn and her Apache-style moccasins for the white uniform—" He glanced at Heather, a quick challenge. "Did you know she used to be a nurse?"

"Yes."

He nodded, giving her credit for doing her homework. "Even if she'd tried to leave it all behind, she was still Lana Kills Crow, and there would always be people who were threatened by that. She only had one kid, and she wanted to keep him alive."

"And far from those who were threatened by her."

"The tribal chairman. The agency superintendent. The FBI. Some people who were interested in mining for uranium on tribal land. She spoke out, and people listened. There were even a couple of congressmen who wanted to shut her up pretty bad. The thing is, technically we occupy federal land. Reservation land is held in trust, and the federal government oversees it." He gave a humorless chuckle. "There's that word again. We're supposed to trust them to do right by us. Like women, right? Like we're a bunch of women trusting the Great White Father to do what's in our best interest."

"I don't know if it's fair to say—"

"What? I thought we decided trust was a woman thing."

"*We?* I think you said . . ." She had to be careful, lest she slip off her seat in the confessional. "Granted, holding the land in trust really is a paternalistic tactic, but—"

"You don't want to compare women with Indians, Little Cherokee?" This time there was a little humor in his chuckle, and something more. Affection, maybe. "Okay, we won't get picky over the pecking order. Civil rights are civil rights."

"But it's more than that, because you have your treaties."

"Oh, yes, we have our treaties. But when they need a place to dump waste, or somebody finds some minerals, or somebody wants a cheap place to run cattle or whatever, well, for a long time Indian people said, just let it go. We've got no way to stop them.

"But people like Lana started finding ways. Get in front of the cameras. Make the news. Alert the environmentalists. Let the church people know. Whatever it takes. You find a few friends, and you make a lot of enemies. But it's not like a war. The enemies don't like to declare themselves. You know who they are, but they act like they're not really threatened by you. You're not that important. A nuisance, like a mosquito. It gets bothersome, you whack it."

"Which worries you more—getting caught by the cops, or being stalked by these undeclared enemies?"

"I'm not being paranoid. You think I'd give that kid up if the threat wasn't real?"

"No, I don't. As you say, your choices were . . ." Her timing was off. She realized she'd injected the question too soon. "It's hard to imagine those choices."

"That's exactly what makes you different."

"No," she repeated, more forcefully than she intended. "You're trying to trump me with a race card here, and it won't take the trick, my friend."

"Kola."

"Whatever." Confessional be damned; they were two people—a man and a woman—rambling down the road in a house on wheels.

"Maybe I'm just plain *human*," she suggested, trying not to sound too defensive. Failing badly. "Maybe I'm too self-centered to do what Savannah did—too selfish to take on somebody else's child. And maybe I'm too self-righteous to imagine giving one up."

"You're judging me?"

"*You're* judging *me*. I know I've been privileged in some ways, but just maybe you have, too. I've never had a child. Never even wanted one."

He looked at her, his eyes inviting her to tell him about it.

Did he think she'd switch seats that easily?

She stared at the road ahead, two beams of light blending into one. Long road, she thought. Long night. What's one little confession?

"When Savannah told me she'd gone on a trip and come back with a baby, I told her she was nuts. What are you going to do with a baby all of a sudden? But I watched that baby change her life. And when she got sick, and she'd start to say, 'If anything happens to me,' I'd cut her off. I wouldn't let her ask. I'd say, 'You're going to be fine.'

"And then I'd go home and think about it." She reached down, felt around her feet for her purse. "I'd think up excuses. I'm not a baby person. I don't know anything about taking care of kids. I have to be free to travel," she recited. "Sometimes I'm gone for weeks at a time. I love Claudia, but I don't know if I have it in me to be her mother. *Anybody's* mother. I can't imagine it." Finally she found something she hadn't missed in a while—a cigarette. "Do you mind?"

"Not if you don't," he said, nodding toward the pack as he rolled his window down partway.

She struck a match and gave herself a light and a deep, soothing drag before reaching across the seats and letting him take the cigarette between his lips. She struck another match and lighted a second one.

"I'm trying to quit, so don't let me get you started."

"Again," he amended after savoring what was clearly his first smoke in a long time. "How many times has it been for you?"

"I used to tell Savannah I smoked for the love of it. I don't love it anymore, so I'm quitting. Simple as that."

"Really?"

"Really." She laughed. Who was she trying to fool? "She said the only time in her life she ever smoked was when you offered it to her. She thought you were the epitome of cool." Another quick puff galvanized her with equivalent cool. "So tell. What did you really think of her?"

"Too beautiful for her own good." He took another deep pull on the cigarette before running down the rest of his list. "Too young for me, too smart, too ambitious. Too willing. Way too white. I loved her too much to screw with any of that, so I left her alone." He glanced at Heather. "Every one of those adjectives fits you, too."

"But you didn't leave me alone."

"Yeah, I did. Remember? Even gave you my bed."

"You did screw with me."

"Honey, *you* screwed with *me*."

"I love you too much not to."

The confession came so shyly, so softly, she hardly recognized the voice as her own. The truth, yes. She recognized it, and she wanted him to recognize it. More than ever she wanted recognition for telling the truth. But the feeling, which was also her own, was new and strange, and so much bigger than she'd made it sound. Big and solid and fragile, like some poor fat woman who had just dropped all her clothes on the floor in front of a two-way mirror. The soft word, the all-important feeling, her gift to him was left hanging there in the air, in the dark, clouded by the smoke from the cigarettes neither of them wanted to want or needed to need.

He put his out.

"Are you still workin' on this story?" he finally asked her. "You wanna hear about my more heroic exploits? You know, we did get compensation for the Utes for a chunk of land they lost for weapons testing. They live right down the road there. They put me up for six months after I busted out of the pen."

He was signaling for another gearshift, waking her up from a dream. Yes, she was still working on a story. His story, not hers. She loved to write; she loved the exploration it required of her, the discovery, the revelation. She loved doing what she did well, and she believed it counted for something. She loved . . .

"Who?"

"I don't know their names. I don't know any names. Just some Indians, gave me a safe place to stay in exchange for some of my best advice."

"Which was . . ."

"If it works good for a bomb, get out of the way and make them pay." He looked at her, gave her time to put his life in order before he confirmed, "Best advice I ever ignored."

"You can never tell, can you? Which tiny triumph is on its way to becoming life's next bitter irony?"

"Hey, I like that," he said. "Wish I'd'a said it so you could put it in the book."

"It's not too late. Repeat after me." She grinned, her premature declaration all but forgotten. "You never can tell . . . which little triumph . . . will become—"

"Let's stick with the triumphs. We figure it's a victory for us if we can just hang tough year after year, refuse to sell out. Try to keep the land and the water alive instead of killing it off with a dam or a mine. You know about the Western Shoshone people?"

She nodded. "But I want to hear your version. I want you to keep talking as long as you insist on driving."

"Ain't shuttin' down till the sun comes up."

"And then what?"

"Then we shut up and go to sleep. The plan is in the hands of our man, Jack. He'll catch up."

The sensible diversion was working pretty well until the camper broke down less than an hour later. Kole managed to coast off the road and park on the shoulder. He didn't look at Heather, but he knew she was looking at him. To her credit she kept all her stupid questions to herself, at least for the moment. He was about to pay for all the "woman thing" remarks he'd been tossing out. Grabbing a flashlight and shoving his head under the hood was an obligation. Cussing was an immediate requirement. After that, he was stuck.

She joined him in hanging her head over the engine, but still she said nothing. When he looked up, she smiled, as though this incident was just as interesting as the story he'd just told her about scrawny Jack getting them into a brawl with some loggers in a bar. Or just as absurd, but she didn't say which. The night breeze lifted her hair back from her face, and she simply smiled.

"Any ideas?" he demanded.

"A few, but they're all theoretical. Let's hear yours first."

"I hate like hell to disappoint you, but all I know about cars is you run 'em till they quit. You never heard of an Indian car?"

"I assumed that meant you always found a way to keep it running."

"And I thought you said you'd been to the rez. Backyards full of dead metal ponies." He pointed the flashlight at the plug wires, which were all tied to their posts.

"Your backyard isn't."

"That's because my ponies always die in places like this. If you're lookin' for Mr. Fixit, go back to the ranch. Clay can fix anything." He spared her a quick, fixed smile. "Including women."

"I don't need fixing. Haven't you noticed?" She folded her arms, bunching her sweater up around her breasts. "Everything about me is perfectly sound."

"Except your judgment." He had every intention of setting her a good example, but somehow he got his signals crossed—closed the hood and opened his damn mouth. "What do you mean, *you love me too much not to*? What the hell kind of judgment is that?"

"It's not a judgment; it's a feeling," she explained, all cocky. Didn't even have the brains to take it back or tell him never mind. "But I wouldn't expect you to know the difference."

"The last time somebody suggested I get in touch with my feelings, I invited him to kiss my ass. His eyes kinda lit up, so I took my invitation back right away."

"This happened in prison?"

"Yeah, but don't strike up the violins. He was a shrink. I only saw him once. He was either totally satisfied with my answers or totally disappointed. I never found out which."

"Maybe that's because you didn't wait to find out." She hugged herself tighter and peered up at him in the dark. "Do you really want to know what I meant?"

"No, but I'll bet you're gonna tell me anyway."

"You *wish*," she shot back. "Who are you betting against, Kole? Yourself? And why ask if you don't want an answer?"

"I don't know. I wasn't thinking. Guess I've been around you too long." He slammed his fist on the hood. "Damn it, woman, now you're screwing with my head."

"Ha! What possible satisfaction could I get out of that?"

"How would I know?" His hand smarted. Ordinarily he would have been laughing at himself by this time. He was setting her up, and she was racking up points by the handful. "It doesn't matter what you meant, Heather. This is a dead-end road. You know that as well as I do."

"For us?"

"For me."

She leaned toward him slightly.

He stepped back. "Yeah, honey, for us, but not for you. You're just getting started. You've got miles to go." *Without him.* He didn't much like that thought, and he wanted to tell her so. He hung his head so he couldn't see into her eyes and be tempted by them. "Look, I'm giving you my moccasins."

"We're going to walk?" She laughed. He looked up and joined in when she added, "*Honey?* I have a feeling it'll be a little more than a mile."

"I don't want you to wear them—they'll get you into too much trouble. I just want you to *imagine* wearing them. Maybe you'll get some other people to do the same."

"I'm not sure I want to." She moved in on him, slipped her arms around him and claimed him. "I feel like keeping them all to myself. I want to be—"

"Shhh." He touched one finger to her lips before laying his arm around her shoulders. "Don't say stuff like that anymore, okay?" He jerked his chin toward the camper. "See, this is what happens. Sooner or later the important stuff breaks down, and I can't fix it."

"Maybe if we try—"

"Maybe I don't want to start it up again."

"Oh, for Pete's sake," Heather said, grinning up at him. "Do you realize how silly this is? Who else would talk like this except two—"

"Pie-eyed fools who have no business gettin' this tight with each other." He started pulling her toward the side door. "Let's go to bed."

"Pie-eyed? Tight? Did I miss something? Granted, we started out in a bar, but after that . . ." She offered no resistance. "Except two lovers," she insisted. "Not fools. Lovers."

"I'll give you a break. I won't point out the obvious."

"You can't deny me that much."

"Fine. There's not a damn bit of difference."

"Which makes us lovers." She squeezed him on one side, patted the camper on the other. "Lovers standing beside their dead pony in the middle of the desert."

He nodded toward the ribbon of road they'd already covered, which ended with a slice of crimson on the horizon. "At sunrise."

"Oh, yes, sunrise. On the road to . . ."

He laughed easily now. "See, you can't even say it, it's so foolish."

"Just admit we're lovers. From where the sun now rises, we're lovers. At least until it sets."

"Why stop there?" He opened the camper door. "I'll go you sunrise to sunrise."

"You're on."

"Not yet, but go inside and take your clothes off. I will be back in a minute."

"I have a better idea. Let Woof out for a few minutes, and *you* go inside," she said, ducking under his arm. "You take your clothes off and get in bed. On your back." She smiled at him over her shoulder, sweet as she could possibly please. "And I'll be there in a minute."

He drew the curtains before he started getting undressed. He could hear her talking to the dog and banging around outside, opening and closing doors. This was an open-and-shut case of being stranded on a pretty isolated road. The next car to come along would undoubtedly belong to a state trooper. A white guy, of course. This was Utah. The statie would step right up to the plate, rescue Heather and . . .

The engine turned over.

Kole hung his head over the side of the over-the-cab berth and came face to face, eye to chin, with Heather's triumphant smile. She held up the red can from Bobby's emergency kit.

"The gas gauge seems to be a little off," she said. "The pony couldn't tell us he was hungry."

15

Kole woke up to rude banging outside his cramped quarters. For a moment he thought he had fallen off the end of the road and landed in a cell.

He buried his eyes in the crook of his elbow. He wasn't sure what part of the day it was, but it felt like early afternoon. The air was close and heavy and smelled vaguely of cigarette smoke. He dreaded drawing more than the smallest breath, but with all the banging, barking, and the distant male voices, he knew he'd have to breathe before he could shout them all back down into their pits. The pits of hell.

His chest expanded on a slow, deep breath, and the piquant scent of sex filled his head. *Ahhhh, the passages of heaven.* At the end of the road he'd gone up instead of down. He rolled over and embraced an angel.

"Somebody's outside yelling for Kole," he whispered. "You know anybody by that name?"

"Secret," Heather muttered even before she opened her eyes. "They can't make me reveal my sources." She cocked her arm back in the shape of a wing and stretched, revealing her sweet breast, tempting him to partake of her sources. He smiled.

Nobody really looked like that.

"Anybody in there?" Jack called out. *Bam bam bam.* "Somebody grunt or something so we know you weren't abducted by aliens."

"Did you lock the doors when you came in, Ms. Good Wench?" Kole whispered.

"We're here," Heather shouted as she pulled the covers up to her shoulders.

"But we don't know where that is," Kole said. He slid her a wink as he reached for his jeans. "We don't know what happened. We said we wanted to go to Hollywood—" He pulled a T-shirt over his head and opened the door. "—and just that quick, we're bouncing among the stars."

"I'll bet you were," Jack said as Kole stepped down from the camper. "What's the big hurry? You guys ashamed to be seen with us?"

"Damn straight." Kole folded his arms and eyed the string of vehicles along the side of the road. He couldn't see too many faces, but those who had rolled their windows down or gotten out of their cars didn't look surprised or angry or critical. Bemused, maybe. Passive. Par for the course, they were thinking, and he laughed. "Look at this depressing little circus train."

"What I'm looking at now is one big sitting duck," Jack grumbled. "That *E* on the dash ain't for 'egg,' man; it's for '*empty.*'"

"This pony don't do eggs, and he ain't empty."

"Tell him what the *F* stands for, Kola," said Red Butt as he rounded the front of the van to join them, followed by Abby Wendel.

"*F* is for 'funny,' and here come the clowns." Kole flashed a grin from Red to Jack. "You two wanna quit while I'm still smilin'?"

"Sounds like a good idea." Jack shaded his eyes with his hand as he surveyed the sagebrush flat, rolled out on either side of the blacktop like endless neutral carpet. Another car door slammed as another pilgrim got out for a stretch. "We're probably due for a break now, anyway, since we kinda need to regroup. But you could've scouted out a place with at least one tree."

"*Regroup?*" Kole turned to the string of cars. "Have we grouped yet?" He'd seen more marchers trying out for school band. Of course, he hadn't seen them march halfway across the country to make the grade. But they were going to need more bodies if they expected to impress anybody.

Bodies like Marty Deerfoot, who was marching toward the camper to join in the parley. Marty seriously impressed Kole, always had, but they'd figured out long ago that they couldn't be more than friends. She reminded him too much of his mother. He assumed Marty's reasons were equally compelling, although they'd never discussed any of it. They'd never needed to.

He lent Jack his ear as he watched her approach.

"We haven't gained anybody since Pine Ridge. We kinda lost you back there in Wyoming. You didn't really come out and, uh . . ." Jack glanced warily at Abby, then chose his words carefully. "We need you to pitch our cause, Kola. They'll follow you."

"If nobody wants to sign on, maybe the cause ain't what it used to be."

"We've got forty-two people here. Forty-two somebodys putting their lives on hold to make an important statement. I think it's important, anyway."

"I think so, too, Kola," Marty said, moving to his side.

"C'mon, Marty, did you really sign on with us because you've got a bone to pick with Hollywood?"

"What do you think? You think I've got time to wait in line for the kind of bones you throw out?"

"That was a long time ago."

"Just like a man. Not half as long as you claim."

"Low blow," he said with a chuckle.

"I never miss," she said. "And, yeah, I like the Hollywood target. That's where all eyes are turned these days, and the image they see of us still sucks. I saw this one movie not long ago about some crooks robbing an Indian casino. The only Indians in the movie were a few bit players, either serving drinks or playing the slots. There were a couple of tribal leaders in one scene who had a line or two, sort of representing the Indians getting screwed over by everybody else in the movie. So we go from being savages to victims."

"What part did Barry Wilson play?" Kole wondered.

"Who cares?"

"Which is exactly the point," Jack said. "Who cares about a token?"

"I think I saw that one," Red put in after some obvious rumination. "Wasn't it called Reindeer something?"

" 'Red Man Gets Run Oo-ver by a Rein-deeeer,' " Jack sang to the tune of an old satirical Christmas song.

"That's about it," Marty said as she turned to Kole again. "And you guessed right, too. I came because of you. I heard you'd returned from the grave, and I have to see for myself what you're gonna do next."

"Guess I'd better come up with something good, then." He glanced up at the camper window, looking for Heather. Wasn't she coming out?

Damn, he was a sad case lately. He always seemed to be looking for Heather, missing her when she wasn't right there beside him.

"We'd better come up with a few more bodies," Jack said. "This don't look like no Bonus Army."

"I know where we can pick up a few experienced marchers," Kole said, yanking his attention back to the problem at hand. "Anybody know how far we are from a gas station?"

"Didn't Bear tell you about the gas gauge on this thing?"

"Obviously Bear isn't the only one who could've told me." Kole laid an arm around Jack's slight shoulders. "So how about sharing from your tank, which is really *my* tank? You do the honors with the siphon hose while I take a look at the map."

✦ ✦ ✦

The next stop was the Ute reservation, where the land was coveted for its remote location. The question of what to do with a nation's refuse had been debated for years. To burn, to bury, to box it up and cart it away. The problem had finally made its way to Indian country, which was seen by some as the perfect solution. It was as though the lightbulb had been turned on in various corporate heads simultaneously. Behind the doors of energy companies, waste management companies, city halls, even various cabinet offices, well-dressed men with important titles were behaving like tobacco chewers looking for a place to spit. *Where to put this stuff?* And suddenly, there it was; lots and lots of land lying fallow and forgotten in luscious legal limbo.

Indian country.

From reservation to reservation, the debate had been going on for years. The Ute people, like so many tribes, were divided on the issue of renting out their land for a dump site. The proposal was economically appealing to many of them, of course. It would bring in two things perpetually in short supply—money and jobs. But the idea of taking in someone else's waste rubbed others the wrong way. Their non-Indian neighbors opposed the plan, but the tribal council insisted that it was not a matter for the State of Utah to decide. Still, there were the tribal elders to consider. The old women were particularly adamant about protecting the earth from abuse, and over the years they had not budged on the matter. They stood their ground until they were laid to rest beneath it, but there was no budging.

Kole loved those old women. In their tough and tender faces he saw his mother and grandmother. He would have done anything they asked, and he'd proved it whenever they'd called on him. Their witness was worth his risk.

Mattie Holy Elk had contacted him after he'd published a cautionary piece in *Native Drums* about attempts to bring business to the reservation by partnering up with various industries and investors. It had been one of his best columns.

We've learned some painful lessons. We can deal with them on our terms if we stop thinking like we need them more than they need us. Not true. They don't come knocking on the door unless we have something they really want. (Nowadays at least they knock.) And for them, a want is as urgent as a need. We need to learn everything there is to know about whatever we're thinking about getting our people into. Whoever said that knowledge is power was absolutely right. But wisdom is even more powerful. Put the two together, then make the choice on our terms, based on what we value.

After reading the column, Mattie had called Jack and asked if he could get Kola to help her.

She was glad to see him again, glad he was "back at it" and eager to round him up some sympathizers, whatever his cause. She and her sister made a batch of frybread and brewed a pot of coffee in the community center. The aroma wafted out the kitchen windows and brought people in the door.

"This one helped us run off those men who flew here in their own airplane and told the tribal council they wanted to put their trash here," Mattie announced as she seated Kole at the head of a long table. She kept glancing at Heather and Abby as she told her story, clearly assuming them to be the only people in the room who required additional background. "Some of our councilmen are no good. They get those dollar signs in their eyes, they can't see the forests or the trees."

"*For* the trees," Mattie's younger sister, Anita, put in authoritatively.

"We were sure talking up for the trees. We don't have much forest, but we have pretty good grass, some places. They say some of that trash they wanted to dump out here from some of their factories, some of that stuff is *really* bad for the land. They say it can go from the land into the water."

"Well, you stood up to them and shamed the council into voting against it," Kole recalled. He reached over to shake the hand of a large man wearing galoshes who had just come in. "Good to see you, Ron."

"We had to speak up," Anita said. "If it's bad for the land, it's bad for the people. Anybody knows that. We're all part of the circle."

"They even show that in the schoolbooks," said a statuesque woman who wore her steel-gray hair in a long, thick ponytail. "Those diagrams with the fish in the water, the animals on the land, the birds and the clouds and all those arrows making a circle. They teach this in school, in Earth Science class."

"Mary used to be a dorm matron, back when they had the boarding school here," Anita told the visiting white women.

Mary confirmed with a nod. "I used to help with their homework, and I'd tell the way I learned these things. The old stories about why Turtle walks in two worlds and why we must be alert when Frog's voice goes silent at night. Not all knowledge comes from science."

"Before there was science, we had wisdom, which came from life, which came from the Great Spirit," Mattie said. "If you live a long time, you should learn things from your life, and you put it together with the lives of those who came before, you have wisdom. Some of us have, anyway. So we can say, 'You men listen to us. We've seen a lot of things in our lives.'

"There's a reason why these outsiders want to put this stuff on our land," Mattie went on, shaking her finger at no one in particular. "They don't want it on theirs. We know it has no value. If it did, they wouldn't be trying to leave it with us. Maybe it's as harmless as they say, maybe not. If it's harmful, maybe we won't be living so long, and then what? We have no elders. Maybe we have science but no wisdom."

"I can't think of anything more dangerous," Heather said.

"And now it's started again," Mattie said.

Kole scowled. "They're talking about renting out dumping space again?"

"They sent different ones this time," Anita said.

Mattie nodded as she folded her arms beneath her ample bust. "Mostly old bald-headed men with shiny suits. They say what they want to dispose of here isn't as bad as what that last bunch was pushing. Just some ash from their incinerators where they burn up their trash from two or three big cities. They say we have the right conditions here for them to get rid of this stuff, and we won't even be bothered by it. We can trust them on this, they say."

"We've gained more than a little wisdom on the subject of trusting white men," Kole said.

"Tell that to the council," said Mattie. "They want to take the money from these bald-heads. And to boot they want to pay us to bring in movie people and film one of their movies here. They said they could bring all kinds of big spenders here."

"They said I could be in the movie," Mary reported with a quick laugh. "I have a classic profile, they said."

"How much land are they talking about this time?" Jack wondered. He'd been standing at the kitchen pass-through chewing on frybread, but the minute he'd heard *"it's started again,"* he'd grabbed a napkin and begun taking notes.

"About a fourth of the reservation, but they said we could have it back in a few years," Anita replied. "They'll even clean it up, they said."

"What do you think of all that?" Kole asked.

"I think they use those shiny suits and shiny heads to try to blind people," Anita said. "I'm telling all my relations to go to the next council meeting and to be sure to take some dark glasses."

"You stopped them before."

"Us grandmas," Mary piped up proudly. "One of the good things about getting old is that a person can say just what she thinks. You poison the earth, you poison your grandmother. We had those boys squirming so bad, they couldn't say nothing to us. No choice, they had to turn those poison peddlers away that time." She sighed. "But they keep coming back."

Around the table there were murmurs of agreement, solemn nodding, a shared consciousness of the inescapable. It had been a long struggle.

Was it time to quit?

Suddenly restless, Kole tapped his fingers on the table. "We're headed out to California."

"We heard about it."

He looked up at Mattie. "We need some more strong voices."

"To say what? We heard it was something about some movie. Seems like a long trip for you to make just to talk about movies."

"Nobody listens in Washington, so we thought we'd try Hollywood. Everybody's interested in what goes on in Hollywood."

Mattie took a moment to consider the notion. "We had Marlon Brando speaking up for us for a while, but he doesn't get out much anymore, seems like."

"He's about as old as you and Mary and bigger than both of you put together. That's why. But he's still on our side," Anita claimed. She turned on the visitors. "Eeee, you're not talking against Marlon Brando, are you?"

"We're not talking against anybody in particular," Jack said. "We just want to talk up for ourselves. We want people to know who we really are and where we are and why we're there and what's going on. We want to be able to tell our side of the story."

It was Ron Tree, having shown little interest in anything except greeting Kole and eating frybread, who voiced the question on everyone's mind. "What if nobody wants to hear it?"

"I asked that myself," Kole admitted. He glanced at Heather. "I'm told that some people do want to hear it."

"I wanna hear it," Mattie said.

"I mean, besides us. But whether they do or they don't, I'm still thinking that we have to speak up anyway. And the way we're portrayed . . ." He was beginning to feel like his old self, the man who had passion to spare. "Think about blacks, Jews, Hispanics. Think about women. If you don't demand a say in the way you're presented to the public, then you don't get a say. You know, they don't come around asking, and even if they do . . ." His eyes met Heather's. "Well, they still pick and choose. It's gotta sell. If they can make money on something, they're not—"

"Like cigarettes," Heather put in. "You notice how everybody's smoking in the movies these days? Tobacco companies pay for that. It's a subtle form of advertising. Very effective."

"That's true," Jack said. "But how do they make money on stereotyping people?"

"Maybe they're saving money," Kole said. "People expect the American Indians in any story, be it fact or fantasy, to be the victims, losers, fools, savages, drunks, whatever. So it's easy for them to just plug one of those images in."

"I think those roles also help to relieve the national conscience," Heather suggested. "It's too bad about the Indians, but how can we remedy a lost cause?"

"I'm not looking to guilt anybody," Kole said. "I'm looking for justice."

"Right." Anita laughed. "Judge Judy, here we come."

"I'm thinking they oughta film the next *Survivor* show on the rez," Ron said around a mouthful of frybread. "And I want credit for the idea."

"Don't settle for credit," Kole warned. "Cash only."

Jack laughed. "Hey, how about a show called *Who Wants to Marry a Mystic Lake Mdewaken?*"

"Who knows what a Mdewaken is?"

"Anybody who knows his Indian casinos," Jack said.

"That movie they want to make here, they said they already had a director for it," Mary put in. She nodded toward Kole. "It's your old friend Barry Wilson."

"No shit."

"Who's 'they'?" Heather wanted to know.

"Good Riddance." The gaps in Mattie's grin made it no less appealing. "Yes, that's really the name of the company. Specializing in getting rid of bad stuff in a good way is their motto. They say their methods are environmentally safe and sound."

"So why don't they ask the city council of, say, Palm Springs?" Jack suggested. "Isn't that another little town in the desert?"

Heather laughed. "I don't think they need the money."

"How does Wilson figure in?" Kole wondered quietly. The question had been screaming inside his head since the moment the name came up, but he didn't want to tip his hand. He wasn't sure whether somebody in the room might be playing against him.

Mary explained. "It's his big chance to be a director, and they figure we all want to get behind him. The partners in this Good Riddance outfit are also into the movie business and who knows what else."

" 'What else?' is an excellent question."

"The money's hard to resist," Mary said. "We could really use it. It's hard to think of opening up our land for dumping garbage as economic development, but where we are, we can't compete in the casino business."

"Come with us," Jack implored. "You've got your own Hollywood connection now—you gotta check these people out."

"We couldn't be gone too long. We can't miss the next council meeting."

"But that's not for another week," Ron said.

"It doesn't hurt to check them out," Kole said. "That's the last thing they expect."

"They offered the council a trip to Hollywood to tour the studios and meet some movie stars."

"But not Mary Bigfoot and Mattie Holy Elk. Not the repositories of our communal wisdom."

"What about me?" Anita demanded.

Mattie cackled. "Don't cry, little sister. You can come, too."

"But you can't be a repository until you get older," said Mary.

"And fatter," Anita said. "Like you two."

16

The camper had become a bus, and Heather was in the driver's seat.

She had been instructed to head south, drive slow, waste no time, hit no bumps, play no noisy music, and pick up no more riders because all the seats were full. And those were just Mattie's directives. Anita wanted air-conditioning. Before Heather could apologize for the fact that it didn't work, Mary said air-conditioning made her joints ache. Sounding a little pouty, Anita claimed the bed in the back of the camper for a nap. The two "repositories" found the seats behind the table too tight a fit, but the bench along the opposite wall accommodated them comfortably.

Without apologies, Kole offered warm pop from the nonfunctioning refrigerator and the remains of various packages of chips and crackers. "We'll stock up at the next stop," Heather promised. The borrowed camper was beginning to feel like home, and now she and Kole had guests. *Honored* guests. The strange urge to play hostess was very real, which was really very amusing. She'd inherited her mother's knack for cooking, but not her Southern flair for entertaining.

What she ought to have been doing was taking notes. Kole was involved in an animated discussion with Red Butt, who had turned his borrowed vehicle over to Ron Tree, who had brought his "old lady" and two brothers along. At each stop the travelers were welcomed with a traditonal feed. Kole and Jack explained what the expedition was about and encouraged sympathizers to "join up." Vehicle by vehicle, family by family, community by community, and nation by nation, the caravan was growing.

Enthusiasm was mounting. From one traveler to another the goal varied. Heather had been taking an informal survey, and those who had a point to make had a numerical edge over those who were going along for the ride. But there were many different points, most of them having little to do with the way movies were being made. According to Jack, who had gone ahead to prepare the way in Navajo country, the multiplicity of concerns was not a problem. Shouldn't there be as many points of view as there were people? And shouldn't they all be heard?

Indeed they probably should, Heather had said. But how would they achieve a focus? And without focusing, how would they make their point? But while Heather harped on the need to "focus," Jack kept telling her to watch the process. Look at the whole picture, the gathering of all the parts. This was the essence of deep-rooted tradition. They were really doing it again, demonstrating consensus. They were all moving in the same direction. What a remarkable visual!

Heather wasn't sure the American public would get it without the focusing aspect. After all, the Bonus Marchers had had one clear demand. The World War I veterans wanted the bonus payments they'd been promised. Money. Simple as that. There was nothing simple about Indian policy, especially since it varied so much from one reservation to the next.

"Stick with the stereotype issue," Heather had suggested. "Try to get people to stop digressing into all these other complaints. Nowadays you can't go to war without defining the goals and the exit strategy."

"*You* can't," Jack had said. "The difference is, we have nothing to lose. You have everything to lose. That's what you get for taking it all."

He'd laughed. He'd been kidding her, but there was that *us* and *you* again. Why couldn't she just smile the way she always did and keep in mind that she was a neutral observer?

It was an interesting discussion, and it continued even after Jack had left.

"Maybe that's what we've been missing," Kole was telling the group sitting behind Heather in the camper. "We've called it a movement, but it's been takeovers, occupations, and sit-ins. We're nomads. We function better when there's real movement, an-honest-to-god journey."

"Maybe, but what about the Pueblo people?" Red wondered. Back and forth it went as Mattie dozed and the two men coaxed Mary into playing poker for toothpicks.

Heather was staying out of it for now. She needed to get back to listening without comment. Her job was driving the rig, not influencing the outcome of this escapade.

Up front and eavesdropping along with Heather, Abby turned to her and said, "How's your project coming along?"

"Truthfully, I don't know," Heather confided. "I didn't set out to write about an event. I was interested in the work of one man."

"And now you've let yourself get too involved."

"Maybe. But I know I can still write a good piece, even if it isn't the piece I might have been able to write if I hadn't become . . ."

"One of them?"

Little Cherokee. Heather had to smile, too, hearing it in her head the way he'd said it lately, with teasing affection. She hadn't told Abby about her father's claim that they were part Indian. She wasn't sure she would ever tell anyone again.

Or maybe she would. Maybe she'd sit out in the sun for a while. Then she could head for the beauty parlor and see how much darker they could get her hair without turning her into Morticia. Maybe she'd start wearing more turquoise and beads.

Or maybe not.

She laughed the vision away. "I can't make that claim. That's one of the many things I've learned."

"But you're involved."

"True, but that's not the same." Heather caught herself before she elaborated. *Involved* was one of her own favorite fishing words. She glanced at her new friend and smiled. "How about your project?"

"I'm very much interested in seeing how the event plays out." Abby gave a brief listen to the conversation going on in the back. Then she baited another hook. "Interesting business with Barry Wilson. Didn't he get off on some sort of criminal charges and go from activist to actor?"

"He used to be a college professor. But you must have run across quite a bit about him in the course of your research. He made a name for himself in more ways than one. If you're interested in American Indians . . ."

"I'm more interested in the nineteenth century," Abby said.

"You're interested in the Canton asylum, which was twentieth century. And now this march on Hollywood, which might not even make the news, never mind the history books."

"You were talking about my research," Abby averred. "As far as that goes, I'm focusing on late nineteenth century. I mean, sure, I know Wilson used to be a political activist, but I haven't gotten into the activities of too many *living* American Indian war chiefs. You sort of assume they went the way of all good protesters, right?" She gave a little laugh before breaking into toneless song. "Where have aaaall the flower children gone?"

It was suddenly quiet in the van.

"Sorry, folks." Abby sheepishly turned in her seat. "I promise not to sing anymore."

"Was that you singing? Thought maybe a goose got caught in the grille." Red Butt threw in his hand. "Damn, I was all set for roadkill soup."

"Aw, Red, that's disgusting," Kole said as he claimed his winnings. "You'd ruin a good grilled goose by tossing it in a pot of soup?"

"There's nothing wounded up here but my pride," Abby assured them shyly. "Who's winning?"

"Anybody wants to pick goose meat out of their teeth will have to come to me," Kole crowed as he shuffled the deck.

"You guys are funny." Abby turned toward the front again, muttering to Heather. "Incredible sense of humor. I'm glad I came. I'm really enjoying this trip. It's about time I got to know some of these people after reading so much about their ancestors." She paused, ostensibly for a look at the scenery, which amounted to rock and sky. "That whole activist movement has really all but died, hasn't it?"

"Not in Indian country." Heather liked having a soon-to-be-degreed expert ask for her opinion, but the question seemed a bit basic. "Didn't you say you subscribed to *Native Drums*?"

"There's a difference between decrying injustice within the community and actually taking a stand. That's why this trip is so exciting. More of a nonviolent statement than the old take-over-and-burn action." Abby flashed a between-us glance. "I hope."

"It'll be interesting to see what we're going to do when we get there."

"Aren't you privy to the plan?"

Heather shrugged. "I don't even know whether there is a real plan."

"I keep hearing talk of a sit-in on top of one of the Hollywood landmarks."

"Talk? Or banter?" Time to prick the troller with her own barb. "They have such an incredible sense of humor."

"Which is a good thing. I only meant . . ."

With a quick smile, Heather leaned toward Abby, but raised her voice toward the back. "I wonder what *they* say about *our* sense of humor."

Kole laughed.

"What?" Heather protested. "I didn't say anything funny."

"Maybe not," Kole returned, "but what you said made *me* laugh."

"*What?*"

"Just the idea that you're wondering what we say about you. For a whole lot of reasons, that seems funny. White people can be really funny."

"Ole and Lena are funny," Red Butt said of the Midwestern Norwegian joke couple.

"Och!" Mary scoffed. "They're not real people."

"They could be. They take themselves so damn seriously, and they do such crazy stuff."

"But you take, like, Robin Williams or Steve Martin," Kole said. "Big show-offs. It's all about them. You get sick of it real quick."

"Yeah, but Al Bundy is funny," Red Butt added. "*Married with Children?* He is one funny white guy."

"I *hated* that show," Heather squealed. "I was glad it finally got canceled. For a sitcom, I thought it was actually depressing."

Kole laughed. "See how funny she is when she's serious?"

"Maybe it's just me," Heather tossed back. She was getting pretty tired of being typecast. "Maybe I'm one of a kind. Or maybe I'm not even *any* kind? How about that? Maybe I'm just plain humorless. Transparent. *Colorless.*"

Once again the camper went quiet. The silence was heavy with excuses, retorts, rejoinders, maybe even regrets, but nobody was willing to choose one.

Finally Abby piped up in a small voice. "Would anybody like to hear my version of 'If I Had a Hammer'?"

♦ ♦ ♦

The caravan spent the night in northern Arizona in a small town on the Navaho reservation. Jack had contacted the Southwest reservations before they'd set out from Minnesota, and he expected to more than double their numbers in the last few stops. These were people who'd had all kinds of dealings with Hollywood. From Arizona to California wasn't much more than a trip to the store. All he had to do was get them together. Kole would do the rest.

They were well received, given a gathering, a feed, and places to sleep. The message they brought had been delivered, discussed, and tucked into the heads that were considering it. Several people had come from the Apache and Zuni nations to the south. A poet from one of the pueblos in New Mexico had decided to make the trip, and a renowned Hopi artist had paid Kola the ultimate compliment by offering to trade one of his paintings for a flute.

Kole would have enjoyed it all thoroughly if not for the discomfiture that would not go away. He couldn't forget the hurt he'd seen in Heather's eyes, the indignation in her tone, the little tremor in a voice ordinarily confident, if not always composed.

Her reaction had surprised him. He'd almost said, *Can't you take a joke?* He knew now what a mistake that would have been. She'd been irritatingly distant all evening, spoken to him in a way that made him feel apart from her, lonely and lost. He wasn't sure what to do about it, how to get her back.

He stared at the spider-shaped stain on the camper ceiling, reached up and traced the legs with a forefinger, and listened to her measured breathing. Who was she trying to fool? She wasn't asleep. Their bodies did not touch, but her tension stiffened his limbs. He tried to remember how he might have handled such an incident with Linda, but that didn't help. Linda would have fired right back at him in kind, both barrels. Why hadn't Heather done that? He knew she was capable.

But this thing that separated him from Heather—this prickly thing with so many sharp edges—this thing hadn't been there with Linda, even though, theoretically, it should have been. Their people were ancient adversaries. Their ancestors had hated each other long before they'd ever laid eyes on Heather's forebears. White American society knew both tribes by the insulting names they had hung on each other long ago—the Sioux and the Chippewa.

But Linda was not white. And Heather might have had a little Indian blood in her somewhere, but who didn't these days? Heather was . . .

Heather. She was Heather, the woman who lay beside him in their bed with her back to him. She was detached from him, and he struggled with an off-the-wall but unshakable feeling that he would be worthless until they were reconnected. As long as they were together—and God knew that time was growing short—he was a fool to lie there aching for her when she was so close.

He turned to his side and eased up behind her, half expecting her to fly away at his touch, but mostly hoping for her to turn, melt in his arms, and let him off the hook.

She did neither. She allowed him to press his lips to her shoulder without shrugging away, but in her silence she let him know that it would take more. He was going to have to come up with some words, and God help him if they weren't the right ones.

He went straight for the universal male mantra.

"I'm sorry."

She drew her next breath a little deeper. He thought he detected a bit of a quiver, maybe a little less tension in her after she exhaled. He was on the right track. Might as well spill his guts and be done with it.

"I haven't been laughing too much lately, Heather. Maybe I'm a little out of practice. You came along and got me laughing again. It feels good." Slowly he rubbed her bare arm. "It feels so good, maybe I overdo it sometimes."

He rubbed. He nuzzled. He felt like a tomcat ditching his self-respect for the love of warm milk.

Just when he was about to give up and retreat to the other bed, she flipped over to face him. "Like when?"

It took him a moment to gather his wits. "Okay, like today on the road. I didn't mean to tease that hard. I've been feeling shitty about it ever since."

"Okay."

She turned to her back and took her turn staring at the ceiling.

Okay? Meaning what? It was okay for him to feel shitty? It was okay now *because* he felt shitty? Did he have to do time in the shitter before she'd let him touch her again? What?

"I like it when you tease me, Kole."

Yeah, right. "Not today, you didn't."

"No, not today. I guess I was a little touchy today."

"Did Abby say something?"

"Abby?"

"You two were talking. I just wondered if she said something about me." He propped himself on his elbow. "Or maybe something about you and me."

She lay utterly still, but her eyes shifted in his direction, connecting with his. "What about you and Marty?"

"Me and . . ." He flopped over on his back with a groan. "Honey, that's history. A very short chapter, really ancient history."

"You don't have to explain."

"I just did. That's all there is to say." He remembered standing outside the camper jawing with his friends, all the while watching for Heather, wondering what she was doing inside, wishing she'd come out. "It's not like you to sit behind the curtain and listen in."

"Of course it is. I'm a reporter. Or I used to be." She turned in his direction. "But it isn't like me to be jealous. I'm never jealous. I'm *not* jealous. I need to know these things if I'm going to, you know, portray the complete man. Obviously you've had your share of isolation, but given the choice of whether to take women or leave them, you prefer taking. Under the right circumstances, of course."

She'd suddenly switched from curt sulkiness to chattering like a South Dakota magpie.

He had to chuckle. "Like if they're coming at me with a laptop they want filled."

"Now, see, that's funny, but only because it's just the two of us, just us. But never mind that." She propped herself on her elbow. "Back to Kole Kills Crow. Correct me if I'm wrong, but my impression is that he's not one to sleep around. On the other hand, being tied down doesn't appeal to him, either, even though . . . What?"

His incredulousness was obviously written all over his face. "Is this some guy you read about, or is it straight out of a movie? I'm dying to know where you're getting all this."

"My instincts are very reliable. I stake my reputation as a journalist on them day in and day out."

He tried not to smile, but he loved it when she talked about professionalism in the nude.

"I know, I'm getting too serious. Go ahead and laugh."

"Not a chance," he said softly as he gently laid two appreciative fingers between her breasts. "How about your heart? Correct me if I'm wrong, but my impression is that you rarely risk that." He looked up. Her pale eyes shone in the moonlight that streamed through the small window. "Why are you doing it now?" he asked.

"Because . . . given the choice . . ."

"You have the choice. You've never doubted that, have you?"

"I can choose to go or stay. I can choose to risk what's mine, what I haven't chosen to risk before because I'm choosy."

He smiled, his gaze utterly ensnared.

"I am," she insisted. "Given the choice, I'll go with my instincts. This is the first time they've told me to risk it all. 'You'll never meet his like again,' my instincts are telling me."

" 'His *like*'? What's my *like* like? Is that, like, my mug, which looks like hell half the time? Or is it my ass? Do I have a nice ass?"

Her quick laugh jingled like dance bells. "When did you start asking so many questions?"

"When I started hangin' around white—"

Damn.

He dropped his head back on the pillow. "Tell you what you won't miss about me, and that's my manners. You'll be just as glad never to see their like again."

Her silence pierced him as she eased herself down beside him without a glance, without a touch.

"Clay's mom used to get after me about the way I used to tease him," he told her quietly. "Didn't I realize how much he looked up to me? Didn't I know he took everything I said to heart? She said I had a sharp tongue. I was just kiddin', I'd tell her, but she said I didn't know when to quit. And with Clay the time to quit was, like, two jokes in. That was it. Especially if it was about him being . . ."

"Part of something you don't like," she finished for him. "You don't like it in yourself."

"I don't even think about it," he protested. "I didn't really know about it until Lana—until my mother dropped me off there at the ranch. I knew she'd been with a white guy, but I didn't know *how* white, and I didn't think of him as my father. I didn't know what any of that meant. I grew up Lakota. I was never going to be anything but Lakota."

"So Clay's being white put you at odds, on opposite sides, and that wasn't where he wanted to be. He wanted to be with you—your side, your corner. Your family."

"I try to think of him that way. Related. We're all related."

"You're his brother, Kole. That's the way he thinks of you."

"He's a good man," Kole said firmly. "But I'm Lakota, and he's white."

"So am I."

"You're my little Cherokee."

"I don't know anything about being Cherokee, and I don't often think of myself as white. I think of myself as a woman. I identify myself as a journalist. A New Yorker now, although that's just a matter of having a residence. I missed out on the accent, and I couldn't care less about the Yankees or the Mets. I do love Manhattan, but what's not to love? I'm an American." She turned her head on the pillow to show him her face and look at his. "We're both Americans."

"I'm Lakota. Put that in your book, along with all that it means." He tucked a strand of hair behind her ear. "From your perspective, but try to see mine. It's written in my skin."

"Is my perspective merely white? I'm a woman writing about a man. I've written about a lot of men. I think I prefer to write about an interesting male over a female, to try to discover the strengths and weaknesses he doesn't seem to recognize in himself. Maybe my female perspective enhances the story."

"Does your female perspective make me a hero?" When she didn't answer right away, he pressed. "Who decides who the good guys are? Isn't it the storyteller who decides?"

"If it is, you know where you stand in my book."

"On my side?"

"Whether you want me to or not," she told him as she mirrored his attention to her hair by touching his. "Which is why I get touchy when you lump me in with *them.* I want to be part of *us.* It doesn't matter what color my skin is or yours, not anymore. Does it matter to you?"

"Not now."

"When? In the light of day? In the company of . . . who?"

"Nobody." He turned to her. He was about to say something really sappy—he could just feel it coming—and he didn't want the light in his face. He touched the backs of his fingers to her smooth cheek. "There's nobody but you, Heather. When you stray from my sight, I keep looking for you until you're back. I feed on the sight of you. The sound and the feel and the smell of you nourish me in a way that nothing else, nobody else does."

"Oh."

She sounded a little breathless. He liked that.

"But don't ever expect me to talk like this in the light of day."

"What happens then, Kole? You go back to your coffin?"

"We'll see when we get to California." He cupped her chin and gave it a little shake. "Just remember what I said. Because it's true, even if I never get the chance or take the risk of saying it again. There's nobody else. Just you."

17

After a visit to the Havasupai in northwestern Arizona, the convoy stopped for gas. Kole had decided that the desert was not the place to discover or debate the nature of *E*. He flushed all the camper's tanks and filled those that needed filling while Heather stocked up on bottled water and travel food. Their riders had helped tidy the camper inside, and now they were either queued up at the cash register or the restroom, or they were stretching their legs.

Nobody else seemed to notice the layers of western dust covering the windows until Heather went after them with a squeegee. Kole pulled the other one out of the bucket attached to a gas pump, mumbled something about the windows not being as dirty as the water, and set to work beside her. It felt right, the two of them taking up the chores together. She imagined peeling off each state they'd been through, letting it fall away from the camper in a black runnel.

"I've got my people calling Wilson's people to see if he'll make an appearance at the rally on the Mohave," he told her as he swished his squeegee in a different bucket, searching for cleaner water.

"Maybe he'll bring along some famous friends."

"I'm looking for him to bring one particular friend."

"So far you've kept a low profile." She threw him a pointed look across the hood of the camper. "*I'm* looking for you to keep it that way."

"Jack says we're not getting much national notice."

"Wait till we hit Hollywood and Vine, or Hollywood Hills, or wherever we end up making our stand." She snatched a blue paper towel from the dispenser above the window cleaner bucket. "How does that work? If you're staging a demonstration, do you have to get a permit?"

"Imagine a war party applying for a permit," he said with a chuckle as they crossed paths, heading in opposite directions. "I've always been a strong believer in the element of surprise. The night before, we like to do a sneak-up dance."

"Oh, right."

She heard the camper door open and close on the far side. She smiled, shook her head, wiped her hands, tossed the towel in the trash can, turned and crashed into Kole.

He laughed. "You're not deaf. I've been practicing." He bent low at the waist and demonstrated the step.

She started to imitate him.

"Hold it!" He raised a warning hand. "Women don't do that one; the sneak-up is a men's dance. I know times are changing, but I'm a dyed-in-the-feathers traditionalist. You get women doing men's stuff, everything's liable to turn upside down and ass-backwards."

She punched him in the arm.

"I ain't kiddin', now." He put his hands up in defense. "I'll teach you the wounded warrior dance. That's the one the women do when the men come home draggin' ass."

"Which you won't be, because you're staying back in the hills the way Sitting Bull did at the Little Bighorn." She opened the driver's-side door, reached for her purse, and turned to him. "Isn't that right? He made medicine for the warriors' success in battle?"

"For the protection of the people," he told her. "But I'm no holy man. I'm thinking more of using some of Crazy Horse's best strategy."

"I hope that involves keeping your head down. You have to stay back and let the rest of us smile for the cameras." She flashed her pearly whites, then leaned close to tell a secret. "I'll share a cigarette with you."

"How many have you had today?"

"None since . . . What day is this?"

"We-smoke day," he confided, steering her away from the gas pumps toward a gravel path that led to a picnic table and an over-flowing trash barrel. "We have to figure out a way to make sure we attract a few cameras for the rest of you to smile for. After all this, we want to make sure we're more than a CNN state update running along the bottom of the TV screen."

"I thought you didn't watch TV."

"I don't. Hardly."

"Well, we'll be a lot more than a footnote or filler. Don't forget, I know people."

"Meaning?" Grimacing, he pulled a long, slim cigarette from the jewel-colored pack she offered. "Never thought I'd be salivating for one of these."

"Meaning moochers can't be choosers, but I'll put in some calls."

She searched her purse for matches while she spoke. "And the cameras will be there. And the gas station was all out of my favorite brand of cigars."

"You do cigars?"

"Not anymore, sweetie." She struck a match with a flourish. "That is *so* yesterday."

"Yeah, well, I believe in yesterday." He bent his head for the light she offered, took a long drag on the cigarette, plucked it from his mouth. "This is my story, darlin'. All you get to do is tell it."

"Then all you get is half of this." She claimed the cigarette and helped herself to a puff. "Aren't you glad it's a long one?"

"Size doesn't matter. It's potency that counts."

She laughed, gagged, coughed, and punched him in the gut.

He gave way in the middle, laughing with her. "Damn, you're hard on me."

"*Seriously,*" she insisted, "if Jack isn't having much luck in his attempts to get media—"

"Just let it unfold, okay?" He shook off his turn at the cigarette. "Something I want you to know, Heather. You're not *a* kind, but you're *my* kind. My kind of woman, my kind of person. I like you the way you are. I like the way we go together. When it's just you and me, I feel like we're the right fit."

"And when it's more than just you and me?" She dropped the cigarette in the gravel, ignoring his groan. "We can give this up anytime we want, right? But we do need people. We can't exist in a vacuum."

"Why not? As hard-hearted as you are, woman?" When she looked up at him, he smiled. "*You* can't, but I've been doing it for years."

"That isn't what I see here."

She turned toward the canopied gas pump plaza, where a motley array of pilgrimage vehicles were still taking their turns at the hoses.

The front bumper of a shiny new Chevy pickup kissed the battered bumper of a beat-up old Buick that was attached with baling twine. Two Chevy Novas, one at least twenty years the other's junior, formed unlikely bookends around a pair of red pumps. Parked just beyond the pumps, the stalwart camper stood ready for its riders. Robert "Red Butt" Red Bull held the door for Mary Bigfoot, who cradled a small brown paper bag in one arm and used the other to pull her weight over the high threshold.

Heather's right brain wondered what was in the bag, while her left brain wondered how she could still wonder after spending time with these particular individuals. Or vice versa on the brain sides. She never could remember which half of her wits controlled her subconscious or whatever she was struggling with to get past prejudices she could have sworn she'd never in her life harbored. A scene from a movie flashed through her whole giddy head. A man was talking to a brain he was keeping in a jar.

Steve Martin. Heather stifled a giggle.

"Are you gonna finish that thought, or is what you don't see as far as it goes?"

Heather turned to Kole, smiling.

"I don't know if you noticed," he said quietly, "but I just did get serious."

She nodded, still smiling.

A slight breeze lifted his hair away from his forehead, a streak of silver glinting in the Arizona sun. He was trying to plumb the enigmatic core of her divided brain with his intense gaze. Oh, he was beautiful. He was so much more beautiful than her hero-worshiping heart of long ago could have conceived.

He'd have himself a good laugh if she said that out loud.

"What I see is that you're an important part of many lives besides your own. I think you know that."

"I'm talkin' about us right now. I'm trying to say . . ." He shook his head, his attention drifting westward. "No matter what happens at the end of this road, I wouldn't have missed the trip for anything."

"Me either." She grabbed his hands and held them fast. "And I don't know about you, but I don't trust Barry Wilson, and I don't think he needs to know you're with us. Why don't you let me try to find out what's going on with him and Tom Seal?"

"No." His sharp tone echoed in his eyes. "You stay out of it, Heather. You're supposed to be an observer. If I catch you playing detective, I swear I'll lock you up . . ." He squeezed her hands as he looked around, as though searching for a place ". . . somewhere."

"I'm going to interpret that as a sign of your affection."

"Just don't mistake it for a sign of my incredible sense of humor."

"That was Abby's mistake, not mine."

"She's made one or two more." He grinned at her puzzled expression. "Haven't you noticed? She's got her eye on me."

She rolled her eyes and groaned as he slipped his arm around her shoulders. "You are so incredibly male."

"I'll interpret that as a compliment."

"You know what else?" she said as they headed up the gravel path to resume their journey. "I think Steve Martin is hilarious. And so is Robin Williams when he's not, you know, grabbing himself all the time."

"Yeah? Well, I think you still owe me half a cigarette."

✦ ✦ ✦

The small reservation belonging to the Mojave people, for whom the desert was named, straddled the state line at the southern tip of Nevada, but the tribe's continuing dispute with myriad powers had to do with land on the California side. Supposedly protected by the federal government, the land west of the Mojave reservation was coveted by nuclear power plants across the country for a national nuclear waste storage site. At the community center during the caravan's meeting with the Mojave people, the discussion turned, as it had at each stop, to local concerns.

"We've been fighting off radioactive waste for, what, ten years at least?" said the man taking his turn at the microphone, which stood only a few feet from where Kole sat in the front row. "We get a reprieve with one administration, but pretty soon a new one gets in, and we start all over again."

"The Ward Valley controversy," Kole muttered, leaning close to Heather's ear.

"Some people think the Mojave Desert is the perfect place to dump that stuff," the speaker said. "Or *store* it, like somebody might wanna use it again."

The laughs were as scattered as the listeners, perched on folding chairs or hanging around in the kitchen, waiting for the coffee urns to finish perking.

Heather leaned toward Kole and whispered, "They have to put it somewhere."

Kole straightened, grinning. He could see that the speaker noticed, so he did the polite thing. He shared.

"The lady says . . ." Without taking his eyes off the speaker, he grabbed Heather's hand before she could pound his arm. ". . . that they do have to put it somewhere."

A moment of cool silence was allowed to pass.

"This is what they call a teachable moment, Ed," Kole said as he squeezed her hand. "This one has ears. I'll vouch for her."

"They want to put it underground somewhere," Ed explained. "It's all part of that notion that if you can't see it, it doesn't exist."

"Indians know that story pretty well," a young man contributed from the other side of the room.

"So, what, store it above ground?" Heather asked innocently.

Kole figured she knew more about the issue than she was letting on, but she enjoyed playing devil's advocate. Or maybe she wanted to get the stuff out of the densely populated areas. There was that side, too. In all the talking they'd done, he and Heather hadn't gotten around to this issue yet. They hadn't gotten around to a lot of things he'd like to have time to do with her.

"Seriously," she was saying. "I don't mean to sound facetious, but I've been to Three-Mile Island. I don't know what the answer is, so I'm asking—"

"Damn right, store it above ground," Ed said. "Right next to the statehouse in every state that made the waste. If they have to see it every day, maybe they'll stop making waste they can't take care of. Stuff that can poison lives so far into the future we can't even imagine anything about them."

"Except that they'll be our relatives," Jack, sitting next to Heather, put in.

"You have to keep it right in front of their noses," Ed declared. "What you see is what you get, but what you can't see, you're allowed to *forget*."

"Like they say in the movies," Red Butt piped up. "Fer-get about it."

He earned a round of chuckles with his mobster imitation.

"There it is," Jack exclaimed. "That's what people know. What they see in the movies. Which is why we're making our march on the education capital of the world. Hollywood."

"What difference will that make for Ward Valley?" Ed asked.

"Who's fighting for the life of the Mohave Desert and the habitat of the desert tortoise and the poor, beleaguered Colorado River?" Jack submitted, then quickly gave away the answer. "The Mohave Indians."

"What Mohave Indians?" Kole aped, assuming a pompous pose. "The Mohave's a desert. Are there Indians, too? Hell, everybody knows about the Sioux and the Cheyenne, but didn't the last California Indian die way back when? You know, the last of his tribe?" He snapped his fingers, playing the role of John Q. Public trying to recall something he'd learned from his favorite teacher.

"I know the one you mean," Jack chimed in. "Graham Greene played him. Damn good actor."

"Ishi," came the answer from Jack's far side.

It was Abby. Kole grinned and winked at Heather. He'd had no doubt that one woman or the other would come through.

"But the Colorado River doesn't run through Ward Valley," Heather objected. She glanced at the map of the area that hung on the wall behind the speaker's podium, then turned to Kole, delighting him with rare uncertainty. "Does it?"

"It's like this." Ed planted his finger on the map. "The river is twenty miles from the proposed site. Ward Valley sits on top of a huge aquifer. They want to bury radioactive crap there." He punched at the place on the map with his finger. "Right there. How soon before it starts showing up in the water? I don't ask *if.* I'm askin' *when.*"

"The thing about water—it *moves.*" Jack turned in his chair, and Kole could feel another cute little twist coming on. "Remember *A River Runs Through It?*"

"The movie or the book?" Heather asked. "*A River Runs Through It* was a book first."

"Same difference," Kole told her, slipping her another wink. She was doing fine.

"The operative word is 'runs,' " said Jack, using his hands to demonstrate. "It moves, and it takes stuff with it. The good stuff, the bad, and the ugly."

"Was *The Good, the Bad, and the Ugly* a book, too?" Kole asked Heather.

She leaned behind Jack to catch Abby's eye. "I don't know when to laugh anymore. Do you?"

"Anytime you think something's funny," Kole said. "Or so outrageous you might as well laugh because it's die if you do and die if you don't."

"Everybody's gotta die of something," Jack said. "Right, Ed?"

The man at the microphone laughed. "Okay, okay. We'll pack up our signs and take them to Hollywood. But how do we get anybody to pay attention?"

"For one thing, we have to focus on the issue," Jack instructed. "Leave the Ward Valley signs out of it for now. We need to make this a visual statement, so they have something to show on film."

But Ed's attention had been diverted to the door at the back of the room. One after another, people started turning to see what was going on. But Kole didn't have to. Ed Chase's bright-eyed smile told him that they were now in the presence of celebrity. Jack's soft "Uh-oh" provided confirmation.

"Maybe this guy has some ideas," Ed said. "Come on in and—"

"Enlighten us, Barry."

Heather tried to stop Kole from rising from his chair, but he took her hand from his arm and pressed it firmly back in her own lap as he turned toward the back of the room. He took enormous pleasure in lifting his face slowly.

There was no other way to describe it. The look of shock that transformed his old friend's face made Kole's day.

It also settled his plans for the days to come.

He noted that Wilson was not alone. Tom Seal hadn't changed much since Kole had last seen him. He'd put on a few pounds, and he was dressed considerably better, but he still had the look of a guy who was badly in need of a laxative. Seal glanced at Wilson—probably wondering what he should do next—but Wilson was concentrating on collecting himself and revising his entrance.

Maybe Barry Wilson wasn't such a bad actor after all.

But he had changed. Kole wasn't quite sure what it was, other than the fact that he'd gotten older. But they all had. Did old agitators ever die, he wondered, or was it just their cause? Did they lose power in their voices? Their wills? Their minds?

Both Kole and Wilson had gotten grayer, for sure. Craggier in the face. Unlike Kole, however, Wilson was paunchier around the middle; he'd undoubtedly been eating well in Hollywood. And there was something in his eyes that hadn't been there before.

On second thought, it wasn't a matter of something added. There was something missing.

Wilson doffed the black cowboy hat he was wearing. As he took a couple of steps into the room, his demeanor changed. He squared his shoulders, lifted his chin, started filling the room with his presence the way he had done in the old days.

"Kole Kills Crow," Wilson said with a smile. "Hot damn! You're looking for an attention-grabber for your campaign?" He was already playing the room, striding toward the front. "Picture Kole Kills Crow riding through the Hollywood Hills on horseback." He raised a fist as though posing for the poster for *The Ten Commandments.* "Spear in hand, tilting at the ominous sign of the times."

Kole chortled. "Tilting?"

"Counting coup on it, then. Nobody does it better." Wilson offered a handshake. "How are you, buddy?"

Kole nodded, but he said nothing.

"I hate to see you take this kind of a risk after all this time."

Kole shrugged. "What's is the best time for risk taking?"

"When you're young and crazy," Wilson said with a laugh. "We sure took our share of risks when we were younger, didn't we?"

"Did we?"

"I've . . ." Wilson glanced at his audience, looking for signs of support. When he didn't see too many, he seemed to deflate slightly. "I've tried to carry on. Still speaking up for Indian people, reminding people that, uh . . ." He perched on the front edge of an empty chair on the makeshift aisle and braced a fist on one stout thigh. "Well, like this whole question of sacred sites. I got us a little publicity when I went out to Devil's Tower and took a stand on all that recreational rock climbing, tearing up the face of that holy place. I made the news on, what, two or three networks?"

"Did they plug your latest film?" Jack wanted to know.

"Well, they mentioned the one people remember best. I'm not exactly a household name. But I'm a familiar face, so that gives the cause a nice little boost." He swiveled in the slick seat of the chair, turning to his listeners. "Hey, I'm all for using Indian actors in Indian roles, if that's the point you're trying to make here. And I agree with you about the stereotypes. Hell, the day I get to play a part that doesn't call for an Indian will be the day I feel like a real actor."

"You look like a real actor, Barry. Don't sell yourself short, man, you've always been a real actor." Kole nodded toward Seal, who was leaning against the back wall, wearing a black leather sports coat over a black shirt, looking the part. Whatever his part was. "How did you get in with that guy?"

"Tom works for me." Wilson waved Seal off the wall, but Kole's ex-prisonmate took his time making his way toward his boss.

"As what?" Kole wanted to know.

"He's my assistant."

"An assistant is like a helper, right? Does he help you with your acting?"

"He's kinda like a secretary. But you don't care for that job title, do you, Tom?"

"I guess he wouldn't," Kole threw in, raising his voice to make sure Seal didn't miss a word. "To some of us who don't get around many secretaries it might sound too much like *bitch*."

"Never was nobody's . . ." Seal glanced at Wilson, then settled back into himself, keeping his distance from Kole. "What I do is, I make sure Mr. Wilson's life is pretty much trouble-free. I take care of details and watch out for his safety." He tucked his thumbs into his belt and tipped his head to one side. "And, yeah, he knows about my past, but he gave me a chance to start over."

Kole laughed. "That is so big of you, Barry. So very Barry of you. Does your secretary call you Big Barry?"

"What are you trying to start here?" Wilson asked quietly.

"A revolution. Have you forgotten how it's done?" Kole gestured toward Seal with an open hand. "Did you know this guy's a murderer? He never went to court for it, but the inmate he helped to waste was an Indian guy. And you know how those murders generally go unsolved."

"I helped you—"

"That's right, you did. You helped me escape. Why did you do that, Seal? Why did you take that risk for me?" Kole paused briefly, but the only response was a scowl from the unappreciated Seal. "Maybe it wasn't much of a risk, huh?"

"I didn't wanna see you get screwed is all."

"Is that all?" Kole folded his arms across his chest. "Well, I appreciate that, Tom. I didn't wanna see me get screwed, either. But what about Daryl Two Horn?" Clearly the name didn't ring a bell with Seal, which didn't surprise Kole. "The kid who got killed."

"No matter how many times they asked me, I gave the same answer. Didn't know either one of you. Never saw nothin'."

"That kid didn't do anything but steal some cars, and even that wasn't his idea." Kole looked around. Everyone in the room was on his side, and he knew it. He would shamelessly make the most of it for the sake of a boy whose murderer had gone unpunished. "Poor Daryl didn't have too many original ideas. The only thing he was much good at was doing what he was told.

"His whole life he probably couldn't catch on to much, including a break. But in the end he sure caught that bullet nice, didn't he? I never could figure out whether he was trying to do what he was told, and he got set up, or whether we was just in the wrong place at the wrong time." Kole stared directly at Seal. "What do I owe that boy's memory? Was that bullet meant for me?"

"How the hell should I know?" In meeting Kole's stare, Seal seemed to be able to forget the position he was in, surrounded by Kole's friends. "You people had your own little club. I didn't have nothin' to do with your affairs. Never gave a damn who was in, who was on the outs. I had my own worries."

"Oh, man, didn't we all? But we don't wanna bore these nice folks. We'll reminisce about doin' time some other time. I was just wondering how you two got together." Kole turned to Wilson with a disarming smile. "Coincidence, or connections?"

Neither offered an answer.

"Must've been fate, huh? Maybe somebody had an angel on his shoulder." Kole looked at Jack.

Jack grinned. "Or the devil puttin' a bug in his ear."

"Bingo." Pleased with his friend's apt rejoinder, Kole matched Jack's grin. "Have you guys met Jack Laurent? This man has a nose for news. Be sure you get the whole scoop on Barry's new project, Jack. I hear it has to do with flushing a whole reservation down a huge garbage disposal."

"What part does Barry play?"

"Now that's a damn good question, Jack."

"All right, look," Wilson interposed as he rose from the chair. "I don't know what game you guys are playing, but I didn't come here for games. I heard about this parade of pissed-off 'Skins coming to town, and I came to see if I could help."

"Help who?" Ed Chase wondered.

"Help my people. Obviously Kole can't be riding through Burbank on a white horse, but I could. I could take the point position as a familiar face for the cameras, or I could bring up the rear and—for the benefit of any reporters who might decide to follow—I could explain what we're doing."

"We weren't planning on doing anything to the reporters," Kole said.

"Maybe just scare 'em a little," Jack added. "Then we'll let them keep an inch of hair for every column inch we get from them."

"What column?" Red Butt demanded.

"*Print* column," Jack said. "Like newspaper column. Get your head out of your—"

"They want sex or violence. I say we make a sacrifice," Red Butt suggested, smacking fist to palm. "Sacrifice some skin. Or *a* 'Skin. Guaranteed to get us on the news."

Ed Chase stepped around the podium, an invitation in his eyes. "And since Barry wants to help out . . ."

"You sure you want to let him take center stage?" someone called out.

"I'm offering to bring to bear whatever little bit of celebrity I have," Barry said. "If you don't think I can be useful . . ."

"He could be of some kinda use, maybe," Jack said. "You never know."

Wilson turned toward the exit. "Call me if you think of anything."

Kole grabbed Wilson's arm. "I think you need to stick around, Barry. Knowing you, first thing you'll do when you leave here is call a press conference."

"I'm not the president of anything."

"Yet," Jack said. "An actor is just a politician in training."

The entrance to the room was closed and barred by several Mojave men taking the no-nonsense stance.

Kole released Wilson's arms and folded his own. "Did you know we gave you an Indian name, Barry? In Indian country you're known as Steals Thunder. You weren't there for the naming ceremony, but we know how busy you are, so we just went ahead."

"You can't keep me here," Wilson said. But his fear of what they might do shone in his eyes.

"Who's gonna stop us?" Jack wanted to know. "Your secretary?"

"You're right about a sacrifice, Red," Kole said. He turned to Ed Chase. "Do the Mohave people sacrifice bits of skin like the Lakota people do? That's the kind of medicine Sitting Bull made for Little Bighorn." He cast a pointed glance at Heather. "Sitting Bull understood that sacrifice is necessary."

18

Afafter the meeting, Heather wished aloud for the use of a washing machine and a bathtub. Abby, who had a room at the tiny local motel, was able to offer her both. Heather could use the bathroom while Abby used the laundry facilities in the annex off the motel office, and then they would switch.

The bath was heavenly. As she squeezed the water from her hair, Heather wondered whether she had squeezed her last spit bath out of the camper shower. Whatever happened tomorrow, she promised herself a luxurious Hollywood hotel room tomorrow night. Soaking and humming, she imagined stretching out in a comfortable king beside Kole. Not-so-old Kole, a merry sole. One hell of a humorist was he.

His kind of woman was she.

Such a pair they would make, for heaven's sake. . . .

She smiled, remembering the way he'd finally told her how he felt. She was not just any old kind; she was Kole's kind. They were traveling together, and he liked being with her, liked the way they fit together. He wouldn't have missed this trip for anything.

No matter what happens at the end.

Put him in a prison cell, and there they'd keep him very well.

Unfair. He was innocent.

All right, he wasn't completely innocent, but he wasn't totally guilty. Which made him human. He was a man, *her* man. And he was picking the wrong time to play the hero. She was writing a story about a man, not a hero. If she'd given him the impression she was looking for heroics, she hadn't meant to.

She needed a man, not a hero.

Heather slid down in the tub until her chin touched the water.

Why was sacrifice necessary? Did anybody ever think to ask that little question? Any male body? Every female living on or buried under God's green earth had surely asked. She wasn't looking for pain-free, but wasn't it just possible that there might be a less painful way?

Silly question.

He called for his horse, and he called for his spear, and he called for the nails and the tree.

◆ ◆ ◆

She had added his clothes to the wash only because she needed to make up two loads. She had folded them all neatly only because it made sense. She went back to Abby's room only because she still had the key but not to the camper. She wasn't waiting on him, nor was she looking for him, nor did she expect to find Abby and Kole sitting side by side on the bed in Abby's motel room.

And she didn't mean to blurt out the first ridiculous question that came to her mind.

"What are you two doing?"

Nobody jumped except Woof, who got up from the floor to greet Heather with tail wagging and head bowed. Only Kole looked at Heather directly.

"Nothing for you to worry about, honey." Oddly, he appeared to be smiling though some kind of pain as—she was just noticing—he drew his hand back from the phone on the nightstand.

"I'm not worried." She carefully set the two stacks of clothing on the unoccupied bed. She didn't want them coming unfolded. There was already enough undoing in the works, so she returned his smile and gave his dog a more hands-on hello. "I'm curious. Why would I worry about you having a tête-à-tête with somebody you don't even like?" She ignored Abby's rude snigger. "If I wanted to worry, I'd pick something really worrisome to worry about—like whatever it is you're *thinking* about doing—but I choose to be curious about what the two of you were just doing on the phone."

"Heather's a sharp observer, but in her line of work you never want to be too quick to jump to conclusions," he told Abby as he rose from the bed. Then he looked across the other to the side where Heather stood. "We were just talking."

"After what went on at that meeting, don't try to be funny, mister."

"That's a good line for your friend here. I'll bet she's used it a time or two." He glanced at the phone. "Actually, I was just giving some-one Abby works with a little firsthand information about the project she's working on."

"What do you know firsthand about history?" Heather demanded of Kole. The so-called student still sitting on the bed was of little interest to her at the moment.

"I *am* history," Kole claimed as he stepped over Abby's feet. "You're lookin' at a genuine relic."

Heather spared Abby a glance. "What happened to the history paper?"

"You're all done with that, right?" Kole interjected in Abby's behalf. She answered him with a noncommittal glance, which he translated for Heather. "She has all the missing pieces now. That's what I was just tellin' her advisor."

"Cut the crap, Kills Crow. I'm not *that* slow." Heather turned to Abby in disgust. "Who do you work for?"

"I'll tell you something that really is funny, if you think about it," Kole put in. "We're back to that same question, only now it's you asking."

Damn, Heather thought. "She can't be . . ."

"Sure, she can. They come in all shapes, sizes and colors."

"It's my fault. I would never have . . ." On hands and knees, Heather launched herself across the bed, toppling the stacks of laundry as she scooted to the edge and sat opposite Abby, knees to knees, leaning across the divide to get nose to nose. "Listen, this is a legitimate protest. These people pose no threat to national security or whatever it is you're all about. Surely you've seen that for yourself by now."

Surprisingly, Abby nodded. "Personally, I agree with the concerns you all have."

"Well, who the hell do you work for?" Heather demanded, glaring at Abby.

Abby's return expression was almost apologetic.

"What are you going to do?" Heather asked her. "You can't arrest him, you know. You have no jurisdiction here." She looked up at Kole. "Does she?"

"I wasn't looking for Kole Kills Crow," Abby said quietly.

"She just got lucky. You, on the other hand . . ."

She gave him a good, hard, don't-say-it look.

He laughed as he sat beside her on the bed. ". . . have a much better nose than she does. Maybe you're in the wrong line of work."

"You're safe here, aren't you?" she asked him.

Smiling, Kole lifted a finger to touch the nose he'd just complimented.

She batted his hand away. "*Aren't you?*"

"We're out in the middle of the desert on an Indian reservation, honey. Safest place in the world."

"For you. Right? *Honey?* Don't fuck with me now! I'm serious. And don't you laugh either!" She shoved her fists between her thighs to keep them from punching him. She couldn't imagine what he was enjoying so much. "She can't touch you here, can she?"

Woof sniffed up and down Heather's leg, checking for treats secreted somewhere on her strangely behaving person. Disappointed, the dog moved from threadbare carpet to cool tile and flopped on the floor.

"I'm not going to let her touch me," Kole said. "I promise."

Heather scowled.

"I *could*," Abby said, "but that's not what I'm here for." Sounding entirely too competent, she reached for the closest part of Heather, which was her knee. "I'm sorry I couldn't be up-front with you. I've enjoyed our—"

"Bullshit." Another hand batted away. If they were going to be so unfeeling, she didn't want them touching her. "You don't get to claim anything resembling friendship when it was all done under false pretenses." She turned to Kole. "What are you going to do?"

"We go ahead with the march."

"Who were you talking to?"

"Somebody who works with Abby." He was permitted to touch her now, to cover her clenched hands with his. "I'm going to need you to make some calls for me, Heather. For us."

"And who is *us*?"

"Who are we? We are the people." He shrugged, as though the magnitude of the claim embarrassed him a little.

But not enough to set it aside. He rubbed the tension from her hands, his eyes telling her that in his heart the pronoun included her.

"We're the ones who are going to stand up for ourselves tomorrow and tell the entertainment world in one voice, nothing stereo, that we are not a type, not a kind, not their shallow invention. We're individuals who are alive and well and living in communities all over this country that are distinctive and valuable and have not gone, *will* not go away."

"Meaning you're not history."

"*We're* not. I'm not talking individually. Individually, we become history eventually. But we're saying as a people we're not history. So stop writing us off.

"When they kill us, it's murder," he told Abby, who sat across the divide between the two beds. "When they take from us, it's stealing. When they make us out to be something we're not, it's bearing false witness." He smiled at Heather. "Better known as lying, right? The Big Lie. The one that people swallow like some psychedelic drug when the truth becomes tedious or inconvenient. Or sometimes, maybe once in every generation, the truth becomes so outrageous that decent people don't think they can deal with it anymore. They need that lie." He turned to Abby again. "We're saying *deal with it*. All of us, together, we have to deal with it."

"Us, too?" Heather said, the sound of her own voice surprising her. Her heart was pounding, her throat constricting around emotion that felt at once childish and motherly. When had she gone mushy and hoarse?

He glanced back and forth between them. "You two, too."

"Us *three*." Heather pulled her right hand out of the stack of hands he'd made in her lap and slapped his knee. "We can do this. Tell me who you want me to call and what you want me to say."

"You're gonna let me put words in your mouth? That's an offer I can't refuse, Godmother." He slid closer to her. "I want you to call all your most influential contacts in the media and tell them what we're doing. Give them the whole who, what, where, when, and why, starting with Kole Kills Crow, escaped con—you'll have to embellish this a bit because I doubt that the name means much anymore, but you know the details—that the once notorious Indian activist suspected of—"

"No," she said quietly as the direction this was taking began to dawn on her.

"It's time to use the trump card."

"No." She'd nearly been resigned to the notion that no way was he going to stay behind. But actually setting himself up to get caught was something else entirely.

"I want you to say that Kole Kills Crow has a date with destiny. Doesn't that sound good?"

"It sounds like a ridiculous hyperbole and the worst kind of cliché."

"Exactly. Hollywood-ese. The language of the media. You tell your friends to cover this event because your sources tell you that authorities expect to make an arrest."

"I absolutely will not." Heather shook her head furiously. "You're staying here, Kole. Your job was to get your people to join the march, and you've done that. You've got your people. So now I get to call my people and see if I have all this influence I've been bragging about. Then you'll stay here and watch the march on TV." She grabbed his arm, jerking on it as though his head were a bell. "And wait for me. Because if you take off before I finish this book, I'll find you." Affecting Daniel Day-Lewis's *Last of the Mohicans* accent, she repeated, "I will find you."

Heck, she could do movie lines as well as anyone else in this crazy show.

He laughed. "If you want to be one of us, you're gonna have to follow your man. Three paces behind."

"Not if he's walking into an ambush."

"He's making a choice." Kole allowed the word to resonate for a moment before justifying it. "What we're planning here is an excellent strategy, proven effective by Crazy Horse himself. Use one warrior as a decoy." He used his hands to illustrate. "He rides out in plain sight, easy pickin's. The troops ride up the hill after him. You got your war party waiting for them on the other side." The fingers that had played decoy now touched her face. "We have to find a way to draw people in."

"You're not Crazy Horse."

"Well, he was a full-blood, and I'm only half. The crazy half." His hand slid from her face to grip her shoulder. "It's my choice. It's my one shot at looking like a real hero at the end of your book, and I'm going to take it."

"I'm not writing a novel." She glared at him. "I'm not going to write anything at all if you're going to do something stupid."

"I've done plenty of stupid things—some I haven't even told you about yet. But I will. That's the best part of the story. The funny part."

"The part I don't get."

"Sure you do. It's the part that keeps us humble and helps us survive."

"I'm sorry, but I'm very serious about the security of your . . ." She gave a perfunctory smile. ". . . hide."

"This is where I slip out the side door." Abby rose from the bed. "I'm serious about security, too, but it's important that we keep the serious nature of my business here completely under wraps until this is over. Otherwise, Kole, all bets with respect to your situation are off." She turned to Heather. "As far as Indian history goes, I'm learning as I go."

Heather stared long and hard at the door that had just clicked shut behind Abby. "She's a cop, right?"

"Says she is."

A cop. For the first time in her life, Heather felt sick, used, foolish for befriending a cop.

"What kind?"

"The undercover kind. You know, you're beautiful when you're serious, especially when you're serious about me." He squeezed her shoulder. "I've reached the end of my *hide,* honey. Are you gonna help me make the most of it?"

"What do you mean, she says she is? What bets? What situation? Did she show you some kind of—"

He was nodding. "You should see her ID photo. Looked so tough, I was tempted to check for balls. Secret Agent Man."

"Are we going to make a run for it?"

"A run for what? Popcorn?" He chuckled as he slipped his arms around her and drew her close. "You've got twice as many questions as I have answers, woman."

"What about Wilson and Seal?"

"Wilson knows about Crazy Horse's strategy. But so did Custer. I'm bettin' ol' Barry's ego is at least a match for George A. Custer's. You know what the *A* stands for?"

"I can—"

"No guessing." He leaned away from her, grinning. "Actor. He liked to get together with the guys at the fort and put on plays. No lie. He was practicing up to run for president. We were able to spare you that one."

"I wasn't around then!" At this point she wanted to kill him for laughing or making a joke of any kind. "Will you settle down and get serious for just one minute?"

"Can't mess around now, honey; I'm on a roll."

"How do you spell that?" All right, so his flippancy was contagious. "What kind of a roll are you on, Kole?"

"I'm on a . . . tear. A trip. Does it look like an ego trip? Believe me . . ." He drew her close again. "I don't know what it is. I know it's been a trip. You and me, flyin' down the road together, pickin' up more of our kind along the way."

"*Our* kind?"

"People who care about things we care about. People who care like crazy." He lowered his voice almost to a whisper. "I'm crazy about you. Can you tell?"

She searched his eyes. "I can certainly see the crazy part right now."

"I love you too much not to at least try to be the man you think I am. For one day, anyway."

She was not about to part with the crazy part. The crazy, mad, passionate part was the part he couldn't stop from loving her. She slid her hands over his shoulders, over his chest, his arms—more parts of him that she had no intention of parting with. He smelled of lemon soap and freshly ironed cotton.

"Nice shirt," she said, leaning back, suddenly noticing that he was wearing a handmade, crisp white shirt she hadn't seen before. Blue and red satin ribbons were stitched over the shoulders and down the arms, across the chest and the middle of his back.

"Thanks."

"So what are you going to do? Unfurl your plumage for the starlets in Tinseltown like some horny peacock?"

"This is a gift from Mary Bigfoot. She said it would protect me."

"From what? You might as well paint a target on your forehead while you're at it."

"Gotta have a costume." He rose from the bed, drawing her to her feet. "Maybe I am playing a role, but believe me, it isn't the one I want. I'd much rather be Kola, the blind flute maker."

When his people stood up, Woof took his cue to head for the door.

Always a natural performer, he whined, scratched at the door, urged them to keep moving.

"That's right, boy, I'd rather be ramblin' down the road with Woof the Wonder Wolf-Dog and Heather, the magical storyteller."

"If they put you back in prison, we're going with you."

"I believe you would." He took her hand. "You'll write the story?"

She nodded.

"Can you write it up so they'll pick it up for a miniseries?"

"I'd have to write *down* for that."

"Are you ready to make some calls?"

"What's the scoop I'm supposed to give them?" She scooped his half of the clothes off the bed and loaded them into his arms. "Give me my lines."

19

Before the troops made their stand, Kole had to deal with Wilson. Staking him out in the middle of the desert came to mind. The group would put on a good show, and then Kole would get hauled away, leaving Wilson to languish in the sand as long as Kole was left to rot in a cell. At least half of the idea held some appeal. He'd even be willing to let his old friend have his favorite secretary staked out by his side under the warm California sun.

Rally the troops, Barry used to say, and Kole would reply that it was the other side that had troops. Indians had parties. But troops were organized, and Barry had a gift for organizing in the midst of chaos. Until recently, Kole had held Barry Wilson in a special place in his own often-chaotic mental hierarchy. In all the treachery that had touched Kole's life, he'd wanted to believe that Barry was blameless. He had good memories of being part of a classroom full of students or an auditorium full of supporters or a camp full of rebels hanging on Wilson's every word, taking him to heart, and feeling empowered by the growing perception of their own unity and conviction. Wilson seemed to embody the legitimacy of their cause.

On his way back to the community center, Kole waved Jack down.

"He's waiting for you in the Commodity Building," Jack said, reading Kole's mind, as he so often did. "They say it's the most secure building they've got." Jack grinned. "Specially constructed for guarding the big cheese."

Kole smiled. Everybody loved USDA surplus commodity cheese.

Ah, but did the cheese stand alone?

"Where's Seal?"

"He's around," Jack said with a shrug. "You said you didn't want them scheming anything up together, and we figure he's not going anywhere without his boss."

Jack didn't know Seal. Like most cons, Seal was dedicated to a single principle, and that was his own survival. If the cheese really did stand alone, Seal would happily eat it.

"Did you find a way to get me up on that sign?" Kole asked. It would be dark soon. They were going to have to get moving.

"We're gonna get you *down* onto it. Found us an Indian-owned helicopter."

"No way!" Kole laughed. "Man, how times have changed since Alcatraz."

"Were you there?"

"Damn straight. My mom couldn't find me a sitter."

"We're high tech now, thanks to the little big Indians with the fancy casinos. They're glad to help out." He handed Kole a set of keys. "Damn, I wish I could've been there when we took over Alcatraz, just to be able to say I was there. It's like Woodstock."

"Your kids will be wishing they could've been there when Daddy marched on Hollywood." Kole slid the key into the deadbolt lock on the door to the white Quonset building.

"You think so? You think we can keep the spirit alive that long?"

"This is the spear*head* stage, my friend. We're trying to renew the spirit and maybe spearhead a few changes." He pushed the door open. "Check on Seal, huh?"

"I'm on it."

Kole found Wilson sitting at a desk and working on a plate of food he'd apparently been brought from the feed they were both missing now.

"The smell of home." Wilson gestured with a piece of frybread. "They say it's the sense of smell that really triggers the memories. This stuff sure works for me. Grab a chair and help yourself."

Kole turned the back of a folding chair toward the desk and straddled the seat. The second-to-the-last thing he wanted to do was share a plate of food with Barry Wilson. Dead last on his list was swapping memories, even though he couldn't seem to close the door on his own, couldn't help wishing things were different.

Barry was different, but not in ways Kole might have expected. There was a kind of hollowness about the man that saddened him. The first thing he'd noticed when Barry had approached him at the meeting was that the old swagger had all but disappeared. All that was left was a studied stride that lacked color or character.

Maybe that was the point. Barry Wilson could be anybody now that he was no longer himself.

"What are you going to do with me?" Barry's tone suggested that wondering and caring were two different things.

"Haven't decided yet."

"I didn't know you were with them." Barry put the half-eaten frybread back on his plate and peered across the desk. "You're making a big mistake, Kole. You should stay out of sight, exactly the way you've been doing. Let me lead this march."

"And when they put the microphone in front of you, what do you say?"

"Whatever I'm told to say. That's what I do for a living now."

"How do you like it?"

"I like the way they pay me. I like what the money buys. Living out here is a real kick." But there was no kick in Barry's voice. "Sometimes I miss the old days."

"What do you miss?"

"I miss the integrity we had then. I miss being able to tell it like it was, say what I wanted to say. I felt like I was able to do that because you were there, backing me up."

"Well, now you've got Seal."

"Yeah, now I've got Seal." Barry picked up the frybread again and examined it the way a kid might do if he'd been ordered to finish eating. "You wanna know how I got him?" he asked quietly.

"Not particularly."

"He was assigned to me."

"Is that a contract perk? You get your very own ex-con? That's some kick, Barry." Kole leaned forward. "Tell you what, it was a kick in the teeth the first time I saw the two of you together. I don't know what the deal is, but—"

"Jesus, wake up, *kola*."

"Don't call me that," Kole growled, measuring each word. "We're not friends. I took the rap for both of us, man. No way was I gonna give you up, because I *believed* in you. I thought you would do more on the outside than I ever could. I even told myself that getting into the movies was a way for you to stand up and be heard. I saw celebrities getting attention for good causes sometimes, and I thought, yeah, that's the kind of thing Barry'll do, first chance he gets.

"And then I saw Seal standing behind you in that TV interview. One of our kids was murdered, Barry. Daryl Two Horn was only twenty years old, and he was no threat to anybody. It was a setup, and I know damn well Seal was in on it. I just never figured out why."

"You were right. The kid wasn't the target."

Kole stared at the top of Barry's head. His salt-and-pepper hair had been creased by the black cowboy hat that lay near his plate on the desk.

The kid wasn't the target. No ifs, ands, or buts. Wilson knew.

Kole cleared his throat, kept his words soft and steady. "What about my wife?"

Barry looked up, his sad eyes meeting Kole's cool stare. "Seal told me that your house blew up, but you weren't in it. Just some woman. That's all I heard."

"How did he know it was my house?"

"They know. As long as you aren't making too much trouble, they'll leave you alone. You're a good example to point to whenever an example is required, Kole. Hell, they say you're a terrorist. You escaped from prison, probably after murdering one of your own people. Damn Indians, they're an edgy bunch. You just never know. Try to put 'em to some use, they'll turn on you if they don't turn on each other first. What are you gonna do? Can't depend on 'em, can't quite destroy 'em."

"Where'd you get those lines, Barry? Sounds like a hell of a part."

"Keep your head down, and you won't get hurt; that's all they've been trying to tell you."

"Who?"

"People Seal works for. People who opened doors for me."

"You've been living in La La Land too long, Barry. Jack made me watch reruns of that show you were on once, that *X-Files*. 'Your old buddy's on *X-Files*,' he said, and he proceeded to bore me with the whole story leading up to where you come in. All that conspiracy crap, that's exactly what this sounds like."

"Kole, if you divided the non-Indian population of this country into ten parts—"

"Don't start."

"—eight of those parts would tell you they've never met an American Indian and don't know—"

"—'anything about them except what they've seen in the movies,' " Kole recited. "I know. I also know you gave up the right to call yourself a teacher a long time ago."

"The ninth part would know more about Indians than most Indians do. They think Indians are the eighth wonder of the natural world, and they're pretty sure they were either Indians in a previous life or they would love to enlist now if there's any way possible."

"Only one-tenth hates us?" Kole gave a dry chuckle. He took a pack of Marlboros he'd just bought out of the pocket of his denim jacket. Another good intention biting the dust. "Seems like a little more than that."

"That's a lot of people, and most of them won't say they hate us. We're not evil, but neither are we necessary. We're a nuisance. We're sitting on something they want, or maybe we're saying something they don't like. And whatever it is, if we'd shut up and get out of the way, they could turn a profit. That's all you have to do, Kole," Wilson admitted. "Just shut up, get out of the way, and let them have it all. Sometimes there's a reward in it for you."

"Other times, there's just desserts."

Lacking the will to smile, Wilson acknowledged the point in Kole's favor with a cocked a forefinger.

"I can get my own sweets," Kole assured him as Barry waved off the offer of a cigarette. "And I sure as hell don't wanna be no movie star."

"It's better than prison. Better than a bullet in the back of the head."

Kole squinted at Barry through the cloud of smoke he'd just made. "Who is it you sold out to?"

"I'm not even sure anymore." Wilson sighed. "The names and faces change, but the motivation is consistent. There's money to be made in every phase of energy production, even the waste. You've also got your industrial waste, your medical waste, your everyday consumer waste. People have to pay to make all that waste go away. You don't wanna think about it or ever see it again, you pay somebody, and you don't ask any questions unless it gets back into your air or your water. You don't want that.

"So you separate out your own appetites, make an exception of them, and then you get righteous. You call the factories and the farmers and the federal watchdogs to task. Finally, at the waste end of this whole cycle, somebody gets to collect big if they hide this stuff really well.

"Bottom line: they've figured out another way to make money off tribal land or treaty rights."

"We're not after those guys this time," Kole said. "We're doing this gig to publicize our objections to the way Indians have been stereotyped by the media. Simple demand for some of that political correctness they're willing to throw everybody else's way."

"Well, you're headed in the right direction, and you're almost there." Barry gestured for a drag on Kole's cigarette. "Is that all you plan to say?"

"You never know, do you?" Kole slid the pack across the desk. "Depends on who gets to talk. Give an Indian a microphone, he's gonna say what's on his mind."

"Is that why *you* came here, Kole?"

"Yeah." Kole lifted one shoulder as he tossed out a book of matches. "And I thought I might run into you."

"You were one up on me." Barry struck a match. "I figured it would come, but I didn't know when. I thought I knew how I'd feel about it, but I was wrong."

"Me, too."

Kole stared at Barry's shiny shoes, looking for a reason to feel something besides pity for his old friend, regret for what the man might have done if he'd been the man Kole and so many others had believed he was.

But maybe it was never fair to pin that image on the face of a living man. As long as he was still alive and still human, you couldn't tell what he'd do next. It might be something beautiful, or he might get caught picking his nose.

Jack had a point. Resistance to stereotyping was a damn good cause. Noble or savage, either way it didn't spell human.

Kole took a long, contemplative drag on his cigarette. Finally, he looked up. "You ever had any dealings with a company called Good Riddance?"

"Oh, yeah. But only indirectly."

"How about Seal?"

"Look, Kole, I'm just trying to give you a heads-up for old times' sake. Waste is their business, but these aren't your ordinary garbagemen. If you ride out front, they'll shoot you down."

"You mean I'm likely to get wasted?" Kole laughed. "Remember when we used to get wasted, Barry? Head for the nearest bar and tie one on. Damn, we could raise hell back then. I'd wake up when it was all over and wish you'd shoot me so I wouldn't have to—"

"You're a nuisance to them, Kole."

"*Them. They.* 'Don't shoot till you see the whites of *their* eyes.' " Kole studied his cigarette. "Do we ever get that chance? Do we ever even get to look them in the eye?"

"How do you feel about mirrors?" Barry wondered.

Kole looked up, confused.

Barry smiled indulgently. "I hardly ever go near one anymore, but you don't have that problem, do you?"

"Sometimes I do." He stubbed the cigarette out in an ash-marked mayonnaise jar lid. "I've got a kid. Did you know that?"

Barry nodded. "I heard there might have been a kid, but . . ."

"I figured you had. She's not with me."

"But she's okay?" He sounded hopeful. "Go home to her, Kole. Raise her right."

"It's too late for that. I made sure she was safe and loved. That was the best I could do for her. That and maybe leave a story she can someday tell without hanging her head."

There was a knock on the door. Kole turned, scowling as the door opened and Heather stuck her head inside. "Jack told me where to find you," she said.

Kole waved her in. "Did you get something to eat?"

"I wasn't that hungry, but Ed said I should take some food along for both of us, and I didn't want to be rude. It's in the camper." She glanced at Wilson. "What are you going to do with him? You know, you can't—"

"Let me go with you."

Kole looked at Barry in disbelief.

"Don't worry," Barry responded. "I don't know how to play anything but a supporting role anymore."

"Why should I trust you?"

"You probably shouldn't. God knows I wouldn't." Barry shrugged. "The thing is, you don't know who you're up against. You can't distinguish *them* by the color of their eyes. It's the color of their money that stands out." He waved a quick hand. "No, that's not right. It's what they do with their money. Remember, there are two kinds of people."

"The needy and the greedy," Kole finished for him, remembering. He could probably teach the course himself.

Heather patted her jacket pockets. "Whenever I hear somebody I'm writing about say there are two kinds of people, I grab a pencil."

"Did you make your calls?" Kole asked her.

"I'll tell you about it after I hear the rest of the lesson. The needy . . . ?"

"The needy will do what they have to do to get by, to please," Kole said. He eyed Wilson for confirmation, which was bestowed with a silent nod. "They'll do for you to get you to be their friend."

"And the greedy?" Heather asked.

"It's all about what you can do for them. But no matter what you come up with, it'll never be enough."

"To whom would I attribute this quote?"

Kole turned to the man he would once have followed to the ends of the earth. "Professor Barry Wilson."

20

Somebody seriously screwed up." Jack jogged across the gravel parking lot toward Kole, who had just put Mattie and Anita in Ed Chase's car. "I can't find Seal."

"The SUV they came in is still here," Red Butt said. "We've got that locked down tight. He's gotta be around."

"It's too late to worry about him." Kole had the clock to consider, and the final phase of the journey, and the good people who had come this far. The desert had cooled only slightly with the setting of the sun, but Kole felt an icy calm.

"We're leaving this beast here," he said

of the camper as he turned to Heather. "I want you to stay with Jack."

"Why can't I go with you?"

"Because every time I look at you, I get the urge to back out on this stunt," he told her.

It sounded good, but he knew it was no longer true. He was ready to move. Reluctance had retired, reason had taken a back seat, and pure adrenaline was at the wheel. His ragtag group of reformers was about to take the hill. They would be seen, and they would be heard.

He noticed Abby Wendel, standing at the back of the little group, attending to him like an expectant, beady-eyed raven. He wanted to ask her what the hell she was going to do about Seal. If Jack's announcement hadn't put her ass in gear, she must have had something under her drab-looking outfit besides a service revolver. He hoped it was a whole deck of aces. He had little choice but to count on her, even though his experiences with her type had made him a staunch skeptic.

He caught Abby's eye and nodded toward Heather. "Diplomatic immunity for this one, right?"

"Whatever you want to call it," Abby said. "I've told you what connection I'm looking for, and I'm using what diplomacy I can."

"You look out for these two," he insisted, indicating Jack and Heather. "The only thing they're packin' is the message."

"What about you?" Heather asked.

"Well, you got the word out to the media, so we'll see about me. I sure hope somebody shows up besides us." He urged her toward the pickup Jack would be driving. "In any case, timing is crucial. If the LA cops get wind of what's going on before it's all in place, they could screw up the whole thing."

Nervous excitement colored Jack's laugh. "Like, head us off at the pass?"

"Something like that, yeah." Kole waited until Jack was in the truck before he laid his hands on Heather's shoulders and drew her close. "I'll meet you there. It's gonna be okay. Your friend is determined to get her man, and with any luck . . ."

"You'll be free before—"

"Don't say it out loud, honey. I'm superstitious about jinxing our chances. Whatever happens—"

"Don't *you* say it like that." She touched her finger to his lips. "I love you too much for *whatever* to happen. What's going to happen is that you're going to meet me there." She kissed him quickly. "Safe and sound."

"Safe and sound." He opened the pickup door. "I love you too much, too. You can quote me."

✦ ✦ ✦

A thick, predawn fog blanketed the brown hills overlooking Los Angeles and the familiar landmark that had come to stand for the Hollywood dream. The fog was a godsend for the silent intruders making their way on foot through the brushwood toward the great white letters. The sign had nearly fallen apart in recent years, but celebrity boosters had saved it in traditional Hollywood style—with a facelift, a fence, and the protection of security cameras. Hiking up the hill was no longer permitted. But for a determined native war party, it was possible.

They used the fence to prop up their own signs, expressing their accrued frustrations with everything from sports teams turning them into mascots to the use of derogatory terms like *squaw*. There were "No Dumping" signs, "Don't tread on us," and "Forget the money—Show us some respect."

Several people padlocked themselves to the fence. Heather had doled out generous tips to her contacts in the media. She had made her personal pitch for generous coverage in return. The American Indian convoy—which she had billed as "Hollywood R Not Us"—

would make its charge at dawn, and it would be led by a mystical renegade. If everything worked the way it had been planned, the press would arrive before the police.

✦ ✦ ✦

For the sake of putting on a good show, there were five volunteers who would be dropped inside the security fence from the helicopter. For Kole Kills Crow, Marty Deerfoot, and Barry Wilson, it would be like old times. Novices Robert Red Bull and Carl Shinny sat across from the old hands, their eyes shining with excitement as the helicopter plied the reddening skies over Los Angeles.

"Hey, aren't we supposed to synchronize our watches?" Carl said. "I've got six forty-five."

"Fifteen to seven, me." Marty looked at her watch again. "Yeah, six forty-five. Same thing."

"I've got Danielle." Red Butt thrust the name tattooed on his wrist underneath Kole's nose. "Had her, anyway. Then she started two-timin' me. But this proves I had her, in case she needs any references."

"Here." Barry unbuckled his flashy watch and laid it over the homemade tattoo. "Hide your shame."

"Choice," Red Butt crooned. "How come it says six-thirty?"

"Because it's accurate," Barry said. "Which is why I'm giving it away. Going back to Indian time. It's time to start when everybody's there."

"Just get in place as quick as you can and lock yourselves down," Kole said.

"Hey." Red Butt grinned as he tapped Kole's arm. "Lock and load."

"You're supposed to say, 'Let's rock and roll,' " said Carl.

Kole laughed. "If you guys have to run through every *Top Gun* line you've memorized, maybe we should plan on dawn tomorrow."

"That's all I remember. Show us what you learned in boot camp, Kola."

"*Hoka he!*"

"It's a good day to die." Barry nodded, his smile wistful. He put his black cowboy hat on Kole's head. "My gift to you. My lucky hat. Goes well with your shirt. You always did look better in a hat than I do."

           ♦ ♦ ♦

Heather was delighted with the way everything was clicking into place. The helicopter's timing was perfect. A dark silhouette hovering over the fifty-foot white letters against the red-streaked sky, it made a gorgeous picture for the reporters, who had just arrived. With signs and supporters waiting outside the fence for the pièce de résistance, a ladder lowered Marty onto the top of the first O. Carl and Red Butt were placed on the other two O's. Red missed the top and had to scramble up the scaffold behind his letter.

"Give me a Y!" Heather shouted as Barry and Kole became the centerpieces. The crowd around the fence belted out the letter.

"Because we say so!" Barry shouted.

The crowd cheered and waved the signs bearing some of the words they wanted to say.

           ♦ ♦ ♦

"I could use a stuntman right about now," Kole called out to Barry.

They'd each claimed a point of the letter, which was attached, like the others, to a huge square scaffold made of tubular steel. Heather had suggested finding a way to turn the Y into a peace sign, but the consensus was that Y stood them in better stead as a question.

"Just like the old days." Barry's recovered grin seemed to glint in his eyes. "It feels good."

The cameras were rolling on the ground below. Jack was bending one reporter's ear, Heather another's. As the fog retreated like an ebbing tide, the view of the valley became breathtaking. Every curve of the winding road that led to the top of the hill was visible. Far below, they could see the first of the anticipated squad cars on its way up the hill, lights flashing.

"What do you think the cops will do?" Kole called out to Barry. "Go after us first, or the people on the ground?"

"They'll tell us to get down. While the cameras are on us, they'll load up the people down there. We've got about ten minutes total to convince the public that we're just as interesting as a white Ford Bronco. That we're on the verge of doing something really dramatic."

"You ask me, we just climbed *over* the verge."

"People expect more than just a sit-in. This sign has a history. It's been a springboard for all kinds of stunts, including suicide."

"Springboard?" Kole eyed Wilson across the gulf in the middle of the letter they shared. "We're getting off this thing the same way we got on."

"I should hope so."

Kole nodded. This was no time to be using words like *springboard*. He had taken the man's word that he was truly interested in lending his name to the cause. A moment ago Wilson had seemed elated, back in his element. Suddenly he had a strained look on his face.

Of course, they were sitting on top of a fifty-foot sign, which would put a strain on most people.

"The wind feels cold up here," Kole said. "You should've kept your jacket on."

Barry plucked at his shirt. "White shows up better. From down there we must look like a pair of big birds, huh? Storks, maybe."

"Sitting ducks."

"Snow white doves." Barry waved two fingers. "Peace, brother?"

"Truce," Kole said. He was watching the squad cars wind their way up the hill. They weren't in any hurry, but why would they be? A bunch of people chained to a fence didn't require hot pursuit.

"You'd better get on the phone to that TV station if you want to say your piece," Barry said. "It's gonna get pretty noisy in a minute."

Heather had programmed the phone number into her cell phone. All Kole had to do was push a button and tell the woman at the other end that he was calling from the top of the Hollywood sign.

"We're broadcasting live," she said. "We're told you're staging a Native American protest against, what? The film industry?"

Kole summoned his best speech-maker's voice.

"The people you see here represent more than thirty different nations that are indigenous to the land occupied by the United States."

"In other words, Native Americans."

"Commonly known as American Indians, which is a term most of us have come to accept in the interest of differentiating between us and other native-born Americans. Myself, I'm Lakota, also known as Sioux."

"And would you identify—"

"We have come here"—*Message comes before messenger*, Barry would say—"to the mythmakers' capital of the world to make an important statement about the myths that Hollywood has created. We believe that because we are erroneously portrayed, we are not taken seriously. Our religious beliefs are not respected. Our lands are abused. Our right to determine our own course is denied. We are threatened continually by—"

"Sir, would you tell the viewers who you are?"

He paused. The first squad car was pulling over. "My name is Kole Kills Crow."

"Not that it's a common name, but are you the same—"

"Yes, I'm *that* Kole Kills Crow, but, no, I never killed anybody."

"And what exactly are you trying to—"

"What am I doing?" Kole made the mistake of looking straight down. His knees went rubbery. "Good question. I'm sitting up here on top of a huge *Y*, and I'm saying look at us; see who we really are. Listen to us; we speak for ourselves. Yeah, I know. I'll answer for my crimes, so you guys stay tuned. Once the charges start flying, you'll have plenty of—"

Crack!

Kole froze. He knew that sound. "Gunshot!"

The people below turned their faces up to him. Either they couldn't hear or couldn't make sense of what they heard. In his mind's eye, a young man in a prisoner's uniform crumpled to the ground.

"Somebody's shooting! Get down!"

Kole surveyed the slope. Cops? They weren't out of their squad cars yet. Four of them were still on their way up the hill.

"Get down!" he shouted again. Heather was standing there looking up at him. Jack hadn't moved, either. Good God, people were chained to the fence, perched on . . .

Kole turned. Barry Wilson was doubled over, head slumping toward his knees. He hadn't made a sound. Kole's hands and feet barely touched the scaffolding as he dove to catch him.

✦ ✦ ✦

"What happened?" Heather turned to Jack. "My God, he must be having a heart attack or something."

"Sounds like gunfire," one of the newsmen reported into his microphone. He and his cameraman both squatted near the fence. "Keep the camera rolling! Get the two up there on the Y. Looks like one's hit. I'll try to identify . . ." He pushed the microphone toward Heather. "Miss Reardon, they're telling us that Kole Kills Crow dropped the phone. It's hard to tell who—"

She pushed the microphone away. "Get somebody up there to help them!"

Another shot rang out.

"Everybody get down!" Jack crouched and ran toward the fence. "Get off the sign! Off the fence! Get—"

"You told us not to carry the keys!"

"Shit."

"We have to get him down." All Heather could see was two legs hooked over the white letter, a black hat, a gray head, an arm. Two shots had been fired. Had they come from the police? The demonstrators were unarmed. Except one. "Abby! Where's Abby?"

"Who the hell knows?" Jack shouted over his shoulder. "Just stay down."

"They're not shooting at us. It's—" She hurled herself at the fence, trying for a toehold in the chain link. "Kole needs help, for God's sake. Kole!"

"Can we get hold of the helicopter?"

"We can if we can get to that phone," Heather shouted. One of the sign-sitters had just hit the ground running. "Marty! He dropped the phone! Find it!"

A black policeman trotted up the slope, weapon drawn. "You people are trespassing."

"You shoot people for trespassing?" Jack jabbed a finger skyward. "One of our guys up there just got shot."

At her back, Heather could hear the reporter. "The police are arriving on the scene, but we don't know . . ."

"Who's . . ." The policeman shouted to his backup. "Hold your fire. Did somebody fire a weapon at these people?"

While confusion reigned on the ground, Kole struggled to keep himself and Wilson from falling off the top of the big white Y. He wasn't sure which direction the shots were coming from or exactly where Barry was hit, but he had to get them both on the same side, behind the white letter. He whipped off the cowboy hat and sent it sailing into the wind, toward the crowd.

"Barry, can you hear me?"

Barry groaned.

"Hang on, buddy. Can you hang on to this?" He placed Barry's hand on the top bar beyond the edge of the letter, where he should have been able to take a grip. Barry's left arm was like a rag doll's. "You gotta help me out a little bit. Pull your legs over to this side, and we'll try to slide down this pole."

"Can't feel my legs."

"Can you feel anything?"

"A hole." Barry drew his right hand away from his middle, looked at the blood, clutched himself again. "Not gonna make it, man."

"I'm gonna get us both down, but I need you to help me."

"Can't. Can't feel my . . ."

"Don't worry about it." Kole dragged Barry's left leg off the front of the sign and dropped it in back. Now Barry straddled the top of the sign, and Kole straddled Barry. "Just hang on."

"We know . . . history tells . . . that sacrifice . . . is necessary."

"Yeah, I know all about it. Shut up and smile for the cameras, Professor. But don't . . ." Damn, they were both slipping. He needed to move them toward the middle of the letter, where he could get a better grip. ". . . don't waste your breath. They can't hear . . ." The man felt like a sandbag. "Barry? You with me, man?"

"My big . . ." Barry coughed. There was blood on his lips. ". . . scene, huh?"

"Right. Can't get any more dramatic. You're bleeding all over Hollywood."

"Just the Y."

"You gotta hang on to it a little bit. Right here." Kole curled Barry's hand around an upright stanchion. "Help's on the way, now. Hold it right . . ."

"Got it."

"You got it?" He couldn't feel much tension in the hand beneath his. The scaffolding was slippery with Barry's blood. Kole's was getting shaky, losing his grasp, and Barry was only getting heavier. "We're in this together, man. We've gotta get a grip."

"It's my turn, Kole."

"No, I can do it. I just need . . ."

"It's okay."

Their bloody hands slithered, slipped, came unhooked, fingertip to fingertip, then the final disconnection. Kole shouted his name, but Barry slid away silently. His arms seemed to float above his head, like a man giving over to drowning. Kole closed his eyes against his own quick dizziness. He saw himself following—not jumping, but simply letting go, taking the long ride down in Barry's wake.

The sound of Heather's voice chased the dizziness away. Kole shook off every other thought, blocked out every other voice but hers. Slowly he began his descent, sliding, catching himself, sliding some more, all the while homing in on Heather's voice calling his name.

♦   ♦   ♦

Two ambulances came, but only one was needed. A second wave of squad cars brought more officers to search for shooters, but federal agents already had two in custody. No more were found. The police got to work sawing on padlocks and chains, took names but kicked no ass. Barry's death had diffused an angry atmosphere into one of shock, confusion, and grief.

Jack tried to shield Kole by talking to the reporters, but their questions were for Kole. He said he didn't have too many answers at the moment, but he appreciated their interest. He would tell them what he knew as long as Special Agent Wendel was willing to let him talk. He was in Abby's custody.

"We've arrested Tom Seal and two others," she told him after she'd gotten him and Heather into the back seat of a car one of her partners had provided. "We think we can connect them to Good Riddance and put them all out of business. The EPA has its hands full with companies trying to cut corners on waste management."

"Cutting corners is an understatement."

"They thought they'd shot you," she told Kole.

"I was wearing his hat. His lucky hat, he said." He looked up sadly. "He took that bullet for me, didn't he?"

"They call it neutralizing the leadership," Abby said. "Murder isn't the preferred method, but you wouldn't stay out of the way. They'd much rather buy people and use them to their advantage."

"What now?"

"You escaped from a federal prison. You're turning yourself over to a federal agent. That's me." She got into the front seat and told the driver to head downtown. Then she turned to the pair in back. "I'm no lawyer, but once you're cleared for Darryl Two Horn's murder, I don't think you'll have to serve another day."

"And how do I get cleared?"

"Tom Seal is ready to help you out there."

"Seal's gonna sing?" Heather asked gleefully just as her cell phone rang.

"Forgive my frustrated scriptwriter here," Kole said to Abby. "She obviously has no knowledge of any of my—"

"She's as innocent as the rest of the rabble, I know," Abby said with a smile.

"That garbage outfit must be pretty important to you," Kole said. He knew it wasn't that simple. He figured one federal agent had finally seen the light. It was a start.

Heather handed him the phone. "You have a call from somebody who's pretty important to you."

"Hey." Kole glanced at Heather, but it was the sound of his brother's voice that made him smile. "We're okay. Yeah, it turned sour right away, but Heather and I are okay. Sure." His smile broadened. "Hey, Claudia. You saw me on TV, huh? I was scared, yeah."

His gaze was locked with Heather's while he happily took in the child's scolding. "I know, I wasn't supposed to be up there. Why did I

It was a protest. We were trying to make people think about . . ." He laughed. "No, not sex and violence. You're against sex and violence? Me, too."

Heather laughed.

"No, I think it's better if you write a letter. I hope . . ." He turned serious. He thought about his mother and Claudia's mother, and he remembered how much she had reminded him of both women. "I hope it'll be a better world when you grow up, honey. That's why we . . . That's why." He cleared his throat. "Let me talk to your dad now, okay?"

After the call, he handed the phone back to Heather, but he couldn't let go of her hand. It was bad enough to have to let Claudia go. Heather had become part of him.

"Are you going to lock me up?" he asked Abby.

"If I were going to follow the usual procedure, I would take you into custody and we'd get on a plane." She turned to the back seat, smiling. "But now you've got me in this Hollywood state of mind. I saw this one movie about a skip tracer trying to get this embezzler back in time for a court appearance, and the embezzler doesn't like to fly. He'd rather drive."

A weary smile tugged at Kole's mouth. "An old borrowed camper?"

"That property should be returned safely, along with all the people you dragged out here. You've got the dog and the cat back there with the camper." Abby turned to Heather. "And there's a little matter of a book somebody needs to begin writing. I'm eager to read it. I want to see whether I've earned a mention in the acknowledgments."

Kole shook his head in amazement. Lights were flashing behind them, sirens sounding all around them, but he didn't care. He'd been caught, and so far police custody was looking pretty good. "We could name our first kid Abby, but we'll need time to get married and make one."

"Was I consulted about this?" Heather tucked her cell phone away and took out a pencil. She licked the point and pretended to write on her hand. "Two kinds of women. Needy and greedy."

"That's *people*."

"We're talking marriage here, so that's woman and man. White woman, red man. He's already talking about kids, but we've got two kinds of people here. Which means—"

"Okay." He held up one hand. "It doesn't mean we can't."

"You've got one outlaw and one—"

"Don't go there," Abby warned. "We might have to talk about charges against little Abby's mother. Harboring a fugitive, for starters."

"Actually, I was harboring her," Kole said. "Holding her pretty much against her will."

"Bullshit!" Heather squealed. "You don't get to take credit for my crimes. I actually stalked him. And then I persuaded him to go on this—"

"The hell you did! I made this trip—"

"You're a pair, you know that?" Abby said with a laugh. "You are two of a kind."

Somewhere along the journey back through Indian country in a borrowed camper they would discover what kind they were two of.

Or maybe not. Even for a skilled investigator, it was sometimes hard to tell.